KT-444-347

LITTLE MARVEL

AND OTHER STORIES

By the same author

Absinthe for Elevenses
Cuckoo
After Purple
Born of Woman
The Stillness The Dancing
Sin City
Devils, for a Change
Fifty-Minute Hour
Bird Inside
Michael, Michael
Breaking and Entering
Coupling
Second Skin
Lying
Dreams, Demons and Desire
Tread Softly
Virgin in the Gym and Other Stories
Laughter Class and Other Stories
The Biggest Female in the World and Other Stories

LITTLE MARVEL

AND OTHER STORIES

Wendy Perriam

ROBERT HALE · LONDON

First published in Great Britain 2008

ISBN 978-0-7090-8597-3

Robert Hale Limited
Clerkenwell House
Clerkenwell Green
London EC1R 0HT

www.halebooks.com

2 4 6 8 10 9 7 5 3 1

Typeset in 10/13½ pt New Century Schoolbook
Printed in Great Britain by
Biddles Limited, King's Lynn, Norfolk

For Lee Langley

In appreciation of her treasure-chest mind.
Be it Hollow Men or *lentiggini*, she always provides a eureka.

Contents

Little Marvel

'I'm sorry, girls, I've finally lost patience. You're meant to be civilized young ladies, not a herd of pigs wallowing in the swill.'

A nervous titter escaped from Sally-Anne. She tried to suppress it – too late.

'So you think it's *funny*, do you, Sally-Anne?'

'No, Miss Bates.'

'And do the rest of you think it's funny?'

'No, Miss Bates,' they chorused dutifully, Dolores loudest of all. She had found little to amuse her in her nine years of life to date.

'Well, that's a blessing, I suppose.' Miss Bates paused to blow her thin, arched nose – red and slightly swollen from a cold. 'But since you all seem hell-bent on shovelling in your food like little savages, it's time you were taught a lesson. What I want you to do now is to eat your peas one at a time, which I hope will slow you down.'

A gasp went up from the assembled girls; even a muffled cry: 'Oh, *no*!'

'Oh, *yes*!' Miss Bates retorted. 'Just one pea on the fork. And, Amanda – I've told you already – you're meant to hold your fork the other way up, with the tines pointing down towards the food.'

'What's tines, Miss Bates?'

'Never mind. You ask too many questions, child. Now, is everybody listening?' Her sharp grey eyes swivelled round the refectory, corralling every girl on every table. 'Good. That's the first part of the exercise. The second part is equally important. You are to chew every pea fifty times before you swallow it. Have I made myself clear? Fifty times each pea. *That* should stop you guzzling.'

This new command was greeted with shocked silence, Dolores in particular feeling a surge of deep unease. How could you chew one tiny pea fifty times? Wouldn't it slip down on its own accord after only a couple of bites? And she and all the other girls had been given extra large portions, to compensate for the minuscule ration of meat, and for the fact that Cook had burned the potatoes that morning, tossed them into the waste-bin and refused to peel a second batch.

Staring down at her own substantial pile, she tried to count each individual pea, before giving up in despair as she reached 104. She detested peas in the first place, especially these particular ones, which were overcooked and shrivelled, some with splitting skins. She imagined them filling up her stomach until there was no room for her heart or lungs and all the other squashy things people had inside them. And she hardly dared imagine what might happen the other end. Would they rattle into the toilet bowl in a torrent of green rabbit-droppings?

'Slow down, Theresa! What did I just say?'

'Eat the peas one at a time, and chew each one fifty times. But that's impossible, Miss Bates. No one would could ever do it, not even Superman.'

'I grant it isn't easy, but that's the whole point of the exercise. The trouble with you girls is that you're all far too impatient.'

Forking in her first pea, Dolores began anxiously to chew, but it was ready to be swallowed almost straight away. She would simply have to pretend to go on chewing, even though her mouth was empty. She made exaggerated movements with her jaw, aware that Miss Bates was patrolling the refectory, alert to any slackers.

'Theresa! How many more times do I have to tell you to stop gobbling like a turkey-cock? I don't know why I waste my breath when you ignore every word I say.'

'But I'm hungry, Miss Bates.'

'Hunger's got nothing to do with it. Suppose you had to live through a famine, like your Irish ancestors?'

Dolores closed her ears to the ensuing argument. The worst thing about school was that you could never be alone; swarms and shoals of girls always pressing in on every side. It was bad enough at home, where, as the youngest of eight children, there was never space enough to stretch or sprawl, nor peace enough to hear the sigh of lazy clouds idling their slow way across the sky, or the tiny squeaks of slugs and snails munching on a dandelion. Indeed, with seven brothers and sisters rampaging round the garden, most small creatures – including her – were trampled underfoot. When people mentioned Heaven, she imagined it as a vast expanse of shining space she didn't have to share (as she was forced to share her bed and even bath). It would be hers, and hers alone, with no angels, no dead bodies, not even any God. From what she had heard of God, she knew she wouldn't like Him. He sounded very stern – a tyrant like Miss Bates, constantly thinking up beastly, senseless punishments.

Eleven, twelve, thirteen, fourteen ... She had actually managed to chew a pea fourteen times before it vanished down her throat. That was an improvement, although she had to fake the remaining thirty-six chews as Miss Bates glanced her way. Her jaws were beginning to ache, yet she had eaten only seven peas so far, and the pile on her plate appeared to be getting larger. Worse, the peas were shifting slightly, as if they might erupt in a pea-earthquake. Last week, she had seen an earthquake on the News: bloody bodies everywhere and houses collapsing into dust.

Theresa suddenly nudged her in the ribs. 'Pea-eyes!' she taunted. 'Pea-eyes!'

Dolores flushed. Her green eyes were a source of constant gibes. She had been called an alien, a Martian, a pussy cat, a frog, but Pea-eyes was a new one. The thought of a loathsome pea wedged in each of her eye-sockets made her feel quite panicky. Frantically she rubbed her eyes, to dislodge the green intruders, only to stop herself in horror. Without eyes, she would be totally blind – unable to see the blackboard or read her favourite books. Could she put her eyes on strings, perhaps, like those tiny tots whose gloves were sewn to their coat-sleeves on pieces of elastic? While continuing to chew, she did a little business with an imaginary needle and thread, until her round pea-eyes were bobbing up and down in front of her face on lengths of black elastic.

'Dolores, why do you keep rubbing your eyes? Are you developing a stye?'

'No, Miss Bates.'

'Well, what's the trouble then?'

'Nothing,' she muttered.

'Nothing, *what*?'

'Nothing, Miss Bates.' She forked in another pea. Although ten were gone, several hundred were left. They were definitely increasing. For every one she swallowed, another dozen sprang on to her plate. Things like that kept happening – things beyond all rational explanation; things that made you worry that God was breaking the rules, deliberately and cruelly.

'Miss Bates?' a voice piped up.

'Yes, what it is, Hannah?'

'We have netball at half-past one and it's twenty past already. If we have to chew every pea fifty times, we'll miss it.'

'I'm well aware of the time, Hannah. Perhaps you should have thought about missing netball at the *beginning* of the lunch break rather than the end. I could see you girls were spoiling for a fight the minute you sat down, so now I'm afraid you'll have to take the consequences.'

Dolores let the muffled groans wash over her, along with a further scolding from Miss Bates. She was trying to work out just how long they might be imprisoned in the refectory. It wasn't only netball they'd miss, but all the afternoon lessons (including her favourite, art), then home-time and bedtime and getting-up-in-the-morning-time. In fact, maybe the entire rest of their lives they would be sitting here chewing peas, one by one

one by one
one by one
one by one
one by one
one by
one
by

'Do sit down, Dolores. *May* I call you Dolores?'

'Please do.' She had always been embarrassed by her name, which meant 'sorrowful' in Spanish. Why her parents should have given her a Spanish name was something of a mystery, since they were robustly English and suspicious of most foreigners. As for 'sorrowful', she could only guess that an eighth child (and a sixth girl at that) could well have been a burden rather than a blessing.

'And do call me Willow.'

The name suited its frail owner – a slender, floaty sort of female, with a breathy voice and long rippling hair, who looked as if she might break in half, given a strong breeze.

'Well, what can I do to help?' she asked, seating herself on a floor-cushion and draping her billowy caftan over thin, frail, freckled legs.

Dolores hesitated, wondering where to start. Over the last few years, she had developed several *new* fears, including octophobia, but all of them were related to her underlying pea phobia, which had become increasingly disabling. 'I ... I'm frightened of peas,' she blurted out, at last.

Willow nodded kindly, giving no indication of surprise. Presumably she had heard it all before in her role as therapist. Or *alternative* therapist, as she was listed in the Yellow Pages. Dolores had warmed to that word 'alternative'. In ordinary life there were all too few alternatives.

'Oh, I know it sounds peculiar, or even downright mad. How could anyone be terrified of small, harmless things like peas? But they're *not* harmless – not to me. In fact, there's hardly a place I can go now without a sense of danger. All supermarkets and general stores are out of bounds, of course, along with pubs and restaurants, but I also feel quite jittery in ordinary people's houses. I mean, they're almost certain to have peas in the freezer, or tinned peas in the larder.' She was reasonably safe with Willow, who saw her clients in the Natural Healing Centre – which didn't have a café – rather than at home. (One of the reasons she'd chosen her, in preference to the rest.) 'I think I may have picked up the fear from my mother. She was always terribly anxious and—'

'Just a moment, Dolores,' Willow interrupted. 'I'm not a conventional psychotherapist – I do hope you realize that. I don't examine people's childhood or delve into their past.'

'Oh,' she said, nonplussed. Her childhood was surely relevant, if only in view of the fact that the average number of peas in a pod was eight. When she was growing up in a tiny terraced house, there was just that sense of being squeezed and jostled in a claustrophobic pod, as she and her siblings swelled towards maturity, fighting for breathing space. Though it could have been worse, of course. Some varieties of pea boasted eleven or even twelve peas to the pod. And others were triple-podded, the very thought of which made her feel quite faint.

'Perhaps I should tell you a little about my credentials.' Willow leaned forward eagerly, in danger of overbalancing on the large squashy purple cushion. 'I've trained in several different disciplines, including reiki and shiatsu, but now I practise mainly Chinese medicine.'

Dolores tried to hide her disappointment. Why on earth Chinese, when she and Willow were both living in Crouch End? Her parents had always distrusted China; her father muttering darkly about the dangers of a Yellow Peril. Nor, for that matter, would he have approved of this consulting-room. There were no proper chairs (she herself was sitting on a pouffe-thing), the walls were painted insolent orange, and the only decoration was a large statue of a seated Buddha, who looked worryingly obese.

'Which means I'd treat your fear in general, rather than concentrating on one specific phobia. You see, extreme amounts of fear often indicate a deficiency of kidney energy.'

'There's nothing wrong with my kidneys. My physical health is OK – well, OK-ish, I should say.'

'It's not the kidneys themselves, Dolores, it's your kidney *Qi*.'

'I beg your pardon?'

'*Qi* is energy – the basic life force, you could call it. Everything in the universe has *Qi*.'

'Do *peas* have it?'

Willow appeared to ignore the question, continuing serenely, 'It flows around the body through channels or meridians.'

Like fear itself, thought Dolores, instantly alarmed. Things with foreign names were always best avoided.

'The kidneys are the root of all energy in the body. So if a patient's kidney *Qi* is low, they can experience anxiety, or even full-blown panic. But, of course, in order to make a proper diagnosis, I'll need to take a case history.'

Dolores felt increasingly uneasy. Not only were they were going far too fast, but Willow was now staring at her intently, which was surely impolite. 'What are you looking at?' she demanded, blinking nervously.

'Your eyes.'

'Yes, I know they're green, but I can't help that. It's a family trait. All my—'

'It's not your eye-colour I'm interested in, but the colour of the skin just below your eyes, which can reveal problems or deficiencies. A blackish tinge may indicate a kidney problem.'

'*Blackish*?' Dolores put her hand up to her face. She had extremely fair and fragile skin – the sort that never tanned. Not that she would ever dream of braving the dangers of the sun.

'First I need to establish whether you have a kidney-yang deficiency or a kidney-yin deficiency. Do you tend to feel the cold, or are you always opening windows and complaining that it's too hot?'

'I *never* open windows.' The risks were far too great. Wasps or bugs or sparrows might fly in, on a whim, or pollutants waft their perilous way inside. 'And I'm always cold. Instead of getting *un*dressed at night, I put on several sweaters and two pairs of woolly tights, just to keep warm in bed.'

'In that case, I'd suggest a change of diet. Make sure you eat warming foods like cinnamon bark and cloves, fenugreek seeds, quinoa, star anise ...'

Apart from the cloves, she had never heard of any of them. And they all sounded most peculiar, not to mention foreign again. Although she did like the word 'star anise'. Perhaps she should change her name to Star Anise, which had a certain ring to it, and was definitely an improvement on Dolores. She tried it out under her breath, only to realize to her horror that it rhymed with peas.

'Lobsters can be helpful, too.'

'*Lobsters*?'

'Yes. They're very warming as a food.'

No way would she eat lobster. Any food with eyes or claws was totally taboo. Not to mention the expense. She'd had to pawn her watch just to pay for this appointment.

'Before you leave, I'll supply you with a diet-sheet, but I need to ask you a few more questions first. Do you suffer from weak legs or painful knees?'

'Both,' she said, her mind switching back to peas again. *They* had weak stems but, whatever their fragility, there was instant help to hand, in the shape of sturdy pea-sticks or supportive trellising. You could be jealous of a pea, even while you feared it.

'And do you tend to feel tired or lacking in vitality?'

'Yes, constantly.' Fear was a full-time job, depleting all her energies.

'And do you find you have to get up in the night – you know, to go to the bathroom?'

'I'm up half the night in any case. I have these frightful dreams, you see.' The nightmares featured peas, of course – peas at their malevolent worst. However, she ought to count her blessings. At least she didn't have clinophobia – the fear of going to bed at all – which caused many unfortunate sufferers to lose their partners, health and jobs.

'Well, I'm beginning to get the picture, Dolores, and it's definitely adding up to some sort of kidney deficiency. But I'd like to take your pulses, including the kidney pulse, and also have a look at your tongue. So if you lie down on the couch ...'

Dolores tensed. She hated lying down. A prone position made one much more vulnerable.

'Then, subject to my diagnosis, I'll do some acupuncture, to tonify and warm the kidney energy.'

'Acupuncture?' She sprang up from the pouffe. 'You mean *needles*?'

'Don't worry – they're extremely fine, barely thicker than a human hair. You'll hardly feel them going in, though you *will* feel some sensation once they begin to work. It may be a dull ache, or just a sort of tingling, or it could feel like a mild electric shock.'

Dolores turned on her heel and fled. There were only two things more frightening than peas – needles and electric shocks.

She stood hunched outside Safeway's, staring up at the huge letters of its name, blazoned on the store-front. How could any store be 'SAFE', filled as it was with peas: frozen peas, canned peas, mushy peas, marrowfat peas, not to mention all the deceitful peas lurking in soups and stews and ready-meals? Yet Duncan, her new therapist (Cognitive Behavioural), had set her a task as homework. She had actually to enter this shop, phobia or no, and stand for three full minutes beside the frozen peas, before leaving slowly and quietly, without giving way to panic.

She consulted her watch. Ten past four. She had been here since 1.30, trying to pluck up courage, flurries of snow falling on her flimsy anorak. Several times she had advanced towards the automatic doors, only to retreat again. Better to die of hypothermia than come face to face with the source of her most overwhelming fear.

'Excuse me, madam,' said a deep male voice. 'I was wondering if you needed any help?'

She jumped. A tall man in a smart grey suit, with a Safeway's nametag clipped to the lapel, had sidled up to her. One of the store-managers, no doubt, come to nab her as a shoplifter.

'No,' she muttered. 'I'm, er, just waiting for someone. Ah – here they are, at last!' She smiled broadly at a total stranger: a kindly looking matron in a pink padded coat and woolly hat, who was just entering the store. 'Hello, Sally-Anne!' she cried, tagging in after the woman, only to dart out of sight along the fruit and vegetable aisle, before 'Sally-Anne' could accost her.

She stood trembling in front of a pile of clementines, struggling to compose herself. She must remember Duncan's advice. 'Ignore the panic. Accept the physical symptoms, but don't give way to them. Fear can't kill you, Dolores.'

There, of course, he was wrong. Just yesterday she had read a piece in the *Daily Mail* about a young man dying of shock at London Zoo, because he'd ventured into the Invertebrates House in an attempt to cure his arachnophobia.

None the less, she had to complete this exercise, especially now that she'd surmounted the first hurdle of actually entering the shop. She had sold half her mother's jewellery – the emerald brooch, the diamond ring – in order to pay for Duncan's programme, so if she backed out halfway through, it would be like chucking precious stones away. (And she had already wasted large amounts of money on a Jungian and a Rogerian, following the fiasco with Willow.)

Still fighting for breath, she ventured down the aisle, looking neither to right nor left, in case she saw that dreaded word. Even 'pears' could induce the panic, or 'peanuts' or 'pearl barley', just because they shared three letters with the most terrifying food of all.

And, as she approached the frozen foods section, she felt so over-wrought, the floor appeared to be buckling under her feet, and the fluorescent ceiling-lights glaring down as ruthlessly as search-lamps.

Within minutes she was face to face with the huge, swollen sacks of peas. It was all she could do not to turn tail and run, but somehow she found the courage to follow Duncan's orders: stand her ground and examine them. Their hideous green faces were pictured all over the packets, accompanied by such wicked untruths as 'extra sweet and tender'. At least she didn't have to touch the things – that was next week's challenge – but just looking at them brought on a pounding headache, as if a metal hammer was smashing into her skull. It was the sheer numbers that appalled – thousands upon thousands of peas swarming in the photographs, and actually reproducing as she watched.

She tried to get a grip on herself and note down all the details, as Duncan had instructed. 'A rich source of folic acid,' she spelt out. Yes, acid was the word. Peas by their very nature were sour, acerbic, spiteful. Their sweetness was just a façade, like those smarmy people who wooed you with false smiles, only to stab you in the back. Spinach was more honest. It didn't even pretend to be benign. And Brussels sprouts made no attempt to disguise their innate bitterness. Although, in actual fact, she ate neither sprouts nor spinach any more – ate nothing green at all, nor anything with scales or shells, eyes or feet or tails. Her preferred foods were swedes and parsnips, which were solid and dependable, not to mention cheap. She had lost a lot of weight, of course, but that was a small price to pay for avoiding extremes of fear.

'From field to frozen in just two hours.'

That she did believe. There'd been a programme on the radio about new blast-freezing techniques, which could reduce the temperature of a single pea to minus fifteen centigrade in less than sixty seconds. The process was clearly traumatic – the peas were subjected to blasts of freezing air at a very high velocity, which would make them even more neurotic than they were in their natural state. And neurosis bred maliciousness. She knew that from her own case. Easy to be kind and cheery when you weren't assailed by continual panics, or forced to stay awake each night to avoid dread-inducing nightmares. And, of course, the more your fears increased, the more you feared fear itself, until you landed up with full-blown phobophobia.

Summoning her last dregs of courage, she made herself proceed, inch by terrifying inch, along the line of freezers, all crammed to the brim with peas: Birds Eye, Findus, Safeway's own, Oaken Farm Organic – each more vile and threatening than its neighbour. The names of the actual pea varieties weren't printed on the packets, but she knew them off by heart – boastful and deceitful names, forever sneaking through her mind, however hard she tried to block them out: Perfection, Maestro, Kelvedon Wonder, Sparkle, Pioneer. Worst was Little Marvel, comprising *two* lies in its name. How could anything with such monstrous power be classified as 'Little'?

Stomach churning, she stopped to read a recipe for Pea and Coriander Soup, featured on a so-called 'Bumper Pack'. The peas had first to be simmered with an onion and the herbs, then liquidized to a purée. She could actually see them whizzing through the mixer in a tidal wave of spitting green-hot fury, along with all the pests and grubs that pea-plants seemed to attract: aphids, weevils, midges, thrips … People claimed that peas were good for you, but they were in fact polluted; prey to vile diseases such as downy mildew, root rot, fusarium wilt and leaf spot.

A surge of nausea was rising in her gorge. Clamping her hand to her throat, she careered along the aisle, desperate to remove herself from the source of the contagion, colliding in her frantic haste with trolleys, shoppers, children, prams, and only stopping in blind panic as she approached the canned vegetable section – *more* splenetic peas leering at her, mobbing her, trying to waylay her.

'*No*!' she screamed, veering towards the automatic doors, darting wildly through them, then running for dear life, away from peas

peas
peas
peas
peas …

She slumped on a bench in the park. The snow was heavier now, shrouding her in white, turning the trees to shadowy spectres, closing in around her. Her feet were freezing, her fingers numb, yet the cold was nothing compared with the ice-sharp grip of fear. Duncan was over and done with, like all the other therapists. His tasks were just too perilous for someone of her temperament who might land up in a locked psychiatric ward if she pushed herself too far. Even going home posed a major obstacle, since it involved returning to the High Street and passing not just Safeway's but Sainsbury's and the Co-op, all of which sold peas. And there were at least four different cafés – Nick's Diner offering chips and peas with every single item on the menu, and even the upmarket *Dominique's* serving pea purée and *mangetouts*.

An ordeal like that was beyond her failing powers. She would have to stay here in the park – all night, if necessary. Dusk was already falling, the park about to close, but she could conceal herself in the bushes until the park-keeper had done his rounds and padlocked both the gates. It would be terrifying, of course, to spend twelve hours in eerie darkness, with only ghosts for company and the relentless snow laying cruel hands on her heart. And what about the morning? Would it be any easier *then* to face that hazardous stretch of the High Street? Or would she be confined to this small municipal park for the remainder of her life, living like a squirrel on odd scraps and mouldy crusts?

Well, if the alternative was death by peas, there wasn't any choice.

She tried to raise her head to look around her, but even the smallest movement seemed physically impossible. Where *was* she? Everything was dark and quiet, although she knew she wasn't alone. There was a sense of other presences, a feeling of being gently squeezed both sides.

Her thinking process had slowed to the faintest flicker, but she eventually began to wonder *who* she was – perhaps a more important question than 'where'. But however long she pondered, she couldn't seem to remember her name, apart from the vaguest recollection that it began with P. Or Pea, maybe. Certainly she had fallen into a vegetative state, in which the life force burned extremely low.

She *liked* the state. It was restful, very soothing. Never before had she felt so imperturbable, so blissfully inert. Nothing seemed to matter any more. True, she was rooted to the spot, but that, too, was a blessing. No more need to brave the shops or venture anywhere; no more threat from sunburn, thunder, crowds. She was exquisitely protected by an impregnable green envelope: wind-proof, rain-proof, fear-proof. In fact, fear was now impossible. Her mind was ticking over at such an elementary level, all exaggerated emotions were naturally suppressed. She couldn't fret or agonize because she possessed a pea-sized brain.

She let that fact sink in, although it seemed to take some time, Not that she was bothered. She had all the time in the world. There were no more pressures, no more colours, even. Everything was simple, everything was green. All she had to do was bask in her green pod in a state of blank acceptance: safe, and snug, and slow, and sweet – and completely free of worry for the first time in her life.

Slowly, very slowly, a phrase was creeping into consciousness, a phrase describing her new state. At first, it failed to register. The letters were hazy, the concept indistinct, but gradually, eventually, and, with a faint twitch of low-key pleasure, she finally grasped the happy truth.

She had become a … a … a …

Little Marvel.

Germans

Alice emerged blinking from the gloom into the cold stare of the December afternoon. The day seemed cruelly bright, the sun glaring in her eyes, mocking the glum nakedness of the spindly, shivering trees. The sky was an unseasonable blue – the blue of peace and summer; a smug reproof to the cold war in her mind. Almost automatically she crossed the road, turned right, then right again. How odd that she should remember the way after an interval of forty-four years, as if the directions from the tube station to her Aunt Patricia's house had been indelibly imprinted on her child-brain.

'Come back, this *minute*, Alice! If you go skipping on ahead like that, anything could happen.'

Her mother's voice, anxious and reproving; her father's hand clamping her shoulder, as he steered her back to the family group. In those days, Clapham had been dangerous (or exotic, as *she* saw it), a different country from their own safe, salubrious suburb. There were no foreigners in Esher, and certainly no 'darkies', as people used to call them. Whereas in Clapham, in the fifties, you saw every shade of skin from butterscotch to Bournville. Aunt Patricia had half a tribe of Indians living right next door, and an Indian doctor who wore a yellow turban and had two gold teeth that flashed. Their own Dr Barnes seemed boring by comparison, with his balding head and tweedy jacket and off-white English teeth.

Clearly, the area had been transformed in the intervening decades. The houses she was passing had been gentrified, upgraded, and were probably worth a fortune now, judging by the cars outside: Mercedes, BMWs, even the occasional Porsche. And chi-chi restaurants and wine bars appeared to have sprung up everywhere, a distinct improvement on the dingy caffs she remembered from her childhood.

All at once, a wave of panic stopped her in her tracks. Was she crazy to have come? Suppose her aunt refused to see her, slammed the door in her face? The whole thing was Derek's fault. Easy for *him*, as the beloved, favoured nephew who had always kept in touch, to take the moral high ground; harangue her about healing the rift before it was too late. It was *already* too late. She hadn't spoken to her aunt for close on half a century, so how could she just pick up the phone and say, 'Hello. I'm coming round'? In the end, Derek had done it for her, made the phone-call, fixed a date and time, and presented it as a *fait accompli*. Yet her overwhelming instinct was to bolt straight back home and abort this mission before it had begun. Except then she would have Derek to contend with – the sanctimonious elder brother bitterly disappointed in his errant little sister.

Hardly 'little' now, she thought, peering at her reflection in a window. Would Patricia even recognize her, with greying hair and crowsfeet? The last time they'd met, back in 1963, she'd been something of a swinger, in brief mini-skirts and thigh-length silver boots, and with a mane of bleached-blonde hair. Rather different from her present attire: staid grey suit and 'sensible' shoes.

'Look, get a move on,' she muttered to herself. It was twenty-five to three, and Patricia was expecting her at two. Yet her legs had turned to cardboard, as if she had travelled not from Lincolnshire, but from Mongolia or Timbuktu, trekking thousands of dusty miles on foot, rather than lounging on a train. Normally, a rail journey was something of a luxury, but she had sat jittery and irresolute, barely reading a sentence of the new novel open on her lap. The drama on the page kept changing into the real-life quarrel she still remembered word for word.

'A *German*? But you can't possibly marry a German! Not after what happened to Tom.'

'Look, Aunt, it's peacetime now. The war ended twenty years ago.'

'That's not the point. Tom was killed by those bastards. And killed in the most inhuman way.'

'I'm sorry – really I am. But you can't expect me to give up my fiancé for the sake of an uncle I've never even met.'

'He was my *brother*, Alice – and a quite outstanding man.'

'Well, Stefan's outstanding, too. You'd like him if you'd only agree to meet him.'

'I've told you already – if you bring that fellow within yards of me, I can't be held responsible for what I do or say.'

'That's totally unreasonable – an act of war in itself. You can't blame Stefan for what his country did.'

'I *do*. I blame them all. And the thought of my own niece sharing a German's bed makes me literally sick.'

Next, they had got on to the Holocaust. One of Patricia's Jewish friends had been burned to a crisp in Belsen – horrific and unpardonable, but nothing to do with Stefan, who had been a babe in arms at the time. But her aunt refused to relent, and finally she, the execrable niece, had slammed out of the house, never to return. Her aunt was conspicuously absent at the wedding – *and* at the christening the following year. No card, no present, no congratulatory phone-call. She had pretended not to mind; gradually hardened her heart until she came to regard her aunt as a prejudiced old woman she was better off without.

As she turned into Patricia's road, memories came surging up again. When she'd first heard the name, Wildwood Grove, she had imagined it a scene from *Sleeping Beauty*: a magic forest, overgrown with briars, choking a royal palace full of sleeping, cobwebbed souls. She'd even pictured the handsome prince, hacking his way through the undergrowth to wake his bride-to-be. The reality had been something of a let-down – a boring street of sullen, squashed-up houses, with nothing in the way of vegetation save a few heroic dandelions in the scrappy squares of garden at the front. As for handsome princes, the only contenders for that role were a huddle of seedy-looking men, standing on the corner, arguing in some alien tongue.

Once she'd been ushered in, however, by sturdy Aunt Patricia and scraggy Uncle Bertram, there were definite compensations: a massive grand piano, which took up most of the living-room and provided the perfect hiding-place beneath its black embrace. And a real parrot in a cage, with green and yellow feathers and black eyes like shiny beads, which always cried, 'Don't *go!*' in a beseeching, almost frantic tone – even if you had only just arrived. And a fantastic spooky cellar, whose damp stone steps led down, down, down, to rats and thrills and shadows. And an attic crammed with treasures, where you could spend all afternoon admiring cabin trunks festooned with foreign labels, or rummaging through piles of ancient books, or nursing battered teddy bears, or dancing to an old musical box that played the *Skaters' Waltz*. And no one said, 'Don't touch!' or cared if you got dirty, or made you wash your hands. And she mustn't forget the kitchen – a kitchen full of smells and foods they didn't have at home – goulash, garlic, poppyseed cake and great cauldrons of red cabbage (which wasn't red but purple, and had apples in and raisins, totally different from the pale soggy stuff her mother served at home).

She stumbled on a loose paving stone and almost lost her footing, but at least it jolted her back to the present. Fixated on the past, she had been blind to her surroundings, but now she noticed with surprise that even Wildwood Grove had definitely come up in the world. Burglar alarms bristled from the houses, and almost every door boasted solid brass fittings and elaborate holly wreaths. Bay trees preened in fancy tubs, and even pairs of smug stone lions lent status to the properties, whereas in her childhood, all that stood outside front doors were shabby prams or empty milk bottles.

As she reached Aunt Patricia's house, she could feel her heart pounding through her chest. Staring up at the brick façade, she seemed to fall into a time warp. The place looked just the *same*, its small square of cracked and dingy paving a shameful contrast to the terracotta tiling that graced the two adjoining homes. And instead of carriage lamps or fancy Roman numerals, a dirty, plastic figure 9 hung on the unpainted door, lurching to the left, as if drunk or incapacitated.

She turned abruptly on her heel and made to walk away. Why try to make amends, when her only crime was to marry someone her aunt had never met but still despised? And she had no wish to confess that the marriage hadn't lasted; that Stefan had gone running back to Hamburg with a younger female in tow. Or – hardest blow of all – that Stefan Junior had joined him, at the age of twenty-one. Her aunt would crow in triumph: 'I told you so! You can't trust bloody Germans.'

The thought of her lost son and husband brought the usual flood of sadness, overlaid with guilt. Was something basically wrong with her, that she couldn't maintain close relationships? If so, why scupper the chance of repairing one that, once, had meant so much? As a child, she had often secretly wished that Aunt Patricia were her mother. Her real mother was a stickler for small suburban proprieties: clean handkerchiefs and tidy rooms; hats and gloves for shopping trips; no elbows on the table or talking with one's mouth full. Patricia, on the other hand, was a rebel and eccentric who carved her idiosyncratic way through the blazing jungle of life. Now, she was less convinced. Surely a rebel wouldn't condemn the entire German race? Yet, however ambivalent her feelings, she had to go through with this ordeal and at least see her aunt once more.

She smoothed her hair, took in a few deep breaths, then opened the gate and walked up to the front step. The doorbell made no sound, not the faintest trill. Was it out of order? She rang again, heard nothing but a lazy plane droning overhead. Confused, she seized the knocker, gave it an emphatic rat-tat-tat. At least two minutes passed – two centuries, by the feel of them. Her aunt *must* be there, expecting her – Derek had phoned again, just yesterday, confirming the arrangements.

She was about to try next door, in the hope they might possess a key, when a tall, dishevelled, boyish figure flung open the front door. 'Alice?' he enquired, thrusting out his hand. 'Derek told me you were coming. I'm very happy to meet you. My name is Hans – Hans Kaufmann.'

Immediately she recognized the accent. How could she not, when it was so similar to Stefan's? And a German name, of course. But why a German in the house, for heaven's sake, when Patricia detested their whole nation? She knew her aunt had lodgers. Derek had explained that they paid a peppercorn rent in return for helping out, since Patricia was now widowed and had become increasingly frail. But she had assumed the lodgers were female – conventional English matrons, probably getting on in years – so the sight of this barefoot young Bohemian, with his dirty T-shirt and mop of greasy hair, was something of a shock.

'Come in, come in,' he was urging, holding open the door.

His English was near-perfect, yet his intonation – *Stefan's* intonation – made her all but weep. 'Where do you come from, Hans?'

'Hamburg.'

Stranger by the minute. Should she *tell* him she'd been married to one of his fellow citizens? Or had Patricia already informed him of the fact? 'How *is* my aunt?' she asked, deliberately changing tack.

'In her mind, she's extremely well. But her legs are very weak.'

As he steered her through the hall, she looked around in amazement. Like the outside of the house, it seemed totally unchanged: the same dark claustrophobic paintwork and claret-coloured carpet she remembered from her childhood. But how *could* it be the same? Carpets wouldn't last sixty years without fraying into holes.

'She can't walk upstairs, so she lives in the back room now. Me and Gerhard moved her bed down about two months ago.'

'Gerhard?'

'My friend. From Cologne.'

Almost unbelievable. *Two* Germans in the house!

'Gerhard's out. He's working. But would you like to meet Yasameen?'

'Er, yes ... No ...' She was babbling from sheer nerves. Shouldn't she greet her aunt first? And who on earth was Yasameen?

As if in answer, a small, dark-haired, sallow-skinned young girl came gliding down the stairs and shyly shook her hand.

'Yasameen's from Afghanistan,' Hans explained. 'She's trying to get asylum here. But her English isn't good.'

'So how many of you *are* there?'

'Four.' He counted on his fingers. 'Me, Gerhard, Yasameen and Oxana. Oxana's from the Ukraine. She's out, too. She works in a bar.'

A veritable United Nations. Yet, now she came to think of it, her aunt had always been hospitable – Germans excepted, of course. One of the attractions of the house to a young impressionable child was the extraordinary mix of people gathered round the table. Although her mother might disparage these 'lame ducks', to *her* they had seemed wonderfully exotic: Hungarian refugees, Jewish rabbis, with barbarous accents and beards to match, Polish escapees, South African freedom fighters. Her aunt and uncle were childless (whether from choice or misfortune she was never to find out), but they filled their house with *adult* children: benighted souls without homes or lands or bearings, who needed food and shelter. Only now did she realize how much it must have cost – and not only in terms of cash. Patricia and Bertram might be bigoted, but they were generous to a fault – invited the whole world for Christmas, not just relatives. She recalled the babble of different accents, all interrupting each other; the comfy, black-garbed females who sat her on their knee; the whiskery old gaffer who'd sing Romanian carols; the weird chap from God knew where, who always brought his violin.

'Shall we go and see Patricia now?' Hans asked.

'Yes. Yes, of course.' Could he *tell* how nervous she felt, hear the tremor in her voice?

He gave a gentle tap on the door of the back room. That had been the dining-room, scene of the festivities. Entering it now, she was startled by the change. No big mahogany table or broad-shouldered, generous sideboard, laden with Calvados and Cointreau, slivovitz and schnapps: gifts from all the guests. Just a shabby old armchair, a chest of drawers, a bed – and, in the bed, a small, shrunken woman with thistledown white hair and watery blue eyes.

'*Aunt*,' she whispered, tiptoeing over, as if the slightest noise might snuff the remaining life from this fragile figure in its long-sleeved flannel nightgown. Where was the big-boned rebel she recalled, with her flamboyant jet-black hair, piercing gaze, high-pitched, bossy voice?

That voice was muffled now, a mere shadow of a voice, yet its warmth was unmistakable. 'Alice, what a wonderful surprise!'

She nodded, too overcome to speak, sat gingerly on the edge of the bed and reached for the scrawny hand.

The fingers gripped her own, as if in reconciliation. 'I've been looking forward to seeing you so much.'

'Me, too,' said Alice. It no longer seemed a lie.

'And you look just the same, you know.'

Alice laughed – a startling sound. 'Oh, Aunt! How *could* I? I've had my bus-pass now for six whole years.'

'To me you'll always be young.'

Alice sat in silence, struggling to accept the fact that her aunt's former vast domain (job, house, husband, tribe) had shrunk to this one room. An ugly plastic trolley stood beside the bed, cluttered with jars and bottles – mainly medicines, as far as she could tell – along with toiletries, a box of tissues, a bag of sweets and a packet of incontinence pads. She felt a surge of outrage on Aunt Patricia's behalf – to have lost control of her bladder as well as of the house. Yet her aunt smelled pleasantly fragrant, of some floral talc or potion. Had Hans applied it, she wondered, washed the wrinkled face, combed the wispy hair, even changed the pad? A *German* performing such intimate tasks? The mere thought was blasphemous.

'I've bought you a present,' Patricia was saying. 'No, that's a fib. Gerhard went to the shops for me. I can't get out these days, you see. But I wanted you to have a little something.'

Alice blushed in shame. *She* had come empty-handed.

'I'm afraid it's only a token.' Patricia handed over a chunky package, wrapped in Christmas paper, with a red rosette on top.

'Am I allowed to open it now? It's still ten days till Christmas.'

'Of course.'

Alice tore off the paper to reveal a square-shaped candle in a frosted-glass container, which had a pewter angel appliquéd on each side. 'Oh, Aunt – it's gorgeous. Where did Gerhard find it?'

'There's this special shop called *Zeitgeist*, right near Clapham Common. I saw these there last Christmas, when I still had the use of my legs, and by some lucky chance they were in stock again this year. You were very taken with angels as a child.'

'*Was* I?'

'Oh, yes. And fairies – anything with wings.'

She suddenly saw herself as a kid of eight or nine, jumping from the low brick wall in their neat suburban garden, hoping to take off and fly; soar away from her mother's close-cut lawn and regimented flowerbeds to a tumultuous, tangled, wilder world. 'Thank you,' she said, touching the outstretched pewter wing. 'It's lovely, Aunt. You were always good at presents.'

'Remember those Christmas boxes I used to make for you and Derek?'

Alice nodded slowly. She *did* remember, now that she'd been prompted, although in the intervening years she had deliberately suppressed all evidence of Aunt Patricia's kindness. Yet those boxes had been works of art, first covered with coloured paper, then decorated by hand with stick-on silver stars and crescent moons, and even fir-cones and sprigs of evergreen, with a final layer of glitter sprinkled over everything. And inside each box would be at least twenty different items, all individually wrapped – skipping ropes and humming tops and dominoes and picture books and exotic sweets they never had at home. She and Derek had looked forward to those boxes for months and months and months; preferring them to any other present they received. Yet, somehow, she had blanked them out, forgotten them entirely: the love in them, the thought, the sheer amount of time required to shop and choose and wrap. That was truly remiss – to have given nothing back in return for such rich bounty, save forty years of silence and resentment. If she and Patricia hadn't both persisted in their obstinacy, they could have re-established contact several decades ago. Perhaps she was more like her aunt than she realized: obdurate, stiff-necked and too proud to admit to being in the wrong. Now, though, she was determined to make the first overture, whatever it required.

'Aunt,' she said, looking down in embarrassment – apologies weren't easy – 'there's something I want to say.'

She positioned the sprig of evergreen in the centre of the box-lid, attached it securely with sticky tape, then applied a spray of glitter. She had to admit the box looked quite professional, almost on a par with Aunt Patricia's. All four sides were shining with silver stars and moons; a contrast to the scarlet foil covering the cardboard. She'd also stuck on some miniature fir-cones found in the local park, first adorning each with a tiny scarlet bow. Now all she had to do was fill the box. She had already wrapped the presents in the same luxurious foil; spent all week selecting them: a manicure set in a smart pink leather case, a book of twentieth-century verse, a complicated jigsaw puzzle, a pair of velvet slippers in a fetching shade of purple, a box of Turkish Delight, lavender cologne, with matching talc and hand-cream, and a few silly things like sugar mice and joke-books, to make Patricia laugh. She laid each one in the box, adding layers of coloured tissue in between.

Straightening up, she eased her aching back, peering out of the window at the black and starless sky. It was still only six o'clock, but she'd decided to make an early start, in the hope of beating the traffic. As she carried the box out to the car, the cold pounced on her and nipped. Shivering, she went back for the other things: her overnight case, the bottle of champagne, the large freezer-bag of home-cooked food. As far as she could ascertain from her first visit some eight days ago, Patricia and her household lived on snacks. None of the four lodgers seemed blessed with any culinary skills, and none appeared to realize that a woman in her nineties might find it hard to cope with a diet of crisps and nuts.

Buttoning up her coat, she double-locked the front door and finally made her get-away, accelerating slowly down the road, so as not to wake the neighbours at this unsociable hour. She was relieved to see the streets half-empty and, even when she turned on to the motorway, the traffic was comparatively light.

Switching on the radio, she caught the beginning of a piano recital: Beethoven's *Pathetique*. She recalled Patricia playing it, while she and Derek crouched beneath the Bechstein, giggling, as her aunt's big feet pounded away at the pedals. Obviously Patricia's strong antipathy to Germans hadn't extended to their music. But had her feelings changed since then and, if so, why and when? They still hadn't broached the subject, despite the fact that they had each expressed regret for the war of words and long years of estrangement. After their mutual apologies (both halting and abashed), they were about to explore the whole reason for the rift, but at that very moment Hans had knocked, with a tea tray, then Gerhard came in from work, followed by Oxana, and soon it had turned into a party. Although she'd been glad to see how attentive and obliging all four lodgers were, she was still none the wiser about why her aunt had enlisted help from this decidedly strange quartet. Was she ashamed of her earlier prejudice and so had deliberately let rooms to Hans and Gerhard, in atonement for her attitude to Stefan? Or had it simply come about through chance? Unlikely. There would be plenty of different nationalities responding to the advertisement, so Patricia could have had her pick.

Alice braked hurriedly, as she realized that the cars in front were slowing to a halt. Despite the promising start, she now appeared to have run into congestion, and after a frustrating series of stop-starts, stop-starts, she came to a total standstill and sat stranded in a stream of angry motorists. There must have been an accident, or were these normal conditions for the day before Christmas Eve? She re-tuned the radio – the *Pathetique* had given way to a discordant modern piece – and tried to calm herself by listening to a talk on Scandinavian folk tales. After all, there wasn't any rush. Hans was expecting her this morning, but she hadn't told him any particular time and, as far as Aunt Patricia was concerned, the visit was to be a surprise – another sort of Christmas gift.

After half an hour of barely perceptible progress, she decided to cut her losses and pull into the next service station, to allow the traffic to clear. Besides, she could do with a proper breakfast, having eaten nothing before setting out save one small bowl of muesli.

She ordered the full English and sat lingering over her bacon and eggs, still pondering the issue of the Germans. As yet, she hadn't had a chance to mention it to Derek, because he'd been unusually busy preparing for his Christmas trip to Melbourne. In fact, at this very moment he'd be driving to the airport; he heading north from Arundel as she went south from Lincoln. Since the middle of the sixties, the pair of them had lived miles from each other, as if her own rupture with Patricia had affected him as well, extinguishing their former bond. Still, he had arranged to phone her on Boxing Day and she intended asking a few questions: when had Hans and Gerhard actually moved in? And, if their presence in the house indicated a total change of attitude on Aunt Patricia's part, then how had this occurred?

She all but broke a nail on the plastic pot of marmalade – timid jellied stuff, without a shred of peel. Her aunt's marmalade was more robust altogether, a concoction of Scotch whisky, Seville oranges and demerara sugar, which Bertram claimed could make you slightly sozzled. Perhaps she would ask Patricia for the recipe, re-create the old traditions. Whatever her aunt's views might be, prejudiced or not, she was resolved to make this second visit as happy as she could. And, as she returned to her car to resume the long, slow drive, the sun suddenly broke through, at last, as if reflecting that resolve. Instead of sullen murk and lowering sky, everything was now shining and sparkling like the glitter on the Christmas box.

'I'm so sorry, Alice. I don't know what to say.' Hans was actually crying, the tears running down his face, soaking into his sweat-shirt. 'We tried to make them wait until you got here, but they said they had to take the ... body to the hospital.'

'It's all right. I understand.'

'This morning she was fine. Yasameen got her up, as usual, and she even had her breakfast. Then, suddenly—' He broke off, mopped his eyes. 'Gerhard rang 999, but I think it was too late. I couldn't feel any pulse. When they came, they tried to – how do you say?'

'Resuscitate her?'

'Yes.' He shrugged, 'But it wasn't any good. I didn't know how to reach you. I rang your mobile, but—'

'It's turned off when I'm driving.'

'Of course. And you were much later than we expected.'

'The traffic was appalling.'

'Then we tried to phone Derek, but—'

'He's on the plane.'

'Yes. And there was no one else to phone.'

Where, she wondered, were all those people who had once thronged this house at every major festival? Did none of them still keep in touch, or were *they* all dead, as well?

'When the ambulance had gone, we just sat around, not knowing what to do. Then the police arrived and asked us lots of questions.'

'Oh, I'm sorry, Hans. How awful!'

'They left a number for you to call.' He fumbled in his pocket, withdrew a scrap of paper.

She took it without reading it, unable to cope with the police as yet.

'Shall I make you a cup of tea?' Hans asked.

'No, thank you.'

'Or would you like me to go and leave you on your own?'

She nodded. 'Just for a while.'

She needed time to take it in; hardly knew what she was feeling: grief, shock, disbelief, all curdled and confused. Hans was openly weeping, yet *she*, the niece, the relative, was sitting there dry-eyed. She glanced around the room. The bed was dishevelled, the curtains were still undrawn, and Patricia's plastic trolley had been shoved into a corner. Things had fallen to the floor: a tube of hand-cream, a hairbrush, the packet of incontinence pads. Mechanically she began to tidy up, stripping the bed, drawing the curtains, clearing the clutter from the trolley and putting everything away. Best to keep busy – that had always been her policy – and with Derek gone for a fortnight, there would certainly be a huge amount to do. She'd had enough experience of death to know the grim routine: death certificate, funeral, solicitors, estate agents ... But what about the lodgers? How could she sell the house, evict them?

Appalled, she sank into her aunt's armchair. She had better phone Derek as soon as he touched down and discuss a plan of action. Except that would make him worry; spoil his longed-for trip. And it would be pretty pointless anyway, since neither of them could achieve much when everything was shutting down for Christmas. In fact, her wisest course of action might be to drive straight home and return next week, when things were back to normal. No – she couldn't face the thought of being stuck in all that traffic again. Besides, it was hardly fair to leave the lodgers in limbo, uncertain of their future. She knew they had no plans for Christmas – Hans had mentioned it on the phone last week – none of them returning home, or visiting friends or relatives.

Uncertainly she rose to her feet and stumbled to the door. As she pushed it open, she all but collided with a tall, curvaceous girl, dressed in leggings and a sweater.

'Hi,' the girl said, her accent noticeably similar to Hans's. 'I was just coming to see if I could help in any way.'

'No, thank you,' Alice said politely, wondering who this stranger was.

The girl supplied the answer. 'I'm Gerhard's girlfriend – Ingeborg, and I've just arrived from Cologne. Your Aunt Patricia said I could stay for Christmas. But, of course, things are very different now, so, if you like, I'll leave.'

Alice shook her head vehemently. Nobody must leave. All at once, she knew what she must do, as if Patricia's voice were speaking to her from some realm beyond the grave.

'*You* must host Christmas, Alice, here in this house, as I did every year.'

Alice stood stock-still. This was the *old* Patricia – her voice forceful and insistent, a voice that had to be obeyed.

'Invite anyone who wants to come; anyone with nowhere else to go.'

'Including *Germans*?' Alice asked, with just the ghost of a smile.

'Germans in particular. Make them welcome. Share everything you have.'

Immediately Alice began running through the plans; her previous indecision having vanished now entirely. The food she had brought from home would do for Christmas Eve, and the gifts in Patricia's Christmas box could be shared among the lodgers. And she would go out early tomorrow, to buy *more* food, *more* gifts; buy a turkey and a Christmas tree, tinsel, holly, evergreens – return in time to make mince pies, dress the tree, wrap the extra presents.

Ingeborg was looking at her, clearly bewildered by the silence.

Alice flashed her a smile, although her head was whirling with questions: would she find a table big enough and half-a-dozen chairs? Was she too late to get a decent turkey, and where was the best place to try? Would the kitchen boast a carving knife and a large-sized baking tin? Should she make her usual sausagemeat stuffing, or something more adventurous like cranberry-and-chestnut?

'I'm sorry,' she said finally. 'I was just thinking about Christmas. 'Please do stay, Ingeborg. I hate the thought of you leaving when you've only just arrived. In any case, I want to cook a proper Christmas dinner for us all – you and Gerhard and the other three, and any of your friends who'd like to come.'

'But are you sure? I mean, you must be very … sad.'

Alice nodded. Of course she was sad. Yet also desperately relieved to have this chance to make proper expiation. Christmas was the season for rejoicing, so death and grief would simply have to wait.

'I'm absolutely sure,' she said, moving into the hall. Hans and

Gerhard were standing by the staircase, both looking apprehensive. Perhaps they feared she was going to banish them; play the role of greedy, selfish relative, whose sole concern was to get her hands on any assets going.

'I've just explained to Ingeborg,' she said, 'that I think we should all spend Christmas together. Then we can talk about the future. Patricia would want what's best for you – I know that.'

And she extended both her hands in welcome, acclaiming, on her aunt's behalf, these charming, guiltless, blameless, harmless *Germans*.

Thirty-nine

Brian watched the parade of cases circle round the baggage carousel, praying to his new-found God: 'Don't let mine come! Don't let mine come!' If, by some kind stroke of fate, his old, blue, battered suitcase had been left behind in Italy, he would have the perfect reason to return – to wing back to Sorrento. To Firorella. To love, romance.

A cruel two seconds later, the wretched thing came bumping along, clumsily jostling its sleek aristocrat of a neighbour: a stylish case in oyster-grey, without a single scuffmark. Number One priority: invest in some new luggage. Number Two: splash out on new clothes – a pair of dangerous jeans, maybe, and an arty polo neck, black and daringly tight – even a smart cream linen suit, if he could rob a bank or two. In truth, he needed a complete makeover, to be worthy of Fiorella – the most enchanting female he had ever met; ever even dreamed of in his most uncensored fantasies.

As he grabbed the case, his mobile rang. *Fiorella*! Ringing him. Missing him. Gutted that he'd left. Abandoning the case, he scrabbled for the phone and strode away a good few paces to a quiet corner of the concourse. Whatever happened, his colleagues mustn't overhear, and two of them were standing perilously close. Having kept his liaison secret for the duration of the trip, he had no intention of blowing it, now that they were all about to disperse. He could imagine their sense of disbelief if they discovered that their credit-controller, reputed for his dogged hard work and marital fidelity, had actually spent the last three nights making tempestuous love to an Italian girl barely out of school.

'Darling,' he whispered, once safely out of earshot, 'I just can't tell you how— Oh … Audrey. It's *you*.'

'What d'you mean, *me*? Who did you think it was?'

His cheeks were flaming as he tried to explain away the 'darling'. His wife wasn't a suspicious type, thank God. Why should she be, indeed, when never, in their seventeen years, had he so much as looked at another woman? Fortunately, she soon dropped the subject and moved to safer territory. How had he got on? Had he enjoyed the break? Managed to relax, for once?

'*I'd* say! It was fantastic, the whole thing. They laid on a full programme – coach excursions, boat trips, a dinner-dance on Saturday night, and a really swish cocktail reception, the first evening. You should have seen the drinks – stuffed with chunks of fruit and stuff, and so strong they left you reeling! Such a shame you couldn't come.'

To think he had actually been nervous about going on his own – a travel-virgin, who hadn't ventured further than the Isle of Wight, braving the perils of 'abroad' without the comforting presence of his wife! Yet if Audrey *had* accompanied him, he wouldn't have strolled out for a breath of air on that first lonely Friday night (too shy to socialize, and shit-scared of getting smashed), and met the young Italian *signorina* weeping on the terrace. Tears had always moved him, made him feel protective, duty-bound to help.

'Yes, I should be home quite soon – say, forty minutes, by the time I've got through Customs and waited for the bus.' 'Home', he mused, where *was* it now? The answer came immediately: in Fiorella's arms.

'No, of course I haven't forgotten it's my birthday.' He had been dreading it all year – the big four-O – and certainly hadn't mentioned his age to Fiorella. Thirty-nine would sound like Methuselah to a girl of just nineteen. He'd been terrified she'd notice the fold of flesh around his stomach (he hated the word 'paunch'), and had done his best to hold it in, pass it off as muscle. Although, once he was in bed with her, nothing mattered any more save the miraculous fact that a short, sandy-haired, freckled bloke, with no language skills – no skills at all apart from checking invoices and chasing crafty debtors – was actually pleasuring an exotic girl twenty years his junior, who not only spoke good English but had clearly studied the *Kama Sutra* as one of her set texts.

'Yes, of course I've missed you. Tell the kids I can't wait to see them.' Extraordinary – and shaming – how skilled he'd become at lying, in just the last few minutes. He hadn't so much as thought about his family, not after Friday night.

'Love you, too.' He *did* love Audrey – loved her as he'd love an affectionate cocker spaniel, or a comfortable old coat. Which meant he should be feeling hideous guilt at betraying such a decent, dependable wife. Instead, his mind was exploding with passionate eruptions on the scale of Mount Vesuvius, so full of gushing steam-jets and wild volcanic fire, there wasn't room for guilt. And, yes, he had actually seen Vesuvius – he, the boy from Peckham, who had grown up in a family where a holiday meant a day-trip to Southend – gazing out at its brooding bulk across the fabled Bay of Naples.

'Look, I'd better go, dear, or I'll be late for supper. And actually I'm starving.' That was true, at least. Starving for Fiorella; hungry for her silky thighs; ravenous for her breasts, voracious for her shaggy bush, so provocatively dense and dark.

He clicked the phone off and returned to find his suitcase, now one of the few stragglers, circling round disconsolately, as if it had lost all hope of being united with its owner.

'Hi, Brian! We thought you'd gone.'

He turned to see his boss, Rebecca – a tough, terrifying blonde – still lingering by the baggage carousel, with Len, the office manager.

'Er, no,' he mumbled, blushing. 'I had to ring my wife.'

'Well, it was great to have you with us. And thanks for contributing so much to the weekend.'

Much? He couldn't recall contributing anything at all – to Fiorella, certainly, but not to Hawkes Recruitment. Was Rebecca being sarcastic? She was renowned for her sharp tongue.

'See you tomorrow – and make sure you're on time. It's no good pleading jet-lag!'

He gave a nervous smile, assuming she was joking. He had never, once, been late for work. The entire company was aware of the fact; teased him for his plodding punctuality.

'Yes, back to the grindstone,' Len bantered, waving goodbye, as the pair sauntered off together. Thank God, thought Brian, dallying a while, to ensure he wouldn't run into them again. It had been something of a strain, consorting with the top brass for every meal and excursion, as well as at the seminars. To tell the truth, he'd been amazed to have been invited on the trip at all. Normally, these 'feel-good' jaunts were reserved for the top fee-earners, to reward them for the business they brought in. *He* had been included on account of his long service, and it was indeed a rarity to stick around for fifteen years in the same consultancy, although in his particular case, it was due more to lack of ambition than to undivided loyalty. All that had changed, however – and changed in one weekend. Now he was *fiercely* ambitious: ambitious for Fiorella and some kind of future with her. Whatever the obstacles (all but insurmountable), he had somehow to transform a fleeting holiday romance into a permanent – but secret – part of a new enterprising life.

Having found his way to Customs, he stumbled through the channel marked 'Nothing to Declare'. Another huge deception. He had so much to declare, he was becoming distinctly worried about how he would sit through his birthday dinner without arousing suspicion. Surely, the moment they laid eyes on him, Audrey and the kids would notice he was different: taller, younger, fitter, more imposing.

He spent the bus-ride trying to compose himself – not easy, when everything he saw sparked memories of Sorrento, if only in sad contrast. The sullen clouds and spitting rain were so different from the unwavering smile of the South Italian sky, and these mean, grey, shabby streets seemed a world away from the radiant Amalfi coast. He had never seen such colours: the rich, wild, shouting crimson of hibiscus; the emphatic blue of the sea; the gold and scarlet dazzle of the sunsets, paling to mingled amethyst and amber. Even Fiorella's underwear was an astounding bright-hued pink, which set off to perfection her exotic olive skin.

As he alighted from the bus and trudged, head down, through the drizzle, he strove valiantly to drop the role of lover, and resume that of husband and father; to wing away from Italy and ground himself in Hounslow, in puny Nuffield Close.

His steps faltered as he neared his house. Only now did he notice how small and cramped it was, compared with the Hotel Paradiso: a spectacular white building, perched high up on the cliff top and looking down at a grandly rugged coastline. It truly had been Paradise; now he was plunged back into purgatory.

He stood motionless a moment as a plane roared overhead. People often pitied him for living near Heathrow, although he had become so immune to the constant noise, he barely even heard it any more. Only today did he keep craning his neck to watch every passing aircraft, imagining himself on board again, flying back to Fiorella, and remembering quite different sounds: motor launches purring across the bay; music throbbing from moonlit bars; Fiorella's laughter: a gorgeous, girlish giggle he longed to bottle like the rarest wine.

Arranging his features in what he hoped was a dutiful expression, he inserted his key in the door. How dark and narrow the hallway seemed, after the palatial hotel foyer, with its antiques, its gilt-framed paintings, its mosaic floor and dramatic marble staircase. The staircase *here* was carpeted with cheap and well-worn cord, and the only picture to be seen was an unflattering wedding photograph in a tacky fake-wood frame.

'Happy birthday!' Audrey cried, rushing out to greet him. She, too, had changed – extraordinarily. When he'd left her on Friday morning, she hadn't looked so matronly and mousy. But, of course, now he was judging her by completely different standards. Fiorella was elegantly slim, and her hair was so assertively dark it would make any average blackbird fly off in despair.

'Welcome back, Brian! Gosh, you're drenched. Let me take your coat, dear.'

Kindly, caring Audrey, shaking out his mac, then fetching him a towel to dry his hair. And all he was thinking was did she *have* to wear such unflattering old shoes, when Fiorella pranced about on daring red stilettos?

'Hi, Dad! Good trip?'

His son had now come slouching into the hall; a fresh crop of acne covering his chin. 'Yes, fine,' Brian said, averting his eyes. Italian children were beautiful. He had seen them in the cafés, with their lustrous eyes and shining jet-black hair. *No* one – he would swear to it – had acne in Sorrento. 'How's things?'

'OK,' Gary mumbled. His son wasn't one for words.

'Where's Mags?'

'Messing around with your birthday cake.'

'Sshh, Gary, you weren't meant to say,' Audrey intervened. 'The cake's a surprise, remember.'

'Don't worry,' Brian said tactfully. 'I didn't hear a thing.' Grabbing his case, he dragged himself upstairs. 'I'll just have a wash – won't be long.'

'Yes, supper's ready when you are. I'm longing to hear about your trip!'

Once in the bedroom, he glanced with distaste at the skimpy curtains and faded candlewick bedspread. Where were the floor-length velvet drapes, looped with golden tassels; the goose-feather duvet and luxurious counterpane; the awe-inspiring ocean-view? And why were things on such a puny scale? In the Hotel Paradiso, the bed was so vast there was room for him and a *dozen* Fiorellas. And a bevy of staff, to fulfil his every need, addressing him as *Signor*, which made him feel that he was, indeed, the owner of a harem.

'Dad! Dad!' Mags burst in and flung herself upon him. 'Happy birthday! Your present's downstairs. D'you want to open it now?'

'Let's do presents after supper, shall we?' He realized, with a niggle of shame, that he should have bought gifts for *them*. He'd neglected his own family, while showering his girlfriend with long-stemmed scarlet roses and the most expensive chocolates in the shop. 'See you in a moment. Go and keep my chair warm!'

Alone again, he stared at his reflection in the mirror. Strange how all the things he usually disliked about himself no longer bothered him in the slightest. Fiorella *liked* his freckles; called them by their Italian names: *efelidi* and *lentiggini*. Yes, two separate words for freckles in Italian, which surely imbued them with importance. Indeed, both words had such a ring to them that what had seemed a blemish in mere English became instantly attractive, a source of actual charm. And his sandy hair had also been transformed and was now as near as dammit to auburn. Even his flabby chest and stomach had become, magically, a six-pack.

Wiping the smug grin from his face, he trudged downstairs and took his place at the table, which Audrey had laid up with a festive cloth. But no obsequious waiters were bustling back and forth, pulling out his chair, fetching his aperitif, spreading a damask napkin on his lap. And the bowl of plastic fruits, as centrepiece, seemed almost an affront, compared with the impressive cornucopia that graced the marble sideboard in the Hotel Paradiso:

melons, mangos, pomegranates, piled high in wild abandon, topped with nectarines and passion fruit, entwined with fresh green vine-leaves. He stared disconsolately at the podgy plastic banana in a lurid shade of yellow, the brick-red plastic apple. This very morning, at breakfast, he'd been presented with a platter of ripely fragrant papaya – a far cry from his usual porridge oats.

'Gary! Don't pick your nose at table,' Audrey reproved. 'It's disgusting!'

'Worse when he picks his spots.' Mags made a rude face at her brother.

'Fuck off!' Gary muttered, giving her a swipe.

'*Language*!' Audrey reproved. 'And be quiet, the pair of you. Dad doesn't want you bickering.'

Dead right, thought Brian. Wasn't he too young to have these uncouth teenage children? In just the last three days, he'd become a bachelor again – a lad, a stud, a Romeo.

'I got all your favourite things for supper,' Audrey said, setting down four small glass dishes. 'Prawn cocktail for starters and …'

Prawn cocktail – his favourite? His tastes had clearly changed since staying at the Hotel Paradiso. *There*, prawns were the size of small lobsters and came sizzling hot, and giddy with garlic, whereas these were tiny, cold and tasteless, and coated in an unpleasant pinkish sauce, the texture of unset blancmange. 'Great!' he enthused, swallowing a mouthful. As well as running the house and coping with the kids, Audrey worked in their local hardware shop six half-days a week, so the least he could do was show a bit of gratitude.

'Now let's hear all about your jaunt,' she said. 'How was Italy?'

'Really great! And *hot*! I can't believe how chilly it seems here.'

'The coldest May since 1941,' Mags put in, wiping her hands on the tablecloth.

'No, since 1902,' Gary contradicted.

'1941. I heard it on the News.'

'I did, too. You're wrong.'

'Stop it, children. Can't you ever agree?'

'No,' said Gary. 'And we're *not* children.'

'Well, you behave like babies, a lot of the time. And, Mags, I don't know why you're eating with your fingers. Can't you use a spoon?'

'I haven't got one. It's Gary's fault. He laid the table.'

Who, Brian wondered, blanking out the dreary exchange, had chosen his children's names? He suspected *he* was the culprit, but, of course, all those years ago, he simply hadn't known about the poetry in language. Fiorella meant 'little flower', and she *was* his flower – his long-stemmed scarlet rose, his hot-pink peony. Her second name was Margarita – again floral and poetic, and a world away from 'Mags'. Italian names were so much more romantic. He should have christened his son Benvenuto, or Massimiliano – something brimming with passion and lush with lilting syllables. And was it too late to change his own name? Perhaps he could become Fiorenzo, by deed-poll, or even Michelangelo – an artist and a genius.

'So what did you do all day, Brian?'

'All day' was safe enough. He and Fiorella had been forced to stay apart till nightfall. 'Well, in the mornings the whole team got together. On the Saturday, we had a sales seminar, and, on the Sunday, all the different departments had to discuss their biggest problems and frustrations, then brainstorm solutions, or come up with more creative ways of tackling them.'

'God! What a yawn.' Gary shovelled in the last of his prawns, a gloop of sauce dribbling down his chin.

'And we also had a session on time-management – you know, how time is money, so we have to set priorities and—'

'It sounds a laugh a minute,' Gary muttered.

He had to agree, it hadn't been exactly life-affirming. The jargon always riled him, for a start. Phrases such as 'hybrid ventures' made him think of roses, and why, he'd wondered, as the discussion ebbed and flowed around him, did people say 'proactive', rather than, simply, 'active', or use words like ideation and synergistic, which he could barely even *spell*? As for the habit of turning nouns into verbs – monetize, multitask, incentivize – it would have earned the firm a sharp rap on the knuckles, had his old, pedantic English teacher been sitting in on the sessions.

To soothe himself, he buzzed back to the restaurant, picked up his glass of water, swilled a little round his mouth, with new-found expertise, then gestured to the waiter to fill his crystal goblet. His weak head for drink had vanished overnight. He could down a bottle of Chianti now, without ending up pie-eyed, and, when it came to *amore*, remain as stiff as the bottle itself.

'And how was Rebecca?' Audrey asked. 'Did she let her hair down for once?'

'Not a chance!' Brian jetted back to Hounslow, feeling slightly dizzy from the changes of venue. 'She kept her beady eye on us all, making sure nobody was slacking, and we were all bonding and—'

'What's "bonding"?' Mags interrupted.

The answer that sprang to his lips was hardly suitable for a thirteen-year-old. Bonding, he'd discovered, was the remarkable sensation of being totally united – body, soul and spirit – with a person of the opposite sex utterly in tune with you; feeling your sweat, your cells, your juices, your so-called bodily fluids, merge and melt together. He cleared his throat, trying to dispel the image of his sperm shooting over Fiorella's breasts, like the triumphant spume cascading from champagne. 'Well, working as a team, and understanding each other's problems.'

'It's all problems, if you ask me,' Gary said disparagingly. 'Didn't you have any *fun*?'

Brian paused a moment, reflecting. Fun had never figured in his life. His own father had taught him, early on, that man was born to work, to scrimp and save, pay his taxes, and make sure he died without leaving any debts. Even with Fiorella, fun wasn't the right word. A transformative experience was more the sort of phrase he'd use. It wasn't just his freckles that had undergone a sea-change.

'Of course we did. We only worked in the mornings. Each afternoon, we went on an excursion. It was a pity you missed it, Audrey, because the wives and husbands were free all day, and had their own special programme in the mornings. On Saturday, they took a boat trip round the bay, and on Sunday they—'

'Don't rub it in! I'm green with envy as it is. But I just couldn't let Jackie down.'

Brian nodded sympathetically. He owed a lot to Jackie. If his sister-in-law hadn't been involved in a court hearing on the very day he'd left, Audrey wouldn't have had to stay behind to comfort and support her. 'Did the hearing go well?' he asked.

'Tell you later,' Audrey mouthed – not that the children were listening. A furore had broken out, on account of Gary pilfering his sister's last three prawns.

'Pipe down, kids! And, Mags, help me bring the steak in. It's sirloin, Brian. I know you really like that. With chips, of course.'

He set his mouth in the semblance of a smile. How could he expect his wife to understand that steak and chips no longer seemed a treat – not since he had sampled the cuisine of the majestic hotel restaurant, with its gourmet menu and flamboyant presentation (sultry waiters clustering in droves, offering pepper mills and parmesan, olives and obeisance)? Dutifully, however, he cut into the meat, although in truth his mind was not on food but on the far more pressing problem of how the hell he would cope tonight. Audrey would be expecting him to shag her – a welcome-home and birthday shag, all rolled into one. Yet he had a florid purple love-bite on his shoulder, and tiny grazes all down his back from Fiorella's over-excitable nails. Besides, suppose he couldn't perform? Fiorella had upped his standards, with her flat stomach and pert breasts, her enthralling micro-knickers. Stealing a glance at *Audrey's* boobs, he felt all desire dry up; his penis seeming to physically recoil as he pictured her dingy underwear. Should he plead a headache? Or indigestion, perhaps? Both seemed cruel, especially indigestion, when his wife had taken such pains with the meal.

'It's delicious,' he said, with another dogged smile, deciding he had better praise her efforts until he had worked out what to do. 'And beautifully cooked.'

'*Mine*'s not,' Mags objected. 'It's all black around the edge.'

'You said you wanted it well done.'

'Not burnt.'

'Don't be rude, Mags. Your mother's gone to a lot of trouble.'

'Actually I don't like meat at all,' Mags continued, unabashed. 'Deidre's vegetarian, and she says it's cruel to eat pigs and cows.'

'Oh, don't start that again,' moaned Gary. 'Why d'you have to copy Deidre? She's a prat.'

'She's *not*.'

'*Is*!'

Brian tapped the table with his fork. 'Let's change the subject, OK? Do you want to hear about Mount Vesuvius?'

'No, thanks,' Gary muttered. 'I know about it already. We did it in geography.'

'Did you see it explode?' Mags asked.

'No,' he laughed. 'It hasn't erupted since 1944.' In his mind, he watched *Fiorella* erupt – time after time after time. He had read about multiple orgasms, but never encountered the phenomenon for real. And Fiorella was so *noisy*: gasped and moaned and yowled, and let out strings of Italian words that sounded quite deliciously obscene. Audrey contented herself with a timid little 'Oh!' before turning over and falling fast asleep. He and Fiorella hadn't wasted time on sleep. The nights were short enough for all the things he had to learn, all the new experiences that must be savoured to the full.

'*Dad*!'

'What?'

'I asked you – twice – if you could lend me a fiver?'

He was about to say an emphatic no. Gary had to learn the hard way that every penny spent must be earned by honest work, as *he* had been taught at that age. Yet, remembering the price of Fiorella's long-stemmed roses, not to mention her chocolates (the box extravagantly large and adorned with gold rosettes), the 'no' died on his lips. 'What do you want it for?'

'Dad, you *know* what for. I've told you fifty times. I'm saving up for the new Nintendo Wii.'

Of course he knew. It was just that other things kept getting in the way: Fiorella's nipples – their intriguing milky-coffee colour; the way they sprang to attention at his touch.

'I've almost got enough, you see. I just need ten quid more, then I can buy it next weekend.'

'So how are you going to find the *other* five?'

'I thought I might ask Fred – you know, the old geezer up the road.'

Again, he opened his mouth to give his son a lecture on the evils of borrowing, especially from people outside the family. But his usual moral authority had evaporated overnight. How could he lay down right and wrong, when he was an adulterer, a bare-faced liar? 'What happened to your pocket money?' he asked – a craven bid to play for time.

'I spent it – on your birthday present.'

Chastened, he gave in, promising to go and fetch his wallet after supper.

'It's not fair,' Mags wailed. 'You never lend *me* money.'

'Look, both of you can borrow a fiver, but just this once – is that clear?' He had a worrying premonition that it wouldn't stop at 'just this once'; that he'd be showering endless goodies on them, simply to appease his guilty conscience. Where would it end, he wondered, with a surge of panic? Would he default on the mortgage, get behind with the hire-purchase payments, lose his credit rating?

'You shouldn't spoil them, Brian. I don't know what's got into you.'

He knew all right. Fiorella had got into him – or rather he had got into *her*: into every orifice, every crack and cranny.

'It's his birthday, Mum. Lay off!' Gary leaned over and put his sticky hands across his mother's mouth.

'Which reminds me,' Audrey said, pushing him away. 'If everybody's finished, I think it's time for the—' She mouthed a word to Mags, who immediately got up, giggling in excitement. 'And, Gary, clear the plates, please.'

'I'll do it,' offered Brian.

'No, you sit tight. You're the birthday boy.'

And, all at once, it hit him. He had been born at 8.15 at night, and it was now 7.56. In just nineteen minutes, he would be exactly – and officially – forty years of age: a mature and solid citizen, too old to have *affaires*, too ancient for a young bud of a girl just opening to the springtime of her life.

And yes, even now, Mags was walking triumphantly towards him, holding out a circular glass plate, on which sat a large iced birthday cake, all forty candles mockingly ablaze.

'Quick! Turn the lights out,' Audrey instructed, and Gary ran to do so, then returned to join the others at the table.

'We could hardly fit the candles on!' Mags crowed. 'Forty's a hell of a lot!'

You're telling me, he thought. Each candle seemed to taunt him as its tiny flame flickered in the gloom: 'You'll be past it soon – too old to get it up.' 'She won't fancy an old codger, with saggy skin and creaking joints.' 'She'll leave you for some Italian whippersnapper, pushing twenty-two.'

'If you blow them all out, you get a wish.' Mags had set the plate down on the table and was now hovering by his chair, her whole attention focused on the cake.

'Have you thought of a wish?' his wife asked.

He didn't need to think. He closed his eyes, however, pretending to be lost in reflection, while he spelled out not just one wish, but a whole fertile string of them. I wish for Fiorella. In my life. For ever. I wish to be in Italy. Guiltlessly. And permanently. I wish to hand in my notice at work, and be rewarded with a life-long pension and the biggest bonus on record in the entire history of the firm. I wish to splurge the whole damned lot on a life of non-stop pleasure, never stirring from Fiorella's passionate embrace, in that playground of a bed.

'Wake up, Dad!' Mags shook his arm impatiently. 'And aren't you going to thank me for the cake? I made it all myself. *And* iced it. It took me hours.'

'It's wonderful – fantastic! Thank you, love.'

'And wait till you see your present! It's something you really, really want. I saved up all my pocket money and—'

'Ssh!' Audrey warned. 'Don't spoil the surprise. Now, come on, Brian, blow your candles out.'

He drew in his breath, his whole body seeming to sweat and shake with sheer nerves and desperation. Those wishes *had* to come true. What was the alternative? Twenty-five more tedious years totting up figures, sending out accounts, sweet-talking tardy payers; then evenings spent with Audrey and the kids, doing the dishes, helping out with homework, watching *Coronation Street* (which he didn't even like). And weekends mowing the lawn, lugging back the shopping from Safeway's or the Co-op, mending leaky taps or easing sticking doors. And tepid family holidays at some safe South-Coast resort, the kids bickering and bored to tears as they all huddled in the doorway, waiting for the rain to stop in a low-grade B & B.

'Dad, have you made your wish?' Mags chivvied.

Silently he nodded.

'Well, blow for goodness' sake!'

He blew. Thirty-nine candles shuddered to extinction. One remained alight.

'Bad luck!' Mags groaned. 'Your wish *won't* come true.'

He stared at the lone candle flame. Mags was wrong. Already, his luck was changing – hadn't the candles told him that? He *wasn't* forty, but still only thirty-nine. And he would remain that age, for ever; allow Fiorella to grow a little older, while he stayed in his prime. There *was* a God – he'd found Him, along with Fiorella: God in the sense of bliss. You could believe in God, he'd come to see, only if you had attained a degree of happiness. Before this trip, he had viewed the world as bleak, chaotic, rudderless. Now, though, he had hope; a new sense of purpose, a new firm and radiant Faith. Even the hotel's location, high up on the cliff, had made him feel closer to Heaven, and he had no desire to plummet down to earth.

Dazed, he kicked his chair back, rose slowly to his feet.

'What's wrong?' asked Audrey anxiously. 'Aren't you feeling well?'

Without answering, he stumbled to the door.

'Dad! Come back!' Mags called. 'We're about to cut the cake.'

'Brian, are you OK?' Audrey was eyeing him with deep concern. She had worried about his health since the scare eight months ago, when he had suffered sudden chest-pains. Now, she booked him regular check-ups, stuffed him full of vitamins, insisted he took exercise. 'Where are you going, darling?'

Sorrento, he said silently, staggering into the hall, as if indeed in pain once more. I'm going to live in Italy, leave you all behind.

Gary had caught up with him. He, too, looked alarmed. 'What the hell are you doing, Dad?'

I'm leaving, he repeated, determined to speak up. I'm going back to Heathrow, to catch the next plane out. You'll have to fend without me from now on.

'Dad, *answer*, can't you? What's going on? Mum's worried, can't you see?'

He glanced at Gary's pockmarked face. His plain (and freckled) son – so bad with money, so shy with girls – actually concerned about him. His whole devoted family now clustering around him in the hall.

'Look, if you're upset about your wish,' Mags said. 'We can light the candles again, and you can have another go. I mean, you almost did it last time, Dad, so just blow a bit harder, OK?'

I don't *want* a birthday, he tried desperately to say. I'm thirty-nine, not forty, and I'm involved with someone else – someone really special. You've just got to understand.

The words stuck in his throat, like a wodge of birthday cake – a cake made with love by his uncouth, caring daughter. Or like a lump of steak – steak cooked with love by his dowdy, caring wife. His whole gullet was obstructed, making it impossible to speak – clogged with the presents both his kids had bought: things they'd chosen to surprise him, lavishing their pocket money on a rotter of a Dad.

'You're tired,' soothed Audrey, patting his arm affectionately. 'Come and sit down, Brian, dear. All that travelling must have worn you out.'

Still he didn't answer, just stood staring at the wedding photo; he and Audrey vowing to stay faithful as long as they both should live. In sickness and in health. In Hounslow and Sorrento.

'OK,' he said, at last, his voice so faint and rusty it was the croak of an old man.

Then, shamblingly, forlornly, he let her lead him safely back.

Birth-rage

'Holding on to anger,' Justin said, flicking back his long, fair, greasy hair, 'is like grasping a hot coal in our hands, in order to throw it at someone else. But *we're* the one who gets burned.'

Antonia shifted irritably in her seat. Wasn't that a direct quote from the Buddha? Justin should at least acknowledge his sources, rather than claiming credit for an aphorism uttered two-and-a-half thousand years ago. Frankly, she was beginning to wonder if he was qualified to run the workshop at all. According to his credentials, he was a certified facilitator and trainer (which could mean anything and nothing) and a 'former' psychotherapist. 'Former' seemed suspicious in the extreme. Had he been struck off the register for some unspeakable behaviour?

'Anger affects our health – that's been proved beyond all doubt. A study done quite recently showed that people who hold on to anger are more likely to suffer from heart disease than—'

'But, I *don't* hold on to my anger,' objected the puny little woman sitting at the front, who had been interrupting since the start of the proceedings. 'In fact, I'm always the first to try to make the peace, but the more overtures I make, the more shit I seem to get.'

I'm not surprised, Antonia refrained from saying. Minnie or Ninny (or whatever her fatuous name was) had barely let Justin finish a sentence before jumping in herself.

'Can we deal with that a little later on, Minnie? First, I'd like to explain the damage we can do to ourselves just by being angry.'

'But that's exactly what I'm talking about,' the wretched woman continued, unabashed. 'Remember those migraines I mentioned earlier – well, they invariably come on when my boyfriend makes me blow my top.'

Amazing that she *had* a boyfriend, Antonia reflected, with a disparaging glance at the flat chest and frizzy hair. And they could hardly forget the migraines, which had been described in redundant detail a mere five minutes ago.

'It's important for us all to grasp' – Justin was addressing the group as a whole now – 'that no one *makes* us do anything. We have the freedom to react or not.'

'You don't understand. Steve doesn't give me any choices. What *he* says goes, and that's that.'

'Well, you still have the choice to leave him, Minnie,' Justin said, with a conciliatory smile. 'But, look, this afternoon we'll have time and space to share our personal stories. In this introductory session, I want to focus on the health side.'

Antonia fanned herself with her notebook. Whatever else, she had to credit Justin for his patience. Despite Minnie's insensitivity, he had remained completely calm; his voice so soft and unassertive, it reminded her of uncooked dough – the yeastless kind that would never rise, even in the white heat of an oven.

'Minnie, are you OK with that – postponing your issues till later?'

'I wouldn't call them issues.' Minnie said, in her ululating bleat. 'It's a question of Steve's attitude. If he was less obstinate and selfish, there wouldn't be a problem in the first place.'

Justin contented himself with a nod, this time, before returning to his theme. 'You see, anger is like fire – a powerful force when it's used constructively, but lethally destructive if it rages out of control. As I've said, it causes heart attacks and high blood pressure. It can also lead to violence in the workplace, and destroy relationships.'

'That's what's happening with me and Steve. We're in danger of breaking up, just because he can't control his moods.'

If you mention Steve one more time, Antonia murmured under her breath, we'll *all* have heart attacks. Surely the rest of the group must share her irritation, if they only had the honesty to say. The very fact of signing up for an Anger Workshop pointed to the fact that they had problems with hostility. She tried to exchange a meaningful glance with the woman sitting on her right – a plump sixty-something, with stiff, meringue-like curls and a jutting prow of a bosom. But the matron studiously avoided making eye-contact, as if refusing to judge, or even criticize, as did the sanctimonious redhead on her left. Odd, she mused, that only three of the fourteen participants were male, when most studies proved a link between testosterone and anger. Maybe men denied their fury, or redirected it into aggressive sports.

Justin leaned back in his chair, legs crossed, the very picture of composure, although his outfit left a lot to be desired: a crumpled T-shirt, worn with scruffy denim jeans.

'As I told you, Minnie, you'll have a chance this afternoon to discuss your problems with us.'

In which case, I'm leaving, Antonia vowed. Except it would be nigh-on impossible to make a getaway. They were trapped in this small, stuffy room till six, apart from a brief tea-break when they were allowed to stretch their legs. For some inexplicable reason, the curtains had been drawn, blocking out all natural light, and she was already feeling distinctly claustrophobic. She couldn't even sneak off in the lunch-hour, since the so-called joining instructions had requested they bring food to share, so they could eat together, 'as part of the group dynamics'. Although, judging by the offerings laid out on the table at the back, the meal would hardly be a gastronomic highpoint. Her own asparagus-and-salmon quiche (made at dawn this morning) was in a different league entirely from the others' doorstep sandwiches, soggy packages of tofu, and pots of shop-bought humus. The only other home-made dish was a bowl of sludgy beans, guaranteed to induce instant flatulence, and with an unpleasant scum, like frogspawn, on the top.

'Apart from the threat to our health,' Justin continued serenely, 'we also need to recognize that anger is often a mask for *other* emotions – ones we may be frightened to express, such as fear or insecurity, or jealousy, perhaps.'

'That's definitely true of Steve,' Minnie butted in once more. 'I happen to know he's jealous of the fact that I'm better paid than him.'

'Well, he may have unmet needs, Minnie. And, actually, that's a point of interest to us all. You see, if we lack vital things in life, such as love, or a sense of belonging, or a feeling that we matter, either at work or in our families, we may use anger as a means of defence. But the irony is that if we simply blow our top, we lose any chance of getting those needs fulfilled, and so remain frustrated. What we ought to do, instead, is to recognize those lacks and—'

'I do recognize them, Justin. It's Steve who won't and can't. As far as he's concerned, there isn't any problem and it's me that—'

'For Christ's sake, shut *up*!' Antonia snapped.

Her outburst was greeted with shocked silence. She, too, felt shaken by her own temerity. But if someone didn't put a stop to these constant interruptions, the entire day would prove a write-off. She hadn't shelled out £60 to listen to some loser slagging off her boyfriend. Minnie had already had her money's-worth, whereas she and the other twelve participants were in danger of being severely short-changed. And why did the aggrandising windbag assume she had a monopoly on problems? When it came to unmet needs, she herself could lay claim to quite a few.

'Antonia,' said Justin, now turning his attention to her, 'you're clearly feeling stressed. Would you like to share those feelings with the group?'

'No,' she said brusquely. 'I'd like you to continue.'

'But the way you've just reacted is central to our theme. If we respond to someone with anger and resentment, it can damage a relationship.'

'I don't have a relationship with Minnie,' Antonia muttered defensively. 'She's a stranger, more or less.'

Justin uncurled himself from his chair and came to stand in front of her, trying to disarm her with another of his smiles. 'None of us is a stranger in this room. We've all introduced ourselves – shared our names, shared our reasons for coming here today – and that's already created a bond.'

She felt no sense of a bond – not with any of the group. And even the word 'shared' was beginning to set her teeth on edge. 'Shared' was therapy-speak, and Justin had used it twenty times already. 'I'm sorry,' she mumbled, mortified to have put herself in the spotlight. The others would resent her for holding up the proceedings, as *she* resented Minnie.

'There's no need to be sorry.' Justin's voice had changed from dough to thistledown – an attempt, she realized, to put her at her ease. 'As I told you at the outset, whatever happens in these sessions is perfectly OK. You're *allowed* to be angry, Antonia. We're *all* allowed to be angry.'

'So why did you say it was harmful?' the redhead asked, twisting her legs around the chair-rung, as if embarrassed to be speaking.

'It's harmful if it's not controlled. That's the crux of the matter, Bernadette. Anger can be a healthy force if we use it to overcome some social ill or painful situation. In fact, it's a better approach than a passive sort of helplessness, which simply keeps us stuck. But just letting fly is different altogether....'

Antonia bristled silently. He was probably getting at her, despite all his guff about anger being permitted. She stole a glance at Minnie, who was now emphatically nodding, but hadn't yet cut in. So perhaps her outburst might have done some good, however much she regretted having made it.

'We do have the ability to change the way we react.' Justin returned to his chair, draping himself languorously across it. 'Many bouts of temper are simply ingrained habits, and we can learn to replace those habits with more conscious processes.'

'Mm, mm, mm, mm.' Minnie was still nodding her head, like a mechanical wind-up toy, while letting out an endless stream of 'mm's. It was as if her voice-box lacked an off-switch, so that even if she wasn't forming actual words, it was still compelled to witter on non-stop.

'And that can result in emotional growth, improved communication and far less stress, of course.'

'Yes, yes, yes, yes, yes, yes.'

Antonia restrained herself from retorting 'No, no, *no*!' Although Minnie had now changed her tune, the effect was no less galling. Couldn't the bloody woman simply sit in silence, rather than drive the entire room berserk?

Justin glanced around the circle of faces, to ensure everyone was listening. 'And what we're going to learn today are the Ten Tools of Anger Management.'

'Mm, mm, mm, mm,' Minnie responded on cue.

Antonia gritted her teeth. Did this pest of a female intend to alternate 'mm, mm, mm' with 'yes, yes, yes' for the remainder of the day? Well, perhaps they should be thankful for small mercies. At least it was monosyllables now, rather than whole sentences. Unfortunately, however, she'd become so fixated on Minnie, she could no longer concentrate on what was being said, and had already missed the first of the Ten Tools.

'The second tool is impulse control, which means—'

Antonia jumped as Minnie ripped open a giant-sized packet of crisps. Surely she didn't intend to eat them here and now? Yes, she did – and was. Well, perhaps they'd stopper her mouth, which might silence her, at last.

No such luck. Whilst crunching loudly, the woman managed to resume her strings of 'mms' and 'yes's', only slightly muffled by the crisps. Justin appeared blithely unaware, his voice meandering on in placid, slow-worm fashion.

'And the third tool in our kit is to improve our communication skills, so that—'

'Mm, mm, mm. Yes, yes, yes, yes,' Minnie had now combined both mantras, to an accompaniment of crunch, crunch, crunch.

Antonia glared in her direction, but the woman's eyes were fixated on her bag of Golden Wonder, totally oblivious to others in the group, even to her closest neighbours, who were being sprayed with saliva, along with fragments of crisp.

'You see, unskilled communication often leads to anger. If we put other people down, or keep intruding with our own stuff instead of listening to what they're trying to tell us, it can—'

'That's just what Steve does,' Minnie exclaimed, half-rising from her chair in a fit of indignation. 'He never listens to a word I say.'

Antonia held her breath, in an effort not to scream. The 'mm's' and 'yes's' were bad enough, but now they were back to full-scale interruptions. And, Minnie, needless to say, was supremely unaware that she was demonstrating her own total lack of communication skills.

'He just *has* to be right, whatever we're discussing. If I take a different line from him, he shoots me down immediately and …'

Antonia clenched her fists so tightly the nails were digging into her palms, all but breaking the skin. Her heart was pounding at a savage rate and beads of sweat began trickling down her back, despite the fug of the room. She felt her usual horror at the symptoms, knowing what they meant: once her fury reached a certain level, she was capable of violence – that's why she was here, for pity's sake. When it came to anger, Justin was still in kindergarten. What could such a gentle-Jesus know about real murderous rage? *She* was the expert, yet the brute fact still appalled her.

She stared down at the carpet, desperate to distract herself. She must focus on its colour: a shade of dingy grey. Grey as ash, grey as cinders, grey as a dead pigeon. She wanted *Minnie* dead; knew she could kill her in cold blood. Justin's voice had ceased – ceased for *her*, in any case. All she could hear was Minnie's siren-wail, rising to a crescendo of self-absorbed complaint. In her mind, she took a step towards her, crushed her underfoot, crunched her into fragments, like a crisp.

'Now, I don't want to overload you,' Justin smiled. 'So we'll stop there, for the moment, and do a little exercise before we move on to the last Five Tools. Could you please get into pairs? Bernadette, you pair up with Barbara, Jonathan with Pat, Antonia with Minnie ...'

No, she thought. Impossible. Not to mention perilous. If she had to work with Minnie, it could end in some atrocity. But the woman was already darting towards her, crisp packet in hand.

'Hi!' she said, through a mouthful. 'Are you still mad at me?'

'Er, no,' Antonia replied. Fireworks were exploding in her head, showers of toxic scarlet sparks, burning out to black.

'I want the pairs to sit opposite each other.' Justin was trying to make himself heard above the general hubbub, as people got up from their seats and formed themselves into twos. 'But first fetch an extra chair, so there's an empty chair for every couple. Is that clear?'

Obviously not, as several of the participants looked baffled, especially the two foreigners – Dmitri from Greece and Esmat from Iran. There was further noise and confusion as chairs were fetched and couples struck up conversations. Minnie (of course) had launched, again, into the subject of her heinous boyfriend, continuing in an undertone even after Justin called for quiet.

Antonia shut her eyes. Now that they were sitting face to face, a surge of nausea rippled through her stomach, curdling its queasy contents of breakfast egg and croissant. Yet even with her eyes closed, there was no escaping Minnie: she could smell the whiff of greasy crisps; hear the whispered wail.

'Open your eyes, Antonia.' Justin's voice seemed to come from far away. 'It's essential for this exercise that you keep eye-contact with your partner.'

She forced her lids apart, transferred her gaze to the rungs of Minnie's chair. Eye-contact was a stage too far. Even the woman's ludicrous clothes seemed to drive her to irrational rage: those wide-legged purple pants, with their bands of yellow braid around the hems; the 'I'M A GENIUS' sweatshirt; the ostentatious medallion dangling round the scrawny neck.

'OK,' said Justin. 'Is everybody settled?'

There was a chorus of assent, mixed with nervous giggles. Antonia gripped the arms of her chair, needing all her concentration just not to attack the 'genius'.

'Now, I'd like you all to pick someone in your life who really makes you angry, and put that person in the empty chair. Imagine them sitting there in front of you, while you tell them *why* you're mad. Give them all the reasons. Don't hold back. Just say what's on your mind.'

'Out loud, you mean?' asked a tall girl in a kaftan.

'Yes, out loud, Felicity. It's important that your partner can hear. For example, if you choose your boss, you might shout at him, "You're an utter shit, totally unreasonable. You never listen, never give me a word of praise. However hard I work, you still complain and bawl me out". And so on and so on and so on. Do you get the idea?'

'Yes,' said Minnie. 'So if I choose Steve, I'd say—'

'Minnie, save it for the exercise, OK? Has everyone else got the gist?'

'No,' said Dmitri, in his heavy nasal accent.

Justin explained again, in simpler words, while Minnie returned to her mantra of 'mm, mm, mm, mm, mm.' She had also started fiddling with her medallion – tugging at it, chewing it, twirling it round on its chain. It was clearly quite impossible for the woman to sit still, let alone sit still and hold her tongue.

Antonia pressed her hand across her mouth to prevent herself from screaming. If she chose *Minnie* as the person who most provoked her ire, and tried to tell her why, would it stop at words, or escalate to violence? She dared not take the risk. Safer to choose her mother, or father, or one of her four stepfathers. There was no shortage of suitable candidates – she had been furious with her family since birth. And not wholly without reason. Her father had vanished when she was only two days old, leaving her mother to seek comfort with a drummer in a jazz-band, whilst, she, the new-born infant, had been more or less neglected for the thrills of Dixieland.

Justin was weaving his way between the various pairs, still issuing instructions. 'There's a second part to the exercise, but I don't want to confuse you, so let's get on with the first part, if that's OK with everyone?'

'But which of the pair is meant to start?'

'Good point, Joanne! I should have mentioned it. Whosever name comes earliest in the alphabet is the partner who kicks off. So A before B, C before D, E before F, and so on. And if you share the same first letter of your name, like Bernadette and Barbara here, well, Barbara goes first because it's "Ba" before "Be".'

Again Dmitri and Esmat failed to understand. Antonia welcomed the delay – anything to postpone the moment when she was forced to voice her anger. She had suppressed it almost all her life, save for two occasions (shameful, unforgivable) when it had spiralled out of control, like a flash-flood or forest fire. A repeat of such barbarity would be dangerous in the extreme. In fact, she'd been banking on her partner going first, hoping Minnie would monopolize the exercise, so that she herself could escape the whole palaver. Yet here she was in the hot seat – expected, indeed encouraged, to give vent to her rage.

'Have you chosen your person?' Minnie piped up, now scratching at her underarm in a quite revolting fashion, with no regard to the others' sensibilities.

'No.'

'What about your boyfriend?'

'I don't have a boyfriend.'

'You're lucky, then – spared a lot of aggro.'

Antonia raised an eyebrow, not trusting herself to speak.

'Ever been married?'

She shook her head. Was this an inquisition, or just Minnie's way of making her feel small? There had been *no* men in her life; no marriage, no romance. 'OK, I've chosen now,' she mumbled.

'Who?'

'My mother.'

'Oh, I'd never choose my mother. She's a bloody saint, my mum. In fact, she warned me about Steve, right from the beginning, told me he was trouble with a capital T. No, I'd *have* to choose Steve. He's the one that—'

'Minnie,' she muttered, through clenched teeth, 'if you prefer to go first, that's fine with me.'

'No, we can't do that. You're A, I'm M, and Justin said—'

'We don't have to follow what he said.'

'But he's in charge. And, anyway, he's watching.'

Justin was indeed prowling the room, ensuring that everyone was now ready to participate. There was nothing for it – she would have to take part, or risk drawing unwelcome attention to herself.

She fixed her gaze on the empty chair, which at least blocked her view of Minnie. 'Mother,' she whispered, feeling desperately self-conscious, 'I'm going to tell you why I'm angry.' She paused for a deep intake of breath. This whole rigmarole was quite absurd – fatuous, unnatural, unwise in the extreme. Yet she was aware of Justin's presence; his assiduous eye alert to any slackers.

'Well, to start with,' she resumed, in the lowest possible murmur, 'I consider it your fault that I never found a man.'

'Speak up, Antonia! I can't hear a thing you're saying.'

'Look,' she hissed, furious at the interruption when it was so difficult to form the words at all. 'If I want to speak softly, that's my prerogative.'

'Yes, but Justin said—'

'Bugger Justin!'

'You shouldn't swear. I find it quite offensive.'

'Well, bugger you as well, then.'

'Pack it in, you stuck-up cow! I'm not taking your abuse. I suppose you think ...'

Minnie's last few words were swallowed up in a paroxysm of

coughing. 'Bloody hell!' the woman gasped, between further guttural splutterings. 'I must have got a crisp stuck in my throat.'

All at once, Antonia emitted a long, piercing, violent screech. The pair beside her jumped, as she continued yelling at the top of her voice, 'I hate you, Mother. Everything's your fault. You brought me up to despise the entire male sex. Every relationship you had went sour and you always blamed the men. It was never *your* fault, was it? You had all these different partners, yet not one of them came up to scratch. They were all cads and shits and bastards – according to *you*, anyway. And you made me listen to all the sordid details, even as a kid of eight or nine. I didn't want to hear that stuff, don't you understand? It just frightened me, disgusted me, made me think of men as beasts. How could you expect me ever to find a man myself, when you made it sound so loathsome? I didn't stand a chance. The minute I was old enough for any boy to notice me, you killed the thing stone-dead. "Don't trust the brute, Antonia. He's bound to take advantage. You'll regret it, I assure you. You're much better off on your own." Well, I *am* on my own, and it's bloody lonely, if you really want to know.'

She went on screaming taunts, although her voice was hoarse from shouting above the other seven people also hurling accusations at invisible opponents. And Minnie's storm of coughing hadn't yet let up. Antonia turned it into her mother's cough – the hacking smoker's cough that had snorted through her childhood, frightening her with its choking, hawking, rasping sounds; its bark and snarl of death. That cough had always silenced her, drowning any arguments she had ever dared to make.

'You're completely wrong, Antonia. It's time you took a back seat, instead of thinking you know better than your elders. Anyway, can't you see I'm ill? In fact, you've driven me to this. If you keep defying me and answering back, I'll die of emphysema. Cough, cough, cough, cough, cough, cough, cough.'

'Cut that out!' she shrieked. 'And listen, for a change. I've done everything you said, Mother, kept away from men, distrusted every word they said, shunned half the human race on your account Are you happy now, proud of me – your angry, bitter daughter who's never known a single day of love?'

Somewhere, vaguely, she heard the sound of a brief, emphatic hand-clap, and then a soft voice saying, 'OK, people, draw it to a close now'. It took some time to register that Justin was calling for silence amidst the general uproar, and that she was sitting with a group of strangers in a large, bleak, whitewashed room. Yet some part of her was still alone with Mother, in their small fussy, chintzy lounge, with its reek of cigarette smoke. And, yes, her mother was still coughing, in the same terrifying way she had gasped and choked to death.

'Minnie, do you need a glass of water?' Justin asked.

'Yeah' – cough, cough, cough, cough, cough. 'I got some crisps stuck right down my windpipe. But I didn't want to' – cough, cough, cough – 'interrupt Antonia.'

'That's good of you, but go and fetch a drink now, otherwise no one will hear what I'm saying.'

As Minnie left the room, Antonia sat trembling, aghast at what she'd done. Never in her adult life had she stood up to her mother; never voiced her fury and resentment. Her mother had gone to her grave still self-righteous and reproachful; still not knowing how her only child had felt.

Justin was pacing slowly up and down, including each participant in his famous (disconcerting) eye-contact. 'While we wait for Minnie to return, let's have a little feedback from the rest of you. How was it for you all, voicing your hard feelings instead of bottling them up?'

'Wonderful!' said Jonathan.

'No, horrible,' Pat countered. 'I feel completely knackered, like I've run a marathon.'

'Yes, but there *is* a sense of relief,' Caroline put in. 'I chose my next-door-neighbour, and just to say those things to the selfish, rotten pig really freed me up.'

Her words produced a ripple of laughter, although Antonia sat grim-faced, listening to her mother's voice echoing from some realm beyond the grave, expressing outrage at her daughter's cruel attack.

'Ah, Minnie – good! You're back.'

Hardly good, Antonia thought, as Minnie burst in through the door, slamming it behind her, and immediately launching into some new tirade (though mercifully without the cough).

Justin put his finger to his lips. 'Quiet, please, everyone. We'll have more feedback later on, but right at this moment I want to explain the second part of the exercise. Will the partner who's been silent up to now move into the empty chair and play the part of the person you've just heard attacked – be that lover, brother, next-door-neighbour, colleague or whoever. Try to get into their mind and body, *become* them, if you can. And, once you've taken on their persona, I want you to respond to the charges made against you, speaking from their point of view, of course. You can take any line you choose – deny the accusations out of hand, or excuse yourself on certain grounds, or tell the person you're sorry, or try to make amends, or comfort them, or ...'

Antonia let out a long, shuddering sigh. It was too late for an apology, or comfort, or amends. Besides, Minnie *couldn't* assume the persona of her mother. The differences were just too great. Her mother would never wear captions splashed across her chest, or tinny gold medallions, or purple silk palazzo-pants. Her clothes had been uniformly black – in keeping with her moods. And she had always seemed aggressively tall, standing six foot in her stockinged feet, whereas Minnie was barely four-foot-eleven. But why fuss about such details when it would be constitutionally impossible for Minnie to assume any role but that of injured party? She was so completely self-absorbed, so concerned with 'me, me, me', she was bound to spend the time attacking Steve, despite the fact it wasn't yet her turn. In any case, if her own Mum was a saint, what could she know about a mother who got smashed on cooking sherry, or who hated her own daughter because she had her father's eyes, or kept her short of food because she forgot that children had to eat; even starved her as an infant because she had refused point-blank to breastfeed when involved with a new lover?

'OK, ready?' Justin asked.

'Yeah,' said Minnie, putting on a different voice for the purpose of the exercise – less bleat, more mewling purr. 'Darling little Toni,' she began.

Well, that was nonsense for a start. She had never been addressed as 'darling', not once in forty-seven years, and her mother loathed abbreviations. Even as a babe-in-arms, it was 'Antonia', not 'Toni'.

'I'm sorry I messed up your life, Toni. I can see the harm I've done. But at the time I was so pissed off with everything, I turned my rage on you.'

Even more ridiculous. Her mother was wholly lacking in self-knowledge and regarded apologies as surrender, to be avoided at all costs. And she would never use expressions like 'pissed off'.

'You see, if you live with the wrong bloke – or blokes – you get so cranky and uptight, you're blind to anything else. I know for a fact it can give you awful migraines and ...'

Her mother had never had a migraine in her life – only the sort of headache that accompanied a hangover. But Minnie was back to herself, of course, and the migraines caused by Steve – the only subject of the least concern in her narcissistic world.

'So I want you to understand, my little Toni, that however hard it might have been on you, I think there's some excuse for what I did.'

'No, there is *not*!' Antonia shrieked, suddenly leaping up from her seat. This woman had finally driven her to violence and deserved everything she got. She hurled herself on Minnie, ready to claw, scratch, punch, kick, slash. But Minnie instantly disarmed her by reaching out her arms and enfolding her in an affectionate embrace.

She was so startled, so unnerved, her whole body went limp, as if she'd become a corpse herself. Yet she didn't fall – couldn't fall; was supported by those arms; holding her miraculously tight, miraculously safe and close. She hardly dared to breathe as caressing hands began stroking down her back, then gently drifting up again, to fondle her neck, feather through her hair. A *lover* would feel like that, she realized with a jolt of near-disgust – the tenderness, the intimacy, the warm skin against warm skin. Should she pull away, resist?

Time seemed totally suspended as she struggled between violence and submission. She could *murder* this interfering stranger for reducing her to pap, weakening her defences, making her look foolish with such humiliating advances, such vacuous cosseting. Or she could simply surrender and savour the rare and dangerous feeling of hands gliding across her shoulders, pillowing her head, guiding her starving infant mouth towards generous, willing breasts.

Was there really any choice?

'Mummy,' she wept. 'At last.'

Charlotte Elizabeth

Jane sat, slumped in her armchair, staring out at the brambles. Their spiteful thorns seemed to tear right through her flesh, even from the safety of the sitting-room. The whole garden had changed from benevolent to treacherous, and was now rife with malevolent weeds – stubborn dock, strangulating bindweed, lethal, spiky thistles.

The doorbell was ringing, but she made no move to answer it. She hated people calling.

It rang again – a salvo – but she continued to sit motionless, pretending to be out. In truth, she couldn't bear more awkward, mumbled sympathy, or, worse, vacuous advice: 'It's high time you moved on, Jane, and put the past behind you'.

It *wasn't* the past. Her daughter's broken body had become her only present: the exact colour and configuration of the lacerations, bruises. And the cold air of the morgue seemed to chill her skin continually, even on this warm October day.

'Jane, do forgive me. I'm sorry to barge in, but—'

Startled, she turned to see Fiona from next door, actually walking into the sitting-room, armed with a couple of carrier bags.

'The side door was open and I really felt I ought to come and check on you.'

Check on her? Was she a child? A mental case?

'I've phoned at least a dozen times, but there's never any reply. And, frankly, I've been worried. I know it's early to pop in, but I'm out the rest of the day, you see, so I decided I'd better come before I left – to make sure you're OK.'

'Yes, perfectly,' she said a little brusquely. Fiona was a decent sort – kindly and considerate – all the same, she was bound to take the high line and trot out maddening platitudes: 'Yes, terrible to lose your child, but you just have to come to terms with it and carry on with life, if only for your husband's sake.'

She refused to come to terms with it. Nor did she want to carry on with life – not without her daughter. As for Ralph, he was coping better, but he had his job, of course. In fact, he had become a workaholic, to shut out his weight of grief, but it shut out *her*, as well.

'Don't worry – I shan't stay. I just wanted to bring you this.' Fiona placed one of her bags on the table, and withdrew a bare and spindly plant, wrapped in cellophane. 'I know it doesn't look much, but if you plant it now, it'll be a mass of flower in June.'

'I'm afraid I can't plant anything. Not unless I hire a gang of labourers!' Jane gestured to the thorny scrub spreading beyond the window. When she and Ralph first moved here, in the spring, her number-one priority had been to clear those vicious bushes. Yet, despite her vigorous efforts, the briars were creeping back, beginning to take over, encroaching on the house.

'This isn't just any old plant, Jane. It's a variety of rose called Charlotte Elizabeth.'

Jane tensed. Her daughter's name. She and Ralph had christened their long-awaited only child in honour of both their mothers, who had joined forces to help out, after her three miscarriages. Charlotte was Ralph's mother's name; Elizabeth her own mother's.

'D'you mind if I sit down, Jane, then I can explain?'

'Of course not.' How rude she'd become in just the last few months – keeping people standing, failing to offer tea or coffee, or even say a word of thanks.

Fiona perched on the edge of a chair, as if aware she was intruding. 'There's a variety of rose called simply "Charlotte" and several called "Elizabeth". But I wanted *both* names, to make it more specific.' She gave a sudden laugh. 'I have to say it took some tracking down. Our local nursery hadn't even heard of it, and two others said they didn't stock it. In the end, I had to order it by post from a place in Somerset, who claim to be the sole suppliers in the whole of the UK.' She paused a moment, then continued in an embarrassed rush of words, 'You see, I thought it would be rather nice if you planted it in memory of Charlotte.'

Jane made no response. Everything you planted died, so why bother growing things at all?

'And wouldn't it be a good idea for you to continue work on the garden? I don't want to interfere, Jane, but having a crack at some weeding and planting would at least get you out in the fresh air.'

'Yes, I suppose it would,' she murmured, unconvinced. All the zeal and fervour she had possessed six months ago, in her determination to transform a neglected wilderness into a little patch of Eden, had leached away through the hot and harrowing summer. Fiona didn't understand how grief was like the bindweed in the garden, its constricting tentacles throttling your whole life; choking the point and pleasure from everything you did.

'In fact, if I got you a few more of these, you could make the entire garden a memorial to Charlotte. I'd originally planned to order half-a-dozen, but I didn't want to swamp you, if you weren't keen on the idea. To tell the truth, I felt a bit mean, buying just the one, so if you *would* like more ...'

What her neighbour also failed to grasp was that depression sapped your strength; left energy for little else beyond getting up, getting dressed and going to bed again.

Fiona leaned forward, clearly trying to engage her. 'I remember bumping into Charlotte in the village, just a fortnight after you'd moved here, and she seemed thrilled with the new place. She told me how she'd hated living in London and being cooped up in a flat, and how she'd always wanted a garden, so she could keep rabbits and play shuttlecock and invite her friends for barbecues. And she was full of all the plans you had yourself – how you were going to grow your own vegetables, and build a pond and a rockery, and plant apple trees and ...'

Jane glanced down at the floor. The carpet needed hoovering. Too much to do already, without adding ponds and rockeries.

'You could make those plans a reality – make her dreams come true. Even if she's not here to see it, I have a sort of feeling she'd approve.'

Dreams never did come true. Her hopes of a large family had aborted unequivocally. First, the three failed pregnancies, then the hideous accident. Four lives lost in total. Best not to dream at all.

'Look, I'm sorry, Jane, if I've been too pushy. But promise me you'll think about it?'

'OK.'

'And by the way, I've brought some compost, too.' Fiona unloaded a package from the second plastic bag. 'Special stuff for roses. Now's the ideal time to plant, you see. If you get this rose in by the end of the month, it'll have a chance to settle, and begin to make new roots before the winter. Oh, and here's the catalogue the nursery sent, with a good three hundred roses listed. If there's anything you fancy, just give me a ring and I'll order it.'

'That's really kind.' She ushered Fiona to the door, feeling genuinely touched. Other, less compassionate neighbours might have phoned the council and complained about the jungle adjoining their own tidy, well-groomed plot.

'And, don't forget, if you need a hand clearing the ground, both Ted and I are game. In fact, he could do with a bit of exercise, so you'd be doing him a favour. All you have to do is pick up the phone, OK?'

'Yes, fine. And thanks for everything.'

Returning to the sitting-room, she stood gazing at the plant, with its printed tag: 'Charlotte Elizabeth, *rosa floribunda*.' She knew that roses had names, of course, but she'd somehow always assumed they were pompous, high-falutin names like High Noon and Duke of Windsor. A rose with her own daughter's name was something else entirely. Yet this scrawny, twiggy specimen bore no relation to her chubby, lively child. No, not a child, she reminded herself. Charlotte had been almost fourteen when she was mowed down on her bike. She and Ralph had never blamed the driver of the car. He'd been neither drunk nor careless, but he'd had a seizure and lost control of the wheel, so there was nothing he could do to avoid cannoning into the young girl in his path. He'd actually sent a wreath – one almost as big as theirs.

Listlessly, she started flicking through the pages of the catalogue, surprised by some of the names. The Ingenious Mr Fairchild, for example. Who on earth could *he* be? His rose was shown in colour: a true seductress of a flower, with an exotic head of tight-packed, silky petals in a flagrant shade of pink. There were also many foreign names – *Frühlingsmorgen, Boule de Neige, Variegata di Bologna*. And boastful, self-important names, like Brilliant, Tip Top, Super Star. So what did she do with her unassuming, English Charlotte Elizabeth? Give it away? Leave it to die?

The thought of further death was so abhorrent, she dashed out to the garden, wrenched open the door of the dilapidated shed, and seized the billhook, which had been lying idle since the spring – as *she* had been lying idle, mouldering and rusting while summer frayed to autumn. Pulling on her gauntlets, she began slashing with the great curved blade, scything nettles, dock leaves, bindweed, in a frenzy of destruction.

'Go to hell!' she shouted. 'I don't want you in my life! We moved here for my daughter, to give her space and air, so you've no right to strangle everything, overrun what's hers.'

Out of breath and sweating, she continued hacking at the undergrowth: decapitating thistles, mowing down the docks. Her first wild, bludgeoning movements were settling into a rhythm, as she laid siege to deadly nightshade, lashed out at clumps of couch grass. All her recent fury was dissolving with each stroke – fury with the ambulance for not arriving sooner; fury with the police for their intrusive, senseless questions; fury with the hospital and the officials at the mortuary; even fury with the undertakers, for being so damned *calm*. Her lungs felt as if they'd burst, as she gulped in draughts of air. These last few months, she had barely breathed at all, her body's vital processes turned low and shutting down, as if she were some tiny, feeble creature, skulking in a corner in a state of hibernation. But now life was ebbing back, as she bent and slashed, bent and slashed – her aching back and painful shoulders proof that she was functioning once more.

Forced to stop from sheer exhaustion, she limped back to the shed, fetched half-a-dozen green garden bags and began stuffing them not just with debris, but with her anger and her bitterness, her resentment and self-pity. *They* were weeds, as well, and must be torn up by their roots before they stifled any growth in her; blocked out all the light. And her jealousy of Ralph, because he could lose himself in work, was as deadly as the nightshade, and must also be ripped out. Work was merciful, she'd come to see, in that it demanded the time and energy she had been squandering on grief.

Having tied the bags, she dragged them out to the dustbins, to be collected with the other waste. Good riddance! Next, there were the brambles to defeat. Too long and thorny for the billhook, they required secateurs – and patience. Grabbing each rough stem in turn, she snipped it off and tossed it into another empty bag. Despite the heavy gauntlets, her arms were soon sore and scratched, but she could simply view the scratches as her war-scars. And it *was* a war – a war against chaos and confusion, anarchy, neglect; a war she was winning, as each bramble-stem succumbed, and the once savage, prickly bushes were cut back to the bone.

She paused to wipe the sweat from her face. It had been the warmest October on record, so far, for almost twenty years, and her clammy shirt was now sticking to her back. Her jeans were torn and filthy, and her hair had tumbled from its chignon, but she laboured on, pitting all her new-found strength against the cock-sure briars.

Only after an hour had passed, did she stop to look around her, suddenly struck by the extraordinary fact that, for the first time in her life, she'd scarcely registered the change of seasons. She'd been imprisoned in her own closed cage, while heedless nature stampeded on without her, blazing from April to October, from lush green to fiery gold. The trees in Fiona's garden seemed to be shouting, 'Look at us!', as they displayed their vivid patchwork of burnt orange, burnished copper, brilliant blowsy red. And the fallen leaves in her own patch were equally diverse: some brittle brown, some tawny, some freckled green and bronze.

She tried to inhale the colours, like an iron-rich tonic to overcome the anaemia of grief. And the tonic was demonstrably potent, because all her senses came flooding back in a rush. Her ears, once tuned continually to Radio Adversity, were now ringing with a carillon of sounds: the purr of an electric mower, a manic dog yapping its enthusiasm, a child's sudden shout of laughter from far beyond the fence, and, closer by, the robin's jaunty song. And she was breathing in a potpourri of smells: fresh-dug earth, rotting conkers, smoke from someone's bonfire, the rich fondant scent of late-flowering honeysuckle. And, when she went into the kitchen to pour herself some orange juice, it tingled on her tongue – sharp and sweet and sunny all at once. Everything she'd eaten and drunk since the day of Charlotte's accident had been so much insipid pap, but, as she bit into a ginger nut, she was aware of its strong, spicy taste, its gratifying crunch.

However, she had no intention of sitting munching biscuits, when there was still so much to do: the soil to dig, the tangled roots to clear, the trailing shoots and suckers to grub out and destroy. It would take several days, she realized now, to complete the task and eradicate the remainder of the briars. Today, though, she would concentrate on just one patch of ground: the bed outside the sitting-room, which she would designate her rose-garden.

Selecting the largest garden fork, she plunged it into the soil, dislodging a mass of ground-elder and the white, brittle roots of bindweed. The earth looked dark and moist, once she'd turned it over, writhing with fat worms, and thus perfect for her rose-bed. Attracted by the feast, a robin flew down and perched on a nearby shrub. She watched it with her daughter's eyes. Even as a tiny child, Charlotte had loved birds; always clamouring to feed the ducks or the pigeons in the park. And, once they'd moved, she was delighted by the species she never saw in London: woodpeckers and wagtails, greenfinches and jays, even a rare redwing, back in March. They had planned to build a bird-table and put a nesting-box, for tits, in the bole of the old sycamore.

Desolate at the memory, she rammed her fork into the earth again, using physical exertion to banish mental pain. There was still so much pain, but at least she had the antidote of hard, exacting work. She was also winning back some measure of control; no longer a spineless puppet, whose strings were pulled by grief. Whatever it demanded, she would be mistress of this garden, and would make it lushly fertile, as she had never been herself.

Determinedly, she plied her fork and attacked the obstinate roots, then wrenched them out by hand, dislodging the clumps of earth. The couch grass and the chickweed she tossed behind her, to save for the compost heap. She had begun making compost way back in the spring, then abandoned it, along with everything else. It would need at least a year to mature, but she *had* time now – the stopped clocks in her heart and house had restarted, just this morning.

With renewed energy, she continued digging, until she had cleared a patch of soil large enough for a fine display of roses. Fiona was right – she must buy more, although not of this variety. There could be only one Charlotte Elizabeth: unique, unequalled, singular. But she would surround it with those boastful roses – Brilliant, Tip Top, Superstar – to describe her gifted daughter. This evening, she would study the whole catalogue and pick out other varieties whose names and healing attributes she needed in her life: Grace, Salvation, Blessings, Peace. In fact, she would order *scores* of roses, because she wanted masses spare, to give away to Fiona and all her other neighbours. And she'd take armfuls to the cemetery where Charlotte's body lay – a callous and cold-hearted place, rife with unkempt graves overrun by ragwort and brazen dandelions. Those neglected plots, with no families to tend them, she would care for as her own, weeding them and clearing them, heaping them with roses.

But she must start here, with her own plot; her own distinctive rose. Still very much a novice in the garden, she wasn't sure exactly how to plant it, but she wouldn't ask for help. It must be her private task – an act of reconciliation no one else must witness, not even Ralph. He wasn't expected home till late; was going straight on from the office to a meeting, so she could stay out here till sundown, with no need to change, or cook.

Even so, there wasn't time to waste. Already, the light was fading, and the air less close and clammy. A breeze had sprung up, and was fidgeting through the fallen leaves; providing a personal cooling-fan as it teased her hair, plucked gently at her shirt.

Having removed the last of the weeds from the bed, she went inside to fetch Fiona's compost, together with the rose, ignoring her empty stomach and parched throat. Food and drink must wait – the garden took priority.

Relieved to see instructions on the back of the compost bag, she studied them for several minutes, before returning to her rose-bed to put them into operation. It seemed crucially important to do everything correctly: first, mark out the shrub's position, allowing it room to spread, then dig a fan-shaped hole, packing it with compost, to a depth of several inches. Next, set the rose in place and spread the roots out well, before covering them with compost, mixed with fresh-dug soil. She handled the plant with the greatest possible care, tucking it in tenderly and firming the earth around it, to make it feel cosseted, secure.

She had already filled the watering can, and now she doused the roots, watching with deep satisfaction as the soil soaked up all the moisture. The infant Charlotte, small at birth, had suckled so tenaciously, she'd grown vigorous and sturdy within a matter of months. This plant must do the same. It was essential that the spindly thing took root, grew tall and strong and healthy, enduring here for years. And, in order to ensure that, she must give it constant care: water it and feed it, protect it from disease, ward off every predator. And next spring it must be pruned, so that it would flower by early summer. According to the picture on the tag, the blooms were a deep coral-pink, with tiny yellow centres, the outer petals tinged with red, the inner ones paling into white. Deliberately, she hadn't removed that tag. Imperative to keep it there, spelling out her daughter's name.

Still kneeling on the moist, rich earth, she cupped both hands around the unfledged nursling, lending it support. *This* must be her daughter's resting place – not that hated grave in the weed-infested cemetery. No weed should ever grow here, no briar or dock infest her daughter's cradle, no bindweed choke, nor thistle scratch.

She would devote her life, from this day on, to keeping her daughter safe.

Heart's Desire

'I have this sort of feeling,' Ian said in a shaky voice, as he paused beside the meat counter, 'that I'm not a vegetarian any more.'

His wife stared at him in disbelief. 'But you haven't touched meat in thirty-seven years.'

He moved a little closer, examining the plump, pink, speckled sausages and bloody slabs of steak, the overlapping slices of slimy, blackish liver. In the past, such things had struck him as utterly repellent, yet now they seemed to titillate his taste-buds, as if he'd undergone a fundamental change. 'I know. I can't explain it. Unless it's some side-effect of the drugs.'

'Drugs wouldn't work like that – affect your basic tastes.'

'Maybe not, but some strange interior force seems to be sitting here inside me, dictating how I feel, saying I *need* meat now, and we should have it for the meal tonight.'

'What sort of force? You make it sound quite spooky.'

'I can't put it into words. And you're bound to say I'm a hypocrite, when I've been wittering on all these years about battery farming and cruelty to calves. But now I'm seeing things in a completely different light.'

Rita gave a sudden laugh. 'I'm quite relieved, to tell the truth. You always made me feel so guilty if I ate a chop in front of you, or bought a piece of chicken. And I'm pretty sure the Frasers won't object. They've never been that keen on my aubergine risottos and nut loaves and what-have-you. They're too polite to say, of course, but I can pick up what they're thinking. And I happen to know that Mervyn, in particular, is extremely partial to a roast. So why don't I get a leg of lamb, or—?'

'*I'm* cooking this evening, not you.'

'Ian,' she said, with a touch of scorn, 'you've never so much as boiled an egg, so how on earth are you going to manage to produce a three-course meal?'

'To be honest, I'm not sure. But some basic instinct's telling me that if I only put my mind to it, I will know how to cook.'

'Basic instinct or no basic instinct, the only time you ever tried, it was a complete and utter balls-up. Remember, when I went down with the flu?'

'That was years ago. I'm different now.'

'You can say that again!' Rita stood aside to let some shoppers pass. 'Ever since your op, you've been – well, not the Ian I married. Oh, I know it's understandable, after all you've been through, but I do find it really throws me.'

'It throws me, too. But what the hell can I do? I have to be true to this new self.'

Rita peered down at the array of meats, comparing cuts and prices. 'Well, I suppose it won't hurt if you have a bash at roasting meat. If it all goes pear-shaped, I can always take over and save us from disaster. And I'll certainly make the starter. What had we decided on – stuffed mushrooms?'

'Let's try something more ambitious. I thought perhaps a game terrine.'

'Game? But that's way over the top! Joyce and Mervyn will think we're putting on airs. When we last went to *them* for dinner, we had tinned tomato soup to start with, followed by spaghetti.'

'Well, I'll make a soup – tomato, if you like, with garlic croutons and basil.'

'You *are* getting above yourself!'

'Can I help you, madam?' the girl behind the counter asked.

'No, we haven't quite decided yet.'

'*I* have,' Ian declared. 'I'll have three pounds of best beef tenderloin.'

Rita nudged him in the ribs. 'Ian, for goodness' sake,' she whispered. 'That stuff costs a bomb!'

'Never mind the price. I want to make Beef Wellington.'

Grabbing him by the arm, she steered him away from the counter. 'What's wrong with you today, choosing all these posh things? And Beef Wellington means making pastry, which is bound to end in tears. I'm sorry, Ian, but I just can't picture you with a rolling pin in your hands.'

'That's only because I haven't tried. I always left that side of things to you.'

'But I prefer it that way, don't you see? – especially now I've given up my job. I don't want to go into retirement, at home as well as work.'

'You won't need to, dear. It's only a sort of ... hobby for me. Anyway, you're the one who keeps telling me I should get off my arse and stop mooning around all day.'

'Ian, I never said such a thing! I just worry about your health, that's all. The surgeon said you should be doing regular exercise. Why don't you go back to your gardening and leave me be in the kitchen? I know it's been a pretty dismal summer, but you could pop out there between the showers and—'

'I've lost interest in the garden.'

Rita gave his arm a reassuring squeeze. 'You're not frightened, are you, love – you know, that it might strain your heart if you start digging or mowing or...?'

He shook his head. 'Oh, I admit I was shit-scared at first about even getting out of bed, but this is something different. I just want to use my energies for cooking.'

'Well, let's hope it's only a fad. But, be that as it may, don't you think Beef Wellington's a bit ambitious for a novice?'

'No. I saw it in one of your cookery books and it looked dead simple to me.'

'What on earth were you up to, going through my cookery books?'

'Most women would be glad,' he said, edging back to the meat counter and examining the joints. 'Anne next door is forever complaining that Rodney never lifts a finger in the kitchen.'

'Well, I'm not Anne. I like things to stay the same. We've had more than enough upheaval this last year, so why change our basic roles on top of everything else? I mean, the whole reason I packed in my job was so I'd be at home to help you.'

'You have helped, Rita. I couldn't have managed without you. Christ! When I first came out of hospital, I was a total wreck – you know that.' In fact, he had concealed the worst of his fears from her, especially his constant terror that he wouldn't actually survive.

Death had been his grim companion long before he went under the knife; accompanying him to his first Outpatients appointment; continually hovering by his side during the agonizing wait for a donor; crouching over his comatose form in the operating theatre. And, when he awoke in Intensive Care, unable to eat, drink, breathe or excrete without a whole battery of frightening tubes and wires, the sinister black figure was still cruelly sitting there, whispering in his ear: 'Don't count on coming through, old chap. It's still touch and go. You could snuff it any second.' Every bleep from each of the machines seemed to be a death-cry, warning that his new heart might not function, and that even the drugs meant to guard against rejection might kill him rather than cure him. If you could expire from fear alone, he would have done so, months ago.

'All the meat's quite pricey here,' Rita said disparagingly. 'Tenderloin especially. Let's try the ready-wrapped section. They often have good bargains.'

'I don't want a bargain,' Ian retorted. 'You need top-quality meat for Beef Wellington – it said so in the book. Yes, three pounds of that one, please,' he told the serving girl, watching as it was weighed and parcelled up. 'And do you sell game, by any chance? I'd like some venison, some pheasant and a couple of pigeon breasts—'

'Ian, I draw the line at eating pigeon,' Rita hissed in his ear. 'They're filthy birds. You don't know where they've been.'

'No filthier than chickens, and you eat those without a qualm.'

'Listen, you said you'd make tomato soup.'

'I've changed my mind.'

'You'll need a specialist butcher,' the serving girl was saying, 'if you want venison and suchlike. We don't stock it here, I'm afraid.'

'Thank the Lord for small mercies,' Rita mumbled, *sotto voce*.

Having put the beef in the trolley, Ian strode towards the grocery section, running through his mental shopping list. He'd need flour for the pastry, bacon for the terrine, garlic and green peppercorns, and maybe—

'Hey! Not so fast,' called Rita, following fretfully in his wake. 'I just can't deal with this, Ian. I mean, first of all, you insist on coming shopping with me, when wild horses wouldn't have dragged you to a supermarket all the years I've known you, and now—'

'I might have said I hated shopping, but that was in the past. To tell the truth, this place is a real eye-opener – all these hundreds of foods from every country in the world. And that amazing deli counter. And the bakery and—'

'So you'll be doing the shopping, too, will you?' Rita asked sarcastically. 'Deciding on all the menus, giving me no say in the matter?'

'Let's not argue, dear.' Having disentangled his trolley from the wheels of another, larger one, manoeuvred by an elderly matron in clear breach of the Highway Code, he set off purposefully once more. 'Just let me shop today and cook the meal this evening, and if it doesn't work out, that'll be the end of it, OK?'

'OK, but I'm still worried about Joyce and Mervyn. They'll think we're awfully pretentious serving up Beef Wellington, when she always gives us pasta. And besides, red meat isn't good for you.'

Ian reached up for a packet of organic, stone-ground flour. 'Look, I've been vegetarian since 1971 and it didn't save me from heart trouble. It's genetic, I keep telling you.'

'So you say. But no one else in your family's had a transplant.'

'No, they mostly died, poor sods. I'm the lucky one. Now, let's change the subject, shall we? What do you fancy for pudding?'

'Well, it better be something simple, otherwise you'll still be slaving in the kitchen by the time the Frasers arrive.'

'OK, lemon soufflé.'

'That's not simple. What's wrong with good old apple crumble? In fact, we could buy an instant crumble-mix and a tin of pie filling and just put the two together.'

'No, I want a challenge.'

Rita sighed in exasperation as she struggled to keep up. He was now whizzing the trolley towards the fruit and vegetable aisle. 'Once, I knew exactly where I was with you – a nice cheese and onion pie, followed by rice pudding, and you'd be as happy as a sand-boy. Now you sound like Gordon Ramsay.'

'Actually, I have been thinking recently that I might sign up for a cookery course – Cordon Bleu, or something.'

'Come off it, Ian! Don't run before you can walk. Better wait and see how you get on tonight before signing up for anything. Why don't we let the Frasers be the judge? If they approve of your meal, I'll resign my post in the kitchen and leave you as head chef.'

'OK,' he said, picking out six lemons with the greatest possible care. 'Agreed.'

'It's fantastic, Ian!' Having taken a first exploratory bite, Joyce put her knife and fork down and gazed at him admiringly. 'The lightest pastry I've ever tasted, *and* the most delicious steak. It's as good as the game terrine, and that was out of this world! But, do you honestly mean to tell me that you've never cooked in your life before?'

'He can peel potatoes,' Rita put in. 'But that's about his limit. Or *was*, I should say. He's a changed personality now. And it's not just the cooking, but lots of other things.'

'What sorts of things?' asked Joyce, now sampling the steamed asparagus with obvious satisfaction.

'It's hard to explain, but I sometimes get this peculiar feeling that the Ian who came home from the hospital is not the same as the one who went in.'

'Hey!' said Mervyn, waving his fork in excitement. 'I think I know the reason why.'

'Why?' the others demanded.

'It's that woman's heart you've been given, Ian. She was probably an ace cook and you've taken on her skills in that department, and maybe some of her other characteristics.'

'Mervyn, *please*.' Joyce gave her husband a disapproving frown, to indicate that he was being extremely tactless, if not downright rude.

Mervyn ignored the frown. 'It's true, I swear. I saw this programme on the box about transplant surgery – not just hearts, livers, too, and kidneys. And some boffin from the States was saying how certain aspects of the donor's personality can be transferred with the actual organ.'

'I'm sorry, but that's rubbish,' Rita objected. 'It goes against basic common sense.'

'That's exactly what the chappie thought himself,' Mervyn said, warming to his theme. 'But he heard so many amazing stories, he began researching the whole subject, and now he's come up with pretty convincing evidence.'

'What sorts of stories?' Rita asked.

'Well, transplant patients changing their likes and dislikes; sometimes their whole way of thinking – you know, their politics might take a total u-turn, or they'd go from supporting Millwall to jetting up to Scotland for a little bit of grouse-shooting, as if they'd become a different person overnight.'

Rita shuddered in distaste. 'It sounds really creepy to me, not to mention dangerous. I mean, suppose you were given a criminal's heart. Would it turn you into a murderer or rapist?'

'Well, if the guy's proved right – and lots of people oppose him at the moment – there'd have to be new guidelines. One of the things they discussed on the programme was whether patients had a right to know precisely what they're getting. They reckoned a certain proportion might decline the organ if they didn't like the sound of the donor's personality.'

'Decline!' Rita expostulated, almost choking on her steak. 'Ian was dying, for God's sake! You can't have forgotten, surely? I mean, he was just a wraith by January. He'd made his will, said his farewells to everyone. You *cried*, I remember, Joyce, when you came round to say goodbye. We all assumed it was curtains. And then, bingo, the hospital phones us at ten o'clock at night and tells us to come in right away – they've got a perfect match. Well, by that stage, we were frantic for a donor, so if they'd told us it was Hitler's heart, or Stalin's, we wouldn't have declined!'

'Ian, is this embarrassing you, old chap?' Mervyn asked, man to man.

Ian shook his head. In truth, he had barely heard the rest of the conversation, since Mervyn's first revelatory words struck him to the core.

'So what do *you* think about the theory? Is it just a load of balls?'

Ian gestured to his mouth, indicating it was full, though, in fact, he couldn't speak for shock; silenced by this extraordinary explanation of what had been going on inside him. For the past few weeks, he had been baffled and disoriented by the changes he'd experienced, but now, at last, he understood, courtesy of Mervyn, that he had received not just Lavinia's heart, but her preferences and predilections, her attitudes and skills. *That* must be the reason he had so enjoyed cooking the meal tonight; finding genuine satisfaction in even the smallest things, such as decorating the top of the Beef Wellington with pastry flowers and leaves; whipping up the egg whites for the soufflé, grating the lemon zest. And his delight in learning new 'cookery' words (glaze, sweat, seal, *duxelle*) could be similarly explained, along with his fascination in discovering new ingredients: juniper berries, truffle oil, balsamic vinegar. It would solve the mystery, too, of why he had begun to find shopping so entrancing, instead of tedious and time-wasting, as it had always been before. Strange as it might seem to Rita, he was already looking forward to planning tomorrow's menu, and extending his repertoire in the months to come.

As Mervyn had just pointed out, Lavinia must have been a gourmet cook; someone who cared passionately about the pleasures of the table. Indeed, far from being a criminal – a rapist or a murderer, a Hitler or Pol Pot – she was a highly superior mortal, far outshining him in education and basic rank and status. Of course, when it came to hard facts, he knew frustratingly little about her, apart from her Christian name and the age at which she died (thirty-five), but at another, very different level, he had picked up a whole host of things, as if sensing them in his very bones and marrow. He was extremely lucky, actually, to have been matched up with a donor still only in her thirties. With the heart of a young woman keeping him alive, he felt he had shed two decades overnight, and, if the others hadn't noticed, it was only because they were unaware of these subtle inner processes.

'Ian, we haven't upset you, have we?' Joyce was asking anxiously, aware of his long silence.

'Not at all,' he murmured, finally recovering his voice. 'Tell me more about this programme.'

'You'll have to ask Mervyn. I didn't see it myself.'

Mervyn needed no encouragement. 'Well, they featured some of the patients who felt they'd undergone real changes after surgery. There was this young black guy from Harlem, who was into rap and hip-hop, and wouldn't know a viola from a handgun, but after his transplant, he found himself listening to bloody Beethoven, would you believe? Turns out his donor was a Professor of Harmonics at the Manhattan School of Music and an amateur viola player, to boot.'

'*Weird*!' said Rita, forking in more beef. 'But I still don't understand how the hell it could work.'

'Well, to tell the truth, a lot of it was way above my head. The chap was talking about "feedback loops" and something called systemic memory – or was it cellular memory? I can't remember now, and I didn't really grasp it at the time. But from what I *did* pick up, the gist of it appears to be that whereas people used to think that memories were stored only in the brain, now they reckon they may travel along pathways in the body and actually find their way into cells and organs and tissues and what-have-you.'

Joyce broke her bread-roll in half and sat buttering it reflectively. 'Didn't ancient tribes believe that if you ate the heart of your enemy, you'd be taking in their courage? Maybe they were on to something all that time ago.'

'Maybe,' said Mervyn, through a mouthful of potato. 'Of course, most scientists dismiss the theory as just a load of crap, but the guy does have *some* supporters and their little band are beginning to feel they need a whole new science, to explain this sort of stuff. You'd better watch out, Ian, old chap, or you'll be borrowing Rita's make-up next!'

'That's not funny, Mervyn,' Joyce said tersely. 'It's Ian's *life* we're talking about.'

'I was only joking, for heaven's sake.'

'Don't worry,' Ian said, smiling. 'I don't feel threatened in the slightest. I must admit I'm still listening to Radio 2, but I quite fancy the prospect of graduating to Beethoven.'

Rita looked up in concern. 'But if all your tastes and opinions changed, you'd no longer know who you were.'

'So what? Do any of us? Anyway, I'm bored of being me. After fifty-eight years, isn't it time for a change?'

'No,' she said vehemently. 'I like you the way you are – *were*.'

He glanced across at his wife, only now aware how pale and peaky she looked. The stress of the last year had clearly taken its toll. Her hair was limply grey; her face lined and almost haggard, and she had lost her once voluptuous curves. Hardly surprising, when she was still often in a state of high anxiety, fearing that his new heart might reject – even now, when he'd made such obvious progress. In fact, they checked on it with regular biopsies (ten of them, so far), but she still couldn't quite believe that someone else's organ could function like his own. *He* had every confidence – total trust in Lavinia's flawless heart.

'Oh, I've just remembered another thing,' Mervyn said, taking a swig of his wine. 'Some of the transplant patients had these sorts of ... hunches about how their donors died. One bloke kept having vivid dreams about crashing waves and raging seas, despite the fact he lived in Denver, hundreds of miles from the coast. Anyway, he eventually discovered that his donor had drowned in a boating accident.'

'That could be simply chance, though,' Rita frowned, clearly unconvinced. '*I* had this peculiar dream last night that I was hanging from my ankles, high up in a circus tent, but it doesn't mean I'm walking around with the heart of a trapeze artist. Anyway—'

'Well, what do you think of *this*, then?' Mervyn interrupted. 'A small girl of eight receives the heart of another kid who's actually been murdered. The child has terrible nightmares about the murder, although she's never been told a single word about it. It's all hushed up, of course, to spare her. But the police manage to catch the killer, just from what she says, because every little thing she dreams is proved to be spot-on – the time, the place, the murder weapon, the clothes the bloke was wearing.'

'Is that true?' asked Joyce, impressed.

'Absolutely. The whole case is on record.'

There was silence for a moment, then Joyce leaned forward and touched Ian on the arm. 'Have you any idea how *your* donor died?' she asked him tentatively.

'Not a clue. I did hope to meet the family and find out more about her, but they didn't want to know.' He took a mouthful of pastry, relishing its rich, buttery taste – the first of many successes, he hoped. 'I can understand that, actually. If you lose somebody you love, it must be pretty galling to come face to face with a stranger who's – you know, nabbed their heart.'

'It could be consoling, on the other hand,' Joyce observed, 'feeling their loved one hadn't died in vain.'

'Well, if *I* ever met the family,' Rita said, 'I'd go down on my knees to them in gratitude.'

Maybe she wouldn't, Ian reflected, if she were ever to discover how obsessed with Lavinia he'd become. Ever since the surgeon told him that the match was so perfect, it was like having the heart of a twin, he had felt an extraordinary bond with the woman. As an isolated only child, he had always wanted a twin, and preferably a girl twin. And now, towards the twilight of his life, his dream had come true, in part, at least; turning twilight into the blaze of the midday sun.

'I reckon it was a car crash,' Rita said, refilling Mervyn's glass. 'I mean, to die so young ...'

'Well, it might have been cancer,' Joyce put in. 'My poor sister died of bowel cancer and she was only thirty-three.'

Ian grimaced in distaste. He refused to believe that Lavinia had been smashed to pieces in some gory pile-up on the motorway, or had perished from an unromantic bowel disease, let alone been murdered. No, she had fallen from a horse – a refined, high-spirited Arab – while out hunting or playing polo. She moved in those sorts of circles – he'd gathered that from the vibes he'd been receiving; vibes he couldn't rationally explain, but which carried deep conviction. He also knew that she was exceptionally courageous. He had seen her in his mind, jumping five-bar gates on her magnificent chestnut mare, or galloping flat out over field and furrow; her long, luscious, jet-black hair streaming out behind her.

'Such a shame you couldn't meet her family,' Joyce said with a sigh. 'Then you'd feel more connected.'

I couldn't feel *more* connected, he stopped himself from saying. The others wouldn't understand, and how could he expect them to, when he himself was so bemused by the whole extraordinary process? Even this room, which had always seemed quite adequate in his pre-Lavinia days, was beginning to strike him as an eyesore. That bile-green, squiggled carpet was hardly very tasteful, and the reproduction furniture had never looked more tacky. Lavinia, he felt sure, would own Persian rugs and genuine antiques.

'Yeah,' said Mervyn. 'There was this case of a man with cystic fibrosis, whose lungs were crap, though his heart was in good nick. Apparently, if you're replacing someone's lungs, it's easier to remove their heart as well, and give them a double transplant – heart *and* lungs. So the poor bugger had that done, and his existing heart was transplanted into another chap, who was waiting for a donor. And, to cut a long story short, the two men eventually met and got on like a house on fire – which was only natural really, when one had the other's heart.'

Ian nodded in assent. People talked about the bond between a husband and wife, or a parent and child, but the closest possible tie was, he knew, from personal experience, between donor and recipient.

'In fact, the younger guy got married two years later, and you don't have to guess who he chose as his best man.'

'What a lovely twist,' Ian chuckled. 'I bet it made the papers!'

'Yeah, splashed all over the lot of them. The poor bride played second fiddle.'

'Well, any more for any more?' Rita asked, brandishing the carving knife above the remains of the Beef Wellington.

'I'll do that.' Ian all but snatched the knife from her. Having spent the last three hours cooking with Lavinia's skills, he didn't want his cack-handed wife ruining his artistry.

'Yes, please,' said Joyce. 'It's great! Though it's quite a shock to see you eating meat, Ian, after all these years.'

He himself felt less shocked since Mervyn's explanation. Didn't it all fall into place now? Lavinia's preference for meat matched the image he was slowly building up of her as a strong, red-blooded female, who would have regarded vegetarianism as suited only to wimps and cranks. 'Leave room for dessert,' he warned. 'I've made a lemon soufflé, and though I say it myself, it's really rather special.'

Thanks to Lavinia, he didn't add.

'Well, I have to say, Ian, you did yourself proud. The Frasers were over the moon! Poor Joyce, though. She told me she's terribly worried about ever inviting us back, now you've set the bar so high.'

'Yes, I suppose it wasn't bad for a beginner.'

'Are you really a beginner?' Rita was sitting in front of the mirror, creaming off her make-up. 'Or have you been taking lessons secretly?'

'How could I? You never let me out of your sight. And, by the way, that's got to change, my love. I'm better now, so I don't need all this mollycoddling.'

'Look, the surgeon told you to take it easy.'

'Oh, they all say that. It's sheer self-interest, to stop them being sued.'

'Don't be such a cynic!' Having thrown away the dirty tissues, she re-set the alarm, then folded back the counterpane. 'Are you coming to bed?' she asked, slipping off her dressing gown and diving under the covers. 'I'm knackered!'

'I don't feel the least bit tired.'

'But it's way past midnight and you've been on your feet all day.'

'The night's still young,' he carolled, unbuttoning his shirt and examining his scar in the mirror. Although still red and ridged and angry-looking, it seemed more a badge of triumph now, than a constant worrying sign of his imminent demise. In fact, should anybody comment on it when he was swimming in the public baths or stripping for the shower, he'd pretend he'd taken on a dozen armed assassins, fought them single-handed, and left them all for dead.

'I put your clean pyjamas on the side there.'

'It's too hot for pyjamas. I don't know how you can bear that clammy nylon nightdress on such a sticky night.'

'I don't like sleeping naked, Ian – you know that. I may be prudish, but—'

'*I'd* like it – just this once.'

She sat up in surprise. 'You mean ...'

'Oh, I know we agreed we wouldn't try again until I was feeling more – well, in the mood. But tonight I *am* in the mood!' Peeling off his shirt and trousers, he tossed them over the back of the chair. 'I'll just have a wash. Don't go away!'

In the privacy of the bathroom, he studied his erection. 'Thank you, Lavinia,' he murmured, having satisfied himself that it was no less stiff than before his operation. Lavinia was the woman he'd be pleasuring, of course – not poor old dowdy Rita – since it was Lavinia who had endowed him with this new sexual confidence. For the first eight weeks, he'd been too terrified to try, despite the video issued by the hospital: 'Getting Back To Sex', which aimed to reassure all transplant patients that they weren't doomed to eternal celibacy. But, far from reassuring him, it had generated new fears, by pointing out the risks of certain sexual positions that might restrict his breathing or put a strain on the chest-wound. As he'd sat watching the programme with Rita, Death had come careering back, spewing filthy threats. 'You'll cop it on the job, old chap. One shag and you'll peg out!'

In April, he had tried again, only to find himself ignominiously limp within minutes of stripping off. The same occurred in June, when Rita did her valiant best to stroke him stiff again, finally saying in a motherly tone (guaranteed to stifle all desire) that a nice, loving cuddle would do very nicely instead. Nicely for *her*, perhaps.

Returning from the bathroom, he was relieved to see that she had removed the offending nightdress. Its long sleeves and bilious colour would have made it quite a struggle to turn her into his glamorous, sexy donor.

He switched off the bedside light, so he could see nothing but Lavinia, then straddled her lithe body, ignoring Rita's muttered warning, 'Careful now! Don't overtax yourself.' Far from urging caution, Lavinia was whipping him on, in the same tempestuous way she spurred her hot-blooded mare; coaxing amazing feats from him – the erotic equivalent of jumping five-bar gates. And he was certainly coming up to scratch, judging by her passionate cries as she bucked and thrust beneath him. 'Lavinia, you fantastic little witch!' he yelled in silent tumult, as he exploded in the wildest, most dramatic orgasm he had ever experienced in his life. As he shot his load, he was seeding babies – scores of them – children with Lavinia's beauty and his own new-found macho powers. He and Rita had never managed to conceive – a deep and shaming loss – but at this very instant he was fathering a whole brood of sons and daughters, all with strong and perfect hearts.

'Good gracious, dear!' Rita tutted, finally crawling out from under him. 'You *are* changed.'

'Do turn that racket off, Ian. It's getting on my nerves.'

Ian switched the volume down. 'That "racket",' he said irritably, 'happens to be Beethoven's String Quartet in C sharp minor.'

'Come again?'

'Don't worry – it's out of your league.'

'Don't be so blooming patronizing! Anyway, I preferred it when you listened to Terry Wogan.'

'Retune when I've gone, then.'

'Gone? Gone where? I thought you said *I* was doing the shopping today. Which,' she added tartly, drying the last of the breakfast things and putting them away, 'will certainly make a change.'

'Yes, fine by me. I'm leaving in ten minutes.'

'For your wine-appreciation course?'

'No, that's Thursday. Can't you ever listen?'

'Ian, for heaven's sake! I can't keep up with all you're doing nowadays.'

'Today ...' He enunciated in an exaggerated fashion, as if speaking to a foreigner. 'I'm going to the stables.'

'Stables? Which stables?'

'There's a riding school near Croydon and—'

'A riding school?'

'I wish you wouldn't keep repeating what I say, it's beginning to drive me nuts.'

In unspoken rebuke, she slammed the cupboard door. 'Ian, I've looked after you, hand, foot and finger, the whole of this last awful year, and all you do is snap. Surely I'm allowed to ask where you're going and why?'

Struggling between guilt and irritation, he turned off the radio. 'I've booked a riding lesson, OK?'

'A riding lesson?'

'There – you're doing it again. If I want my words repeated, I'll buy a bloody parrot.'

'Ian, will you please not swear. And I don't think you should go riding. It's a highly dangerous sport.'

'Look, I'm just going for a gentle hack. We're not talking about the Grand National.'

'But you've never been on a horse in your life.'

'All the more reason to start.'

'I just can't understand why you're becoming so stuck-up. Beethoven and riding schools, for God's sake! It'll be Ascot next, or Henley.'

Yes, he thought, why not?

'And I bet it's terribly expensive.'

'So what? I've got my pension, haven't I? And we've paid off the whole of the mortgage, and—'

'But suppose you have a nasty fall?'

'I shan't.' Lavinia's own equestrian skills would stand him in good stead. Besides, he had to follow his heart – *her* heart.

'Look, if you insist on gallivanting around like some John Wayne look-alike, we ought to have a word with the cardiac rehab nurse, before you get *near* a horse.'

He slumped into a chair, glancing around at the small, confining kitchen. Only now did he begin to see how Rita had always cramped his style – long before the transplant, which she was simply using as an excuse. Way back in his thirties, she had warned him not to try for promotion, claiming he'd crumple under the pressures. And, after their failure to conceive, when he had suggested they adopt a child, maybe one from Romania, she had refused even to consider it. On less important matters, too, she invariably clipped his wings, insisting they took their holidays at the same boring Bournemouth hotel, when he ached to climb the Matterhorn or see the Pyramids; even cross the Gobi desert on a camel. People envied them their long and happy marriage, but coupledom, he realized, was a sort of mental anaesthetic, which could force you, for the sake of your spouse, to shrink your natural potential, suppress your inbuilt longings, until you were only semi-living. Life with Lavinia would be a different matter entirely. With their own lively, talented brood, they wouldn't need to adopt. The whole troupe of them would travel the world; take up truly dangerous sports like paragliding, white-water-rafting, mountaineering, rally-driving. And horses would be part of their existence. No need to visit some tame suburban riding stables, when they bred their own thoroughbreds at home.

'Ian, are you *listening*? I said why don't we ask your cardiac nurse?'

'Because I'm not in touch with her these days. Besides, I can't change the lesson now, or they'll charge me anyway.'

'And what *do* they charge, I'd like to know?'

'£50 an hour.'

'Fifty? It's a scandal! Your pension won't last long if you start flinging cash around like that. What *I'd* suggest, if you have so much surplus energy, is that you go back to your job.'

He shuddered in reply. The very thought of spending yet more years as a meticulous drone in the local Council's Rates Department filled him with despair. He'd wasted decades of his life already, chasing up arrears, updating information from semi-literate ratepayers, dealing with complaints from dense, disgruntled tenants, even spending lunch-hours at his desk. That old, staid, tepid self had died with his crappy heart, thank God. His new self was a dazzling entrepreneur, leaping into action as his fellow-worker, Lavinia, bid him scale the heights.

'Look, I'll discuss my future later. But right this minute, I'm going to the stables, and it's quite a drive to Croydon, so I'd better get a move on.'

'Well, I insist on coming with you, so I can explain your medical history to the instructor.'

'*I* can do that, Rita. I don't need you as nanny.'

'You *did* need me,' she said bitterly. 'For every tiny thing, remember – even cutting up your food and—'

He flushed with genuine shame. He had, indeed, been totally dependent on her, clinging like a child. He would never forget his first day home from hospital, when he'd lain groaning on the bed here, imploring Rita not to leave his side, even for a second. The simplest functions seemed more or less impossible – breathing, moving, eating, drinking, were all fraught with risk and pain. And although he no longer had the chest-drains to contend with, or the oxygen mask and catheter, his entire body still felt stiff and sore, as if he'd become a battle casualty. Without Rita as ministering angel, he might well have gone to pieces in the frightening weeks that followed, when he struggled in succession with nausea, depression, constipation, coughing fits and bouts of racking pain.

'Look, I'm sorry, dear. I *am* grateful – more than I can say. But I need a bit of freedom, don't you see?' He owed her a huge debt, yet, as new, intriguing elements of Lavinia's personality transferred themselves to him, he was becoming more free-spirited, less willing to kowtow. So, ministering angel or no ministering angel, Rita must somehow be persuaded to accept the new regime.

'Ian,' she said, arms akimbo, and moving oppressively close, 'it's my duty as your wife to investigate those stables for myself – check out their safety record, make sure they put you on a nice, quiet, gentle horse.'

He sprang up in annoyance. 'OK, let's change the plan and go for a donkey ride on Camber Sands.'

'There's no need to be sarcastic,' she said, taking off her pinny. 'Anyway, I'd enjoy the outing. These last two weeks have been pretty grim, if you really want to know. I mean, I feel at a loose end, with you doing all the shopping and cooking. And I hate staying here alone when you keep gadding off on those high-falutin courses.'

'All right,' he barked. 'Come with me. But only this once – is that clear?'

Rita marched up to a girl in jodhpurs and smart brown riding boots. 'Excuse me,' she declared. 'My husband's booked a lesson here, but there are some important things I need to tell you first.'

Ian dug her in the ribs. 'Shut up!' he whispered. 'I'll deal with this.'

'Sorry,' said the girl. 'Can't help. I don't even work here. You'll need to see Miriam. She's the boss.'

'Where is she?'

'Out on a hack.'

'But my husband's ride is booked for ten o'clock, and it's already quarter past.'

'Oh, she's always late.' The girl shrugged and turned away, clearly losing interest.

'Look,' Ian said to Rita, once they were alone. 'You've seen the place, so why not pop off home, OK? I can get the bus back.'

'I haven't seen a thing, Ian, apart from a few tumbledown buildings, and a disgusting amount of mud. Where are the *horses*, I'd like to know – well, apart from that poor creature who looks fit for the knackers' yard?'

Ian gritted his teeth. 'Do you intend to ruin everything before I've even started?'

'Sshh!' she said. 'Those people will hear.'

'What people?'

'In the cars there.'

'They can hardly hear if they're in their cars.'

'Who do you think they are?'

'No idea. Maybe they're just sheltering until it's time for their rides. And if *you* had any sense, you'd have stayed in the car. You're not dressed for rain. I am.' In truth, he, too, was disappointed with the general ambience, knowing instantly it would fail to meet Lavinia's standards. However, he hadn't had much choice – riding stables were thin on the ground in Camberwell, so he'd had to consult the Yellow Pages and take a chance on something further out.

Just at that moment there was a clattering of hoofs and a string of bedraggled horses came trotting into the stable yard – well, hardly horses, he thought, gazing at the creatures, which were mostly pygmy-size, and ridden by quite tiny children; mounts and riders both soaked to the skin. Having done a quick tally in his head, he realized to his dismay that he was a good five decades older than anyone in sight, with the exception of the instructor. *She*, he assumed, was Miriam, and riding the only horse bigger than a Shetland pony.

'Hi!' she called. 'Are you Ian?'

'That's right.'

'Won't be a jiffy. Just let me get this lot sorted out, then I'll be with you, OK?'

'Yes, fine.'

'Avril!' she screeched, swinging down from her mount and handing the reins to a small, scraggy girl who had come running from the tack-room. People were also emerging from the cars – *parents*, he realized now, who began helping their children dismount, clucking over their sodden state, towelling their wet hair. Well, at least he was in good company. He, too, had a nanny in tow.

'Go on, Ian. Tell them about your operation. And ask if you can borrow a hard hat.'

'I'm not asking anything,' he muttered, 'until this lot have pissed off.'

Unfortunately, that took quite some while, as all the parents seemed to know each other and were using the occasion to catch up with news and gossip, regardless of the rain. It was almost half-past ten before the last of them departed and he was free to approach Miriam.

'Sorry we're a bit behind,' she said. 'But don't worry, we'll have plenty of time. I'm not taking out another ride till noon. Now, I know you booked a private lesson, but before we start I need to get a few things straight. You say you'd never ridden before?'

'Well,' he demurred, feeling a strong objection to the statement arising in his mind – clearly from Lavinia. 'Not ... much.'

'Not at all,' said Rita tartly. 'And my husband's not a well man.'

'In that case, he shouldn't be riding,' Miriam pronounced, tapping her riding crop against her side in a decidedly irritable fashion.

'I'm perfectly well,' Ian snapped. 'OK, I had a heart transplant, but that was a good six months ago and I'm fighting fit at present.'

Rita pushed forward again, stepping distastefully around a pile of still-steaming manure. 'Can you be sure to put him on a really placid horse?'

'Well, seeing how tall your husband is, we won't have a lot of choice. I tend to specialize in children, you see, so I go in more for ponies. So it'll be either Blossom or Tommy – they're our big'uns.'

'And are they both safe?' Rita demanded.

'Listen, love,' Miriam said, with an air of martyred patience, 'no instructor can really guarantee that any horse is safe. They're living creatures, after all, so they might get frightened by a sudden noise, or thrown off-course, or—'

'Told you so!' said Rita, wagging her finger at Ian.

Miriam ignored the interruption. 'But,' she continued, emphatically, 'these particular two are as safe as any horse could be.'

'Satisfied?' Ian muttered, looking daggers at his wife.

Rita now changed tack, though still plugging away in nursemaid style. 'It's essential that my husband wears a hard hat. He doesn't own one, I'm afraid, but—'

'We provide them as a matter of course,' Miriam interjected, now sounding somewhat waspish. An ally, Ian concluded, taking pleasure in the thought.

'Avril, saddle Blossom, will you? And bring a hard hat for this gentleman.'

'Goodbye, Rita,' Ian said pointedly. 'See you later. Thanks for the lift.'

'I'll wait for you in the car,' she said, shaking rain from her hair. 'You can't take the bus in this weather.'

'For Christ's sake!' he exclaimed, finally exploding in fury. 'I'm going to get drenched on the bloody horse, so a bit more wet won't hurt. Now, scat!'

'Don't let your wife put you off,' Miriam advised him, once Rita had, at last, withdrawn. 'Some people just aren't good around horses. Right, let's get you up. This is how you mount, Ian. Put your left foot in the stirrup here, facing Blossom's tail, then swing your right leg up and over. Well done! Most people don't get the hang of that until at least the third or fourth time.'

Once sitting astride Blossom's back, he felt an extraordinary sense of mastery, a sense of coming home, as if he had done this in another life – which, of course, he *had*.

'We'll start off in the paddock, OK, and put you through your paces.' Miriam took hold of Blossom's bridle and led her down a narrow path that opened into a grassy ring enclosed by a wooden fence. 'You have a very good seat, I must say. I noticed it immediately. Most beginners have to be told – and sometimes told continually – to sit up straight, and not to point their toes down, and to keep their hands low on the horse's neck, but you're doing all that naturally. Are you sure you haven't ridden before?'

'Let's put it this way,' he started, then broke off in confusion. Impossible to tell a stranger that one part of him had been in the saddle since the age of two or three.

Fortunately, Miriam was distracted by the task of closing the paddock gate. She had let go of the bridle, thank God. He could manage a horse on his own – indeed, given his present confidence, could manage the Spanish Riding School, or the entire Household Cavalry.

'Now I'm going to stand here in the middle of the field and I want you to get Blossom to walk round and round at a nice controlled and measured pace. Keep the reins fairly taut, but don't pull on her mouth. And remember, *you're* in charge – not her. If she tries to break into a trot, or puts her head down to eat the grass, then pull her up, show her who's the boss.'

'OK,' he said, with a surge of satisfaction at being recognized as boss. And he relished the sensation of sitting so high up, lord of all he surveyed. OK, Blossom wasn't pure Arab – in fact, a pot-bellied, rather clumping mare, the colour of Bisto gravy – but at least this was a beginning and it felt gloriously right.

'You're a natural, Ian – there's no doubt about that. It's like having an ear for music or an aptitude for sport – a knack that people are born with. And I can tell you're really self-assured, which Blossom will pick up, of course. Horses aren't stupid, you know. If a rider gets on their back who's a bag of nerves, or expecting to take a tumble any minute, the horse will sense that instantly and start to get fidgety itself.'

How incredible, he thought, patting Blossom's mane with a proprietorial air, that a timid chap like himself, once so prey to terror, and whose sole experience of horses to date had been the odd flutter on the Derby, was now imbued not just with Lavinia's equestrian skills, but also with her courage.

'Shall we try a trot?' Miriam suggested.

'Fine,' Ian said airily. With Lavinia's valour to call on, he could jump a ten-barred gate.

'Goodbye, dear. Enjoy yourself.'

'Not a hope,' said Rita. 'You know what Trevor's like.'

'At least he's taking you out to lunch.'

'Yes, but only so he can tell me all his troubles.'

'Well,' said Ian, endeavouring to close the door against her, 'eat all you can get, in between giving him advice.'

'Advice!' she snorted stepping back inside the hall. 'When has my wretched brother ever listened to a word I say?'

'Goodbye,' he repeated, doggedly, desperate to get off himself.

'Hey, what about *your* lunch?' Rita made a lunge towards the kitchen.

Ian tried, in vain, to fob her off. 'Don't worry. It's all under control.'

'You seem awfully keen to get rid of me. What are you up to, Ian?'

'Nothing,' he lied. 'Just planning a quiet day indoors.'

'Well, don't forget to bring the washing in, if you see it clouding over. I've never known an August like this – rain, rain, rain, rain, rain.'

'Goodbye,' he said, third time.

'I'll try to be back by early evening.'

'Don't rush,' he said, through gritted teeth.

The moment she had vanished down the street, he dashed

upstairs to change into his riding clothes, which he had hidden in a suitcase in the spare-room. As he pulled on the Mark Todd breeches and buttoned the black hacking jacket, with its inset velvet collar, the outfit seemed consolingly familiar, although he had bought it only last week. And the knee-length leather riding boots added a definite touch of class, admitting him to Lavinia's private circle. In fact, it hurt to have to hide the clothes beneath an old blue plastic packamac, but the neighbours might be watching as he left. His new riding hat was more elegantly concealed in a special leather carrying-case, which he'd purchased with the other gear. He must never, ever, let Rita see the bill. The boots alone had set him back a cool £300. But, Lavinia, he knew, insisted on high quality in every aspect of her life.

Having opened the front door an inch, he gave a cautious glance to right and left, to ensure that Anne and Rodney weren't cleaning the car or weeding the front garden. There was no sign of them, thank God, nor of anybody spying from the houses opposite, so he slipped into his ancient Honda Civic and accelerated away, feeling considerable relief. He had been worrying all morning that Rita's lunch would somehow be called off. Every time the phone rang, he'd imagined it was her brother, calling to say he'd changed his mind or gone down with a bug. But no, she was safely on her way and, with any luck, wouldn't return till seven – maybe even later, since there were problems on the trains.

He, too, had a long journey ahead, but every mile he travelled, away from Camberwell and Rita, brought an increasing sense of calm. And when, at last, he reached his destination, a single glance was enough to confirm that this particular establishment (chosen from a score of others within a radius of sixty-miles) was infinitely superior to the shambles run by Miriam. There was no trace of mud, despite the surly weather, just an immaculately swept yard, surrounded by well-constructed looseboxes, set in an attractive landscape of rolling fields and gently wooded hills. He stood gazing at the horses in the yard – far finer specimens than clumping, cob-like Blossom. OK, Blossom had played her part, the few times he had ridden her, in familiarizing him with this new equestrian world, but it was high time he moved on and became more worthy of Lavinia.

A woman was coming towards him, impeccably turned out in well-cut breeches and an elegant blouson jacket; her honey-blonde hair swept up in a chignon. 'Good morning, sir,' she said, her accent reassuringly top-drawer. 'I'm Caroline Wynn-Jones. We spoke on the phone. You must be Mr Jackson.'

He nodded, swishing his new riding crop with barely contained excitement.

'And you particularly requested a purebred Arab horse.'

'That's right.'

'No problem at all. We're putting you on Azizah.'

'Sorry, I didn't catch the name.'

'Azizah. It means "precious" in Arabic – someone deeply loved and cherished.'

Perfect, he thought, and a definite advance on 'Blossom'.

'She's a wonderful ride – a little highly-strung, perhaps. She may need a bit of holding back. But you did say you're experienced.'

'I've been riding since before I could walk,' he murmured with a self-deprecating shrug.

Caroline opened one of the loosebox doors. Inside was the most stunning horse imaginable, identical in every way to the one he'd always pictured as Lavinia's. A young girl was giving a final buff to the gleaming chestnut coat; a slightly older boy brushing the long, flowing tail.

'Isn't she a beauty?' Caroline smiled, displaying perfect teeth.

'I'd say!' With Lavinia's trained eye, he registered the qualities that made the Arab purebreed so distinctive: the refined head and high-arched neck, the slender fetlocks and deep, well-angled hip, the finely chiselled bone structure. As his eye travelled from the horse to its surroundings, he noted with approval that the loosebox floor was deeply banked with clean and fragrant bedding, not the thin covering of dirty straw Miriam made do with. He also studied the rows of rosettes pinned to a board at the back – more proof, presumably, of Azizah's exceptional prowess.

Caroline led her out, while the young girl and boy vanished into the tack-room. Ian felt particularly gratified that no other riders appeared to be in evidence. If this was Lavinia's livery stable, he didn't want a bunch of kids (or even vulgar grown-ups) ruining the ambience. However, he chafed with ill-disguised impatience as

Caroline lengthened the stirrups and gave a final tightening to the girth. Couldn't he do such things himself?

'Right, she's all yours, Mr Jackson.'

Of *course* she is, he thought, as he gathered up the reins and swung into the saddle. And Azizah knew it, too, giving a long, appreciative whinny, in instant recognition of her master.

'If you take that path' – Caroline pointed beyond the stables to her right – 'it leads to open country after half a mile or so, and you can gallop her along the Downs.'

'Brilliant!'

He had never galloped in his life. At Miriam's place, they'd been restricted to a trot or gentle canter, but in his *other* existence (Lavinia's existence) a vigorous morning gallop had been part of his routine.

He set off at a steady pace, whispering words of endearment to his mount. 'Gorgeous girl! Lovely girl! Precious one. Beloved one.' He was soon aware of the horse's ultra-sensitivity as she reacted to every flutter in the hedge, every smallest noise or movement; her ears flicking back and forth, her fine head tossing skittishly if a bird swooped low, or a fallen branch crunched beneath her feet. His role, as rider, was to reassure her that *he* was in control, that they belonged together – and always had – that, so long as he was on her back, neither of them would experience the slightest twinge of fear.

Admiring her high-stepping stride, he gently urged her on, as the path opened out to a wide expanse of downland, unfurling lushly and enticingly towards the blue smudge of the skyline. Responsive to the lightest touch, she broke into a canter; her fluid, easy movement a world away from Blossom's lumbering gait. As they bowled along, in tandem, the clouds began to lift, and the sun suddenly sailed out, bathing the whole countryside in a triumphant sheen of gold. With another nudge of his heels, he spurred Azizah on again, until she was flat out in a gallop, her thudding hoofs scarcely making contact with the dazed and dizzy ground. They flew across the turf; he and the horse inseparable as they scorched towards the horizon, with no limits, no constraints; unbounded space stretching on all sides. Speed itself was a new potent wonder-drug, in a different league entirely from the shoal of medications he took each day, just to keep alive. That was mere existence – this was living.

As the landscape hurtled past in a blur of green and gold, he and his mount seemed to be lifting off into a new, unfettered land, where the very breeze blew reckless, rampant, rapturous, from some wilder, windswept shore – intoxicating contrast to all his years of caution and restraint; the inertia of his marriage, the tedium of his job. He was taking wing, at last, breaking out, escaping, leaving Rita and the Rates Department far behind in his stolid, stagnant past. There was no going back – he knew that – not to the Council or to Camberwell, not to retirement or to Rita. He would gallop to the ends of the earth, until his heart burst with the bliss of it and he was born again, as *Lavinia* – one with her indissolubly – one spirit, body, mind and flesh, conjoined and fused, for ever.

Sacred Heart

'Trifle for you, madam, or meringues?'

'Meringues, please,' Grace replied, eying the plate with a certain weary distaste. The meringues were heart-shaped – of course – adding to the surfeit of hearts, already, frankly, oppressive. Every table was sprinkled with tiny, glittery ones – a new form of confetti, she presumed. The paper napkins were printed with two joined hearts, while heart-shaped bunches of helium balloons were suspended from the ceiling. And the wedding-anniversary cakes, in pride of place on a separate table, were two elaborate twin hearts, one iced with a large figure six, the other with a nought. Even this hall belonged to the Church of the Sacred Heart, where they had just celebrated a second Nuptial Mass.

As if tuning in to her thoughts, the Reverend Bernard O'Flaherty, sitting on her right, remarked on how magnificently the hall had been transformed – indeed, he barely recognized it.

'Yes, it does look pretty,' she murmured, refusing to add either 'Father' or 'Bernie'; the one too Papist, the other too familiar. This obese and greedy Jesuit was not her favourite priest. In fact, *any* priest provoked her ire these days.

'You should have had some trifle with your meringues,' he said, wiping a white moustache of cream off his face. 'The two go very well together.'

She forbore from saying that he, like her, had been offered one or the other, and not both. Instead, she attacked her rock-hard meringue with the somewhat inadequate dessert-fork, hoping it wouldn't break her teeth. Hardness was on her mind today *'Diamond is the hardest natural substance known to man – fifty-eight times harder than the next hardest mineral on earth.'* One of the facts listed on the large greetings card produced by her great-grandchildren, accompanied by charming (if skewiff) drawings, and made as part of a school-project.

She touched her diamond engagement ring, too tight now for the arthritic finger-joint. The ring was a family heirloom, handed down from Charles's great-great-grandmother, although, secretly, she had always regarded diamonds as cold, unfeeling stones: icicles, frozen tears, splinters of broken glass. Had anyone bothered to consult her, back in 1946, she might have suggested a ruby; something with some life to it, and colour. She had even felt the same about her wedding dress. Why not flamboyant scarlet instead of pallid white?

'Well, you've done us really proud,' Walter observed, draining his wine with a noticeably shaky hand.

Grace glanced from his bald pate and deeply furrowed face to his earlier incarnation in one of the framed wedding photos grouped around the cakes. Sixty years ago, he'd boasted a thatch of thick black hair, a dramatically slimmer silhouette and a rosy complexion with not a single wrinkle. Well, at least he was alive still, unlike many of the guests who'd attended that first ceremony. Besides, who was *she* to talk, when she had aged so much herself? Everything was dropping, drooping, sagging, inside as well as out: eyelids, jowls, breasts, womb, even the arches in her feet.

'Yes, I love the colour scheme,' Marjorie put in, helping herself to a heart-shaped chocolate mint. 'Was that your doing, Grace?'

'No, Elaine's,' she said. In her own opinion, mauve was rather a dreary colour, although she had no intention of criticizing her daughter, who had gone to such great trouble over this Diamond Wedding party. The fact that she herself hadn't actually wanted it was neither here nor there. Her children had always overruled her, simply through sheer force of numbers. Anyway, there was her husband to consider, and Charles was not only a stickler for tradition, but someone who cared deeply about appearances. What would their friends and family think (not to mention the local priests) if they failed to lay on a fitting celebration?

'Well, she's done a wonderful job,' Marjorie persisted, licking melted chocolate off her fingers. 'Even down to the details. I mean,

Charles's tie is exactly the same shade of mauve as those flower-things on your dress.'

'Yes, Elaine's a real perfectionist.' Grace's eye roved around the room, taking in not just the hearts, but the acres of mauve and white: balloons and bunting, flower arrangements, tablecloths, paper streamers, paper napkins, all in the same colour scheme, as well as the icing on the cakes. As for her dress, Elaine had marched her to the shops, rejected every garment that didn't fit the guidelines, and finally found the 'perfect' outfit: white silk, patterned with mauve swirls.

'And she's working like a beaver,' Vera added. 'She hasn't so much as sat down yet, let alone had anything to eat.'

Grace watched her daughter move assiduously from table to table, making sure she spoke to every guest, thanking them for presents, enquiring about their health, commiserating over traffic jams or delayed or draughty trains. As the eldest of eight children, Elaine had always had a strong sense of duty, much in evidence these last few weeks. She it was who had stage-managed the entire proceedings: supervised the guest-list, hired the hall and catering staff, laid on the decorations, arranged the flowers in church, consulted with the organist over the choice of hymns and music, and – since one o'clock today – had been keeping a punctilious eye on the serving of the food. And now she'd started rounding up the waiters to pour the tea and coffee, so that the speeches could begin.

With an inaudible sigh, Grace leaned back in her seat. She longed to be outside, dressed casually in slacks and a sweater – not a corset and silk flounces – shuffling through the fallen leaves with the two new spaniel puppies (which were confined, at present, in a neighbour's tiny flat, and so were probably feeling equally frustrated). A bright autumn sun was burnishing the trees, and the lively, zippy breeze that had dishevelled her stiff hair-do on the way in to the church seemed to be whispering to her through the window, 'Don't waste this glorious afternoon. Leave your guests and join us.'

If only. There would be at least six separate speeches, a poetry recitation by the grandchildren, a piano duet by two of the great-grandchildren, and finally the cutting of the cake. Even then, she wouldn't be able to leave. Some people had travelled hundreds of miles, so she would have to be gracious, like her name, and entertain them as long as they might linger. And several were staying overnight, so that, even tomorrow morning, she would be captive, overdressed, still valiantly smiling, scrupulously polite.

Once the waiters had done the honours with the teapots and the coffee jugs, Elaine clapped her hands for silence. It took some time, in fact, for the hubbub to subside. Stone-deaf Auntie Winnie was halfway through some endless monologue, Paddy and Priscilla were giggling over a joke, and several obstreperous toddlers continued to squawk and squabble. However, at last there was an almost-lull, and Elaine positioned herself in front of the top table and unfurled her three pages of notes.

Grace did her best to concentrate, since she knew Elaine would have rewritten this speech at least a dozen times, agonizing over the exact position of every dot and comma, and probably even recording it on tape, so she could edit out any fluffs or hesitations in advance.

Long it certainly was. Her daughter had raked through their entire sixty years to mine the smallest incidents for suitable material, although Grace could scarcely recognize her life. All the pain and problems had been tactfully erased, leaving only love and loyalty, courage and good humour. Like obituaries, she thought – or at least obituaries in the old days, when brute truth was often distorted for the sake of propriety and decorum.

'And now I'd like to pay tribute to my father's charity work. I'm sure most of you here will know how tireless and unselfish he's been in supporting worthy causes.'

Grace cleared her throat. If only *she*, his wife, had been one of those worthy causes, who deserved as much attention as endangered Brazilian rain forests, or torture-victims in Uzbekistan.

'And I'm sure Bernie will agree that he's been an absolute pillar of this, our local church, giving unstinting time and energy to every parish venture, be it the Children's Mission or the annual summer fête.'

'Hear, hear!' the priest enthused, although still seriously preoccupied with shovelling in his third helping of dessert.

Grace noted with distinct unease that *her* devotion to the parish had received not the barest mention. Surely no one could have stumbled on the truth: that she no longer believed a word of

Catholic doctrine? Indeed, if faith were seen as a flame, hers had always been a puny little nightlight, and was now totally extinguished. But she had long kept up a pretence – for Charles's sake, the family's sake – never voicing her doubts to anyone, least of all to her pious eldest daughter.

She was relieved to see the waiters approaching with bottles of champagne, which meant the speech must be drawing to its close. And, sure enough, Elaine put away her notes and picked up her champagne glass.

'... so I'd like to drink a toast to my parents, to congratulate them on sixty glorious years.'

'To Charles and Grace,' everyone repeated, clinking glasses on each of the twelve tables.

His name had always come first. Just as his father's had and grandfather's. In Charles's circle, women were subservient. He caught her eye and smiled and, as she raised her glass to him, she wondered which was worse: the fact he actually seemed a stranger to her, after all these years, or his lack of emotional insight, which meant he would never realize how she longed for their relationship to be closer and less formal. When she watched her own married children – or, indeed, other couples on television – they seemed so much more relaxed, sharing confidences and pillow-talk, teasing each other, even daring to pick quarrels, if only to make them up in bed. She and Charles remained at arm's length, despite six long decades of so-called intimacy, yet she had never, once, admitted her frustration, except silently, to the furniture.

She took a long, deep draught of champagne, enjoying the sensation of frisky bubbles tickling on her face. Charles had bought *Veuve Clicquot* for each of her eight births, but usually drank it all himself, claiming it wasn't wise for *her* to drink, as it might affect her milk supply. Her milk had never failed, in fact, even with the eighth child. In that respect at least, she had been a model wife.

As Elaine sat down, the priest levered his great bulk from the chair and launched into his own speech. He had spilt cream down his black trousers and flakes of salmon mayonnaise were clinging to his cassock, but he continued, unabashed.

'I've already given a sermon at the Mass, so I'll keep this very brief.'

Unlikely. The sermon itself had lasted half an hour.

'But I would like to say how privileged we are to count Charles and Grace among our friends and family. It's extremely rare these days for marriages to last, let alone endure for sixty years.'

Endure, she thought – *mot juste*. That great stretch of time *had* required endurance.

'And Charles and Grace are doubly blessed in having such a large and loving family. To have brought up eight lovely children, each one of them successful in his or her own right, is a considerable achievement.'

And one he'd value, of course. Priests wanted souls for God – the more the better. Women, in the Church's view, were mere reproduction-machines. It had always struck her as an impertinence that celibate men who knew nothing whatsoever about labour pains or broken nights, leaking breasts or prolapsed wombs, should forbid all forms of contraception, except the rhythm method, which patently didn't work. In the end, she had come to dread Charles's advances, tensing if he so much as kissed her, for fear of yet another pregnancy. Although at least they'd had the wherewithal to afford so many children, whereas some of their fellow fecund parishioners were reduced to penury.

'And all but one are here today,' O'Flaherty continued in his lilting Irish brogue. 'Gemma couldn't join us, but only for the best of reasons. She's just given birth to a lovely baby boy – Charles and Grace's twenty-second grandchild. So let's drink another toast to this newest member of the family.'

Poor Gemma, Grace reflected – her youngest child still fertile at the age of forty-seven. 'Drink all you can get, my darling,' she muttered, *sotto voce*, 'and to hell with your milk supply!' Hugh and Gemma already had six boys, and this seventh child had dashed their hopes of a girl – again. The Church should dish out special medals for all mothers of large broods, whose heroic efforts compensated for the sharp drop in the number of Catholics, now endemic in the Western world. How ironic it was that, having produced so many souls for God, she herself was now a non-believer. In her younger days, when the doubts had first set in, she'd been too terrified of her in-laws (he a member of Opus Dei; she a direct descendant of St Edmund Campion) to admit to apostasy. Right from the start, they had regarded her with a definite distrust, since she was not a cradle Catholic, but had only converted at Charles's insistence. Marriage to an agnostic, or, worse, an atheist, simply didn't figure in their scheme of things – or his.

But, when she'd first met Charles, good sense and rationality had been swept away by those very characteristics she had later come to resent. His masterful authority had seemed wonderfully exciting to a young impressionable girl, and his tall, athletic figure and dark, romantic looks had made it relatively easy to stomach fictitious dogmas or pagan practices. Her parents-in-law had a statue of the Sacred Heart in their living-room at home, and, on her first meeting with the family, as Charles's bride-to-be, they had invited her to kneel before it, and join them in reciting the Litany of the Sacred Heart. She'd been struck at the time by the contrast between her lust for Charles and the chastening words of the Litany:

Heart of Jesus, overwhelmed with reproaches.
Heart of Jesus, bruised for our iniquities.
Heart of Jesus, obedient even unto death.

As for the image of the heart itself, she found it, frankly, barbarous: Christ's gory, pulsing, bleeding heart open to public view, pierced with a lance and surrounded by a crown of thorns. Yet to them it was an object of the most sincere devotion – a symbol of Christ's love: total, fervent, selfless love that had proved itself through suffering and death. Back then, of course, she hadn't breathed a word about her sentiments, and, even now, with her in-laws long since dead and gone, she continued to hold her peace; far too old to rock the boat.

Having praised her and Charles in particular, as a happy, blessed couple, O'Flaherty turned his attention to marriage in general: a holy sacrament designed by God for human welfare and contentment. What did *he* know? Two people yoked in close conjunction for more than half a century could be regarded as human hell. The priest's own state was more conducive to bliss, perhaps, living as he did with an adoring, servile housekeeper and a handsome (neutered) cat.

'And now I call upon Charles himself to speak.'

Quickly, Grace gathered her thoughts. She mustn't wander off while her husband was on his feet, since he was bound to ask her, later, to comment on his delivery or on the content of his speech. Although she had to admit she was finding it hard to concentrate in this stuffy, over-heated hall, and with too much wine coursing through her veins.

He did look very elegant – that she couldn't deny. His silver hair was well-cut; his suit, though old, was Savile Row, and he still retained the military bearing that had distinguished him in his youth. He wouldn't dream of stooping or slouching, and, even at the age of eighty-six, had never suffered the slightest memory-lapse. That was the trouble, really. His own high standards made him unforgiving.

Clearing his throat, he glanced imperiously around, to make sure he had everyone's attention. 'The great St Paul,' he declared in his deep, resonant voice, 'wrote in AD 57, or thereabouts, a great epistle on the nature of love. We all know the words by heart, of course: "I may speak in tongues of men or of angels, but" ...'

Oh, *no*, she thought, not Corinthians 1, 13 again. It had already been read out at the Mass, and, indeed, at every anniversary Mass since 1947 – although the older version which stressed 'charity', not 'love', had been easier to tolerate, especially in Charles's mouth. Charity was his provenance, his forte, but when he talked about love, it was like someone tone-deaf presuming to pronounce on the subtleties of music. Love meant tenderness and closeness, sentiment, romance – all unknown territory for a man of his stern character. And love meant madness, wildness, longing, lust, all of which he regarded as indulgent, if not perilous. And love meant melding, joining, mutual understanding, and a large dose of imaginative sympathy that would permit a wife to be her genuine self; not a cipher or a trophy; not a corporal to his colonel, or acolyte to his Eminence; not, repeat not, a pious Catholic baby-machine.

'There is nothing love cannot face,' Charles continued, now well into his stride. 'There is no limit to its faith, its hope, its endurance.'

That word again and, yes, he, too, had needed endurance, to stand firm against the traumas life had dealt them both. And she certainly couldn't fault him when it came to faith and hope. One was related to the other, of course. Because his faith burnt brightly, his hope was also fervent – hope of virtue rewarded; hope of rejoining his parents in another, better world, along with the whole Community of Saints. But where would *she* be while they sat on God's right hand – rotting in her coffin, eaten by the worms? It seemed another saddening irony that they should be separated eternally, when they had shared a hearth and home for the whole of their adult lives.

Charles appeared to have assumed the role of cleric, his delivery so solemn she couldn't help reflecting that he would have made a first-rate priest. 'Love will never come to an end,' he intoned, still quoting his beloved St Paul.

She would come to an end, though, and probably fairly soon. Thoughts of death were never far away these days. She envied diamonds in that respect – their indestructibility.

'The youngest diamond is 900-million years old,' the great-grand-children had written in their home-made anniversary card. *'They have survived the wrath of nature. Wind, water and extremes of heat and cold were not able to destroy them, nor the force of time itself.'*

Nature's wrath – the phrase seemed joltingly apt when she applied it to her own life: the three miscarriages and two still-births, interspersed between the eight successful pregnancies; the colon cancer, followed by the pneumonia and pleurisy, then Richard's worrying heart condition, Rose's septicaemia and—

She forced her attention back to Charles, who had finally reached the end of his 'sermon', and was now paying tribute to *her*, as wife and mother.

Forget the 'mother', she begged him silently. Even forget the 'wife'. Let's be two madcap lovers, kicking over the traces, running away from all duties and restraints.

She became so involved in the fantasy – she and Charles racing off to some island paradise, flinging themselves down on warm, soft, yielding sand, to make impassioned love – that she missed the rest of his speech, and was only brought to her senses as he proposed a toast to their whole extended family.

She clinked her glass to his. 'Their whole extended family' didn't include many on her side. As the only child of an only child, her relatives were few – perhaps the very reason she had married into such a powerful tribe.

The children were getting restless, she noticed, as Walter got up to speak. In fact, a few of them had left their seats at the table and ventured on to the stage. Her two favourite great-grandsons, Dominic and Jude, had crawled under the piano and were whispering and giggling in fidgety rebellion. She suppressed a smile as their young twin cousins joined them on the stage and started fighting like unruly puppies, rolling over and over on the well-worn wooden boards. Next it was Melissa's turn, although the five-year-old prima donna decided to put the stage to its proper purposes, and, having torn off her lacy sweater and best white party shoes, in a sort of mini-striptease, then embarked on a manic dance, jigging about in her socks and vest, without a trace of self-consciousness. How fortunate these children were to be born in such a free-and-easy age! Grace imagined herself ripping off her tight, constricting corset and hurling it across the room; pulling out her elaborate hair-do (hairpins showering everywhere), then doing her own twist-and-shake, arms flung high, hips shimmying and swaying, long hair flowing loose.

Walter's speech had faded to a drone. All she could hear was the heartbeat of the music – urgent, pulsing, thunderous – and the wild, rampaging rhythm of her feet.

'And now,' said Elaine, 'I call on my parents to cut the cake.'

Grace clutched at Charles's arm. She was feeling strange, light-headed – dare she say it? – drunk. The sea of faces just beyond the cake-table had faded to a blur, and Charles himself had lost his usual sharp, dogmatic outlines, and seemed to be made of mist and froth. Having steered her into position, he placed her hand firmly on top of his, over the handle of the long-bladed knife. Already, she could tell how hard the icing was. Hard like diamonds. Hard like marriage. Diamonds were for ever. Marriage was for ever. No divorce or freedom in the Church.

'Wait a moment!' someone called. 'We need more photographs. Grace, keep still! You're reeling!'

She tried to freeze, tried to smile; Charles's cold, forceful fingers a rebuke to her hot, helpless ones. *He* would do the cutting, of course. She was back to being a cipher once more; her veiny, feeble, arthritic hand a mere adjunct, an appendage. But this restaging of their wedding was crucial to her husband – a matter of duty and decorum, of honouring tradition, keeping up appearances. And from eleven o'clock this morning, when they had repeated their original vows at the solemn Nuptial Mass, she had supported him in her usual compliant fashion.

'Grace Eliza Edgeworth, will you take Charles Augustine Haines, here present, for your lawful husband, according to the rite of our holy Mother the Church?'

'I will.'

Suddenly, impulsively, she seized the lethal knife, and, throwing Charles off-balance, plunged it deep into his heart; kept stabbing, stabbing, stabbing, in a paroxysm of furious delight.

She heard applause, heard muffled cheers; saw flashbulbs popping, people raising glasses. 'To Grace and Charles,' the guests were all repeating, their hands outstretched, their faces wreathed in smiles; 'Grace and Charles,' 'Grace and Charles,' resounding through the room.

They were hailing her, acclaiming her, crowding round to offer their congratulations. She had broken through, at last; won their praise, at last, as a devout and worthy wife. And she *did* feel genuine pride as she stared, entranced, at the brilliant, ardent, crimson blood streaming from her husband's heart – a fervent heart, a tender heart, a pulsing, lance-pierced, open heart – yes, truly a most Sacred Heart that had proved itself through suffering and death.

Treasure Hunt

'Welcome to Manor Park Hotel!'

'Thank you.' Emma cast an apprehensive glance at the three old souls sagging on the leather sofa in the large reception area; their pale and wrinkled flesh a sorry contrast to its stylish black solidity. 'I'm sorry I'm so late.'

'Yes, I'm afraid you've missed the Champagne Welcome Party. *And* the carol singers.'

Don't rub it in, Emma thought. She was in no mood for a party – or for carols, come to that – but a glass or two of bubbly might have helped to lift her spirits.

'If you'll kindly sign the register, I'll get a porter to show you to your room.'

Obediently she scrawled her signature, envying the receptionist her perfect hair-do and radiant smile. Her own hair was, frankly, a mess and, as for smiling, it was all she could do not to burst into floods of tears.

'Dinner's already started, Miss Hunt, but they serve until 9.30, so you've plenty of time for that.'

The very thought of eating resulted in a surge of queasiness. In fact, it was probably total madness to have come here in the first place – especially considering the expense. But after twenty fruitless phone-calls, it had been such a huge relief to find a hotel with a vacancy, she no longer even cared about the price. It was a matter of seeking refuge; somewhere she could lick her wounds and hide, while recovering from the shock of Alexander's announcement. So here she was, lapped in five-star luxury, in a substantial nineteenth-century mansion, tastefully modernized and renovated. What she hadn't realized was how elderly her fellow guests would be – no one under sixty-five, as far as she could tell. Even at this moment, an old crone on two sticks was weaving her precarious way towards the reception desk, accompanied by a skeletal gent who seemed to be visibly wasting and fading as she watched.

At least the porter was young: a strapping, fresh-faced lad, who rushed up to her like a Labrador eager to go walkies. Seizing her heavy bag as if it were made of thistledown, he led her briskly along the passage and up the curving staircase, enquiring about her journey all the while. Had she run into traffic? Were the roads still flooded? Did she have trouble finding the turn-off, as many guests appeared to do?

She replied in monosyllables: yes, no, yes, no. The journey was more or less a blur. She had driven like a zombie, her mind circling round one subject only: the rift with Alexander.

The porter unlocked the door of an elaborately furnished room and, still chatting, ushered her in. Had she travelled far? Where did she live? How long did she intend to stay?

Instead of answering, she all but begged, 'Don't leave me!' tempted to grab the boy by his sage-green waistcoat and drag him back into the room. They could stay here as a couple – infinitely less shameful than an abandoned singleton.

She fumbled in her wallet for a tip, wondering how she would sleep tonight without Alexander's reassuring bulk beside her in the bed, the steady sound of his breathing, the warmth of his naked body melting into hers.

'Thank you, madam,' the porter said, pocketing the coins. 'Merry Christmas!'

'Merry' was hardly the word. The Christmas she had planned with Alexander had promised untold happiness, which made it all the more incredible that he could have changed his mind so suddenly and cruelly, for no reason except he 'needed space to work things out'. Couldn't he have waited until a less emotive time before disrupting everything?

She dived towards the mini-bar, extracted a miniature vodka and a can of diet Coke, sloshed them both into a tooth-glass and took several desperate gulps. If it required Dutch courage to get her through this three-day break, so be it. The alternative was to head straight home, but could she really face Christmas on her own? She had friends, of course, but it was far too late to turn up on their doorstep when they were all busy with their own families and plans. And she had *no* intention of creeping home to her parents, who disliked every boyfriend she'd ever had, and especially Alexander.

Mechanically she began unpacking, laying out her things on the king-size double bed. Single rooms in hotels appeared to have vanished altogether, only emphasizing the point that the world was made for coupledom.

'Stop wallowing in self-pity!' she rebuked her wan reflection in the mirror. Here she was, in a glitzy hotel, awash in a tide of 'madams' and being waited on by attentive staff. If she had any sense, she would try to make an effort to enjoy it. At this very moment, half the nation would be slaving away in the kitchen, stuffing turkeys, making trifles, preparing Brussels sprouts, and tomorrow there'd be a marathon of cooking, followed by Everests of washing-up. And many people would be stuck with squalling kids, tricksy parents or impossible in-laws – all three at once, in some cases – whereas *she* was free to do exactly as she pleased, with no more onerous task on her hands than getting dressed for dinner.

Suddenly decisive, she stripped off her clothes, turned the shower to cold, and tried to shock herself into a less despondent mood. She emerged shivering and glowing both at once and, having put on her best black trouser-suit, spent some time in front of the mirror applying blusher and mascara. If there was no one to admire her, she would simply dress for her own self-respect. And, half an hour later, she had to admit she did feel distinctly better, though probably mainly due to the vodka.

The waiter greeted her at the door of the oak-panelled dining-room. 'Good evening, madam. Would you like a table on your own, or would you prefer to share?'

Share? With whom, for heaven's sake? Did they lay on escorts as part of the service?

'On Christmas Eve and Christmas Day we always set up a couple of tables for people on their own. It's more companionable.' The waiter waved in the direction of two communal tables at the far end of the room.

She glanced quickly at their occupants. One table was already full – of centenarians, by the looks of them, probably swapping childhood memories of the first planes, or even cars. The other seemed more promising: two youngish women and a rather striking fifty-something, all three smartly dressed, and with not a walking-stick or hearing aid between them. The ratio of females to males was roughly twenty to one, but that was probably par for the course.

'OK, I'll share.'

The waiter bowed obsequiously, before ushering her over and pulling out her chair.

'I'm Emma.' she said to the others, dispensing with formality.

The three women gave their names, which she tried to remember by association. Marilyn was blonde, like her more glamorous film-star namesake; Victoria (the older one) looked queenly, and tiny Tina was the smallest of the three.

Tina passed her the menu. 'None of us has ordered yet. We're trying to decide between fillet of sea-bass and breast of guinea fowl.'

'They both sound pretty good,' she said, surprised to realize that she actually felt hungry. An hour ago, it had seemed utterly impossible that she would ever eat again. In fact, she hadn't swallowed a morsel all day, since Alexander's brusque assertion had erupted like a bomb, blitzing breakfast and their relationship in one savage detonation.

'Well, there are loads of other choices, so take your time – don't rush.'

'I'm not sure about the sea-bass,' Victoria put in, arching a well-groomed eyebrow. 'I had monkfish at lunchtime yesterday and it was definitely overcooked. I tried to send it back, but that damn-fool little waitress didn't understand a word I said. *What* is it she calls herself? Ludmilla, or Ludvika, or something equally outlandish. I suppose she imagines she can get away with murder, with that soppy smile and those big brown eyes of hers, but if *I* had any say in the matter, she'd be out on her ear – tonight!'

Victoria's invective was received in edgy silence, but she continued, unabashed.

'I blame the management. A new couple took this place over about eighteen months ago. All they're interested in is money. They put up all the prices, sacked half the existing staff and then took on all these appalling East Europeans. I mean, I *ask* you! How can someone from the Ukraine or Lithuania possibly do a decent job of work, when their English is so basic? Oh, I know they're paid a pittance, but then what do they expect? They're only here because the conditions in their own countries are more or less Third World.'

As Emma opened her mouth to object – and object vociferously and vehemently – the waiter glided up to seat another female at their table. Although the newcomer looked ancient, her presence was a blessing, since the resultant introductions put a stop to Victoria's virulence.

'Have you just arrived?' Emma asked, admiring the old girl's elegant blue suit and elaborately coifed chignon, and her charming name, Rosamund.

'Oh, no, my dear. I *live* here. Since my second hip operation, I just couldn't manage on my own. So I sold my house and booked a suite, on a more or less permanent basis.'

'And how do you find it?' Emma smiled, feeling instant sympathy for anyone on their own.

'Well, it's especially nice at Christmas, because everyone's more friendly. Normally, I have all my meals alone.'

'Actually they've ruined Christmas,' Victoria observed, sounding still more querulous. 'Last year, the turkey was an absolute disgrace – dry and completely tasteless. And as for the Christmas pudding, I could have done better myself!'

'So why do you come?' Emma asked, venting her anger on her roll, which she tore in half, before slapping it with a lump of hard, cold butter.

'Well, I was hoping to spend Christmas with my son. But his wife said she wanted to be alone with him and their new baby. Utterly selfish, don't you think? And my daughter was just as bad – said she had "other plans", whatever *that's* supposed to mean.'

Nobody replied. Emma guessed they were all thinking much the same as her: was it any wonder that neither son nor daughter should welcome such a mother?

'I did try another hotel, but I knew it was a non-starter the minute they answered the phone. The *rudeness* of these receptionists! I don't know where they find them. It's probably the fault of the schools. They don't teach them manners any more – or grammar, for that matter.'

'Shall we order?' Marilyn suggested diplomatically. 'I've decided to go for the guinea fowl.'

'Me, too,' said Tina.

'There's nothing I fancy at all.' Victoria looked disparagingly at the menu. 'The food here's far too rich.'

A minute ago you were complaining it was tasteless, Emma didn't say.

'Perhaps I'll have the vegetarian option, They're less likely to ruin that – although the asparagus risotto they served on Friday was a complete abomination.'

'And what about you?' Emma asked the old lady, deliberately turning her back on Victoria.

'Oh, I'm afraid I have a problem eating more or less *any*thing. I suffer from multiple allergies, you see. I can't touch wheat or dairy, and nuts can be quite treacherous. As for eggs, I wouldn't so much as *look* at them! I mean, I'd be risking my life, with that dreadful salmonella business. Half the flocks are infected, so they say, and it's especially bad in Italy and Spain.'

Emma chewed disconsolately on a piece of buttered roll. First Eastern Europe under attack; now Western.

'The chef usually cooks me something special,' Rosamund informed them all, pushing away the side-plate that contained her own bread roll. 'But he probably won't have time tonight, when the dining-room's so busy.'

'He should *make* time,' retorted Victoria. 'We're paying enough, for Christ's sake!'

Emma let out an audible sigh. Mistake Number One: coming here at all; mistake Number Two: not opting for a table on her own. Sandwiched as she was between Victoria's hypercriticism and Rosamund's hypochondria, this so-called festive dinner looked set to be a washout. 'What shall we have to drink?' she said, seizing the wine-list and opening it with a flourish. 'I don't know about the rest of you, but seeing as it's Christmas Eve, I fancy something special.'

What she *didn't* add was that, in order to endure this meal, she intended to get well and truly smashed.

*

Opening her eyes, she was aware of someone knocking at the door. 'Come in,' she called sleepily, forcing herself to sit up.

As a man in a smart green uniform entered with her breakfast tray, she suddenly realized that her naked breasts were directly in his line of vision. Hastily she covered them with the sheet, blushing in confusion. She didn't actually *own* a nightdress – Alexander hated them. And yesterday she had packed in such a rush, she had forgotten to bring a T-shirt or something to use as a substitute.

'Good morning, madam. Happy Christmas!'

Christmas had completely slipped her mind, although the minute the word was uttered, thoughts of Alexander doused any chance of happiness. Still, she ought to be grateful that she didn't have a hangover. She had actually left the table halfway through the meal last night, as Victoria's decrials had become gradually more global in their scale. (The country was 'overrun by foreigners and scroungers'; the government was both 'dangerous' and 'a farce'; and the whole universe was 'headed for disaster, if not total destruction'.) Nor had Rosamund offered much cause for cheer, recounting in gruesome detail the saga of her hip operations (during both of which she'd landed up on Life Support), followed by the entire history of her husband's various illnesses, starting with his diverticulitis at the age of twenty-four, to his eventual death from bowel cancer.

Bowel cancer and Dover sole didn't mix too well and, in the end, she had pretended to a malady herself (a sudden crippling migraine); left her fish half-eaten and her bottle of Pouilly Fuisse barely touched, and made her getaway. Just as well, perhaps – at least as far as the wine was concerned. She had no wish to start the day with a *genuine* pounding headache, on top of all the rest.

Turning her attention to the breakfast tray, she noticed a crisp white sheet of paper, listing the day's activities, lying beside the croissants and the fruit.

10 a.m. – present-opening round the Christmas tree.

No way! Victoria was bound to find fault with the size, shape, brand and colour of her particular present, while Rosamund would prove allergic to the wrapping paper.

10.30 a.m. – mince pies and mulled wine in the Grosvenor Room.

Again, not a good idea. Since she intended to drink seriously at both lunch and dinner today, better give the mulled wine a miss.

11 a.m. – Treasure Hunt.

Ah – that *did* appeal. Treasure hunts had been an annual feature at her boarding school and, whether by luck or skill, she had nearly always won. She enjoyed deciphering the clues, racing round the grounds from lake to copse to orchard, until finally she was rewarded with some cleverly hidden prize – usually a book. Over the years, she had built up quite a collection: leather-bound volumes of history, anthologies of verse, a whole stack of novels, both classic and contemporary, even a complete set of Jane Austen in a presentation-case. Treasure indeed.

Easing herself out of bed, she went, still naked, to the window and drew the heavy curtains. The extensive grounds looked tempting; the many statues, fountains, arbours, grottoes, all perfect for concealing clues. And it wasn't even raining, which was something of a miracle after the recent heavy downpours – although it would be muddy underfoot, of course. In fact, she had every chance of winning, since the old and the infirm were unlikely to venture out, and, even if they did, would probably be impeded by the puddles and the boggy ground. While they dawdled, she would sprint, glad of some vigorous exercise to distract her from the loss of Alexander (and also work off a few calories before a rich and heavy lunch).

She saw to her surprise that it was already ten past ten. But then she had lain awake for hours last night, agonizing, fretting – alternately blaming Alexander, then herself. Perhaps she *had* been too clingy; too eager for him to make a formal commitment, which she knew to her cost could scare men off, however much she personally might long for it. As she nibbled on a croissant, she wondered for the umpteenth time what he was actually *doing*. Had he stayed alone in the flat, or gone to visit friends? Was he regretting what he'd said? Missing her? Or glad of his new freedom?

She tried to distract herself by getting washed and dressed and, by five to eleven, she was downstairs in the foyer, kitted out in coat and boots and gloves.

'The treasure hunt?' she asked. 'It said meet here in Reception. Is everyone outside already?'

'Oh, it's not *outside*,' the receptionist explained. 'It's in the drawing-room. Just along the passage, madam, first door on the left.'

'The drawing-room?' she repeated, feeling a surge of disappointment. The whole beauty of the treasure hunts at school was the sense of space, of freedom; the challenge of exploring places normally out of bounds; the joy of communing with wild nature instead of being confined to a stuffy classroom. But, due to the bad weather, they were obviously holding it indoors. Still, it needn't be a write-off – not completely – not if they were allowed the run of the house. That would certainly compensate and, after all, the place was big enough, with a whole extensive modern wing she hadn't even glimpsed yet, as well as a billiard-room, a library and an octagonal conservatory, in the older part of the building. With the clues concealed in all those different areas, she could chase about for hours; sprint from room to room, discovering secret snuggeries or hidden glory-holes; climb from cellar to attic; maybe even find her way to the turrets and gaze down at the landscape.

A woman in the Manor Park green uniform was standing in the doorway, ready to welcome all contestants. 'Are you taking part in the treasure hunt?' she asked.

Emma nodded, relieved to see that there was no sign of either Victoria or Rosamund as she peered into the large, high-ceilinged drawing-room.

'Great!' the woman enthused, passing her a biro and a sheet of paper, both printed with the Manor Park insignia.

Seating herself on the sofa beside a couple of greyheads, Emma scanned the sheet.

MANOR PARK TREASURE HUNT was printed in bold capitals, with a typed list of questions underneath – the clues, presumably. However, reading on, she saw to her dismay that it was a completely static pursuit. All you had to do was fill in the answers to the questions, place the first letter of each answer in a numbered box on the sheet, then rearrange the letters to find the hidden word. Far from racing round the house, you didn't move an inch from your seat; the only form of exercise the movement of the pen across the paper.

Of course, she should have had more sense than to imagine that a bunch of octogenarians would go bounding up and down the stairs, risking falls and fractures, let alone scamper round the grounds, climbing trees, or crawling on their stomachs to peer over the edge of streams, as *she* had done at school. This was just an indoor parlour game – or maybe even a marketing ploy, judging by the tenor of the questions.

The tranquil atmosphere at Manor Park Hotel is designed to help you —— (fill in a word of 5 letters).
Manor Park Hotel is renowned for its fine cuisine. Fill in the name of our magnificent restaurant, redesigned this year ——— (11 letters).

Quickly excusing herself to her neighbours, she sneaked towards the door, but the woman with the papers stood blocking her escape.

'Do you need another sheet, madam, or is your pen not working?'

'No, I'm, er, just a bit … overdressed. I'll take my coat and boots off and be back in a couple of minutes.'

Instead, she charged along the corridor and out of the front door. The lounge was stifling, the entire hotel maintained at tropical heat, and she was gasping for some air.

Streaking across the lawn, she turned off into the shrubbery and continued running along the path, gradually calming down as the peace and space and stillness of the grounds enfolded her in their green embrace. Even the raw December weather suited her bleak mood. Who wanted the mocking sun to shine when Alexander was lost to her?

As she slowed her pace, she was struck by an idea: why didn't she go on her own individual treasure hunt – invent the clues, invent the prize? At least it would help to pass the time until the ordeal of Christmas lunch.

She paused a moment, trying to recall the form. She did, in fact, remember a few of the clues from school, including the first she had ever deciphered, as a skinny child of twelve: *three tall, slender ladies have changed their fresh green dress for gold*. Admittedly, it had taken time to solve, but, once it clicked, she'd gone zipping towards the three tall, graceful poplar trees just beyond the sports field, then resplendent in their golden autumn foliage. And, yes, there she found the second clue, hidden in a patch of grass just beneath their trunks.

Twelve had been a perfect age. She'd been independent, carefree, with no periods yet, or breasts, no marks of dangerous womanhood that would ensnare you as an adult in the baited trap of love. OK, she'd *be* a child – pretend to be one, anyway, in order to snuff out Alexander, eradicate the entire male sex. She was in her all-girls' school again, with all-female staff and teachers, and, as for love, it was safe enough for twelve-year-olds, because you only loved your dog and your best friend.

Elated by the memory, she went hurtling on through the shrubbery in search of poplars *here*. She couldn't see a sign of one, but eventually hit upon three slender, feminine-looking trees that would have to do instead, despite the fact they weren't especially tall, and completely bare, not gold. She crawled on her hands and knees around their trunks, looking for the second clue, then imagining she'd found it: *my fruits supply sport for boys*.

That was simple: a conker tree.

Off she rushed again, searching for a horse chestnut, although finally having to settle for a *sweet* chestnut, which didn't fit the clue. She knew she was taking liberties, but the important thing was to keep active; keep her body moving at full stretch; keep inhabiting her child's mind.

There, beneath the sweet chestnut's boughs, she mimed the action of picking up the third clue, again tuning in to her memories of school. Strange how she remembered the words almost off by heart, although she had left the place eight years ago.

If you're sitting down, I'm sitting underneath you.

That had proved quite baffling, until she twigged the fact it was probably a bench, with the next clue taped beneath its seat. Well, there were benches by the dozen here at Manor Park. Swooping back to the main lawn, she crouched down by the first one and scrabbled underneath it, trying to recapture her former child's excitement at discovering a piece of paper, pinned there, as she'd guessed.

She sat on the bench to read it, already out of breath, her upbeat mood suddenly collapsing into deep dejection as she unfolded empty air. What in God's name was she *doing*, rampaging around like a maniac on a completely fictitious treasure hunt, with no prize at the end? Her whole life stretched ahead now, devoid of any prizes – loveless, pointless, empty, without Alexander to share it. It *was* his fault, not hers. He'd been utterly unreasonable, acting on a selfish whim, without any prior discussion. In fact, her parents could even be right in damning him as feckless and irresponsible. If she wasn't so infatuated, she would have seen his faults long ago: the way he drifted round the place without a proper job, never getting up till late, while *she* was in the office on the dot of eight o'clock each day. And his untidiness and messiness – dirty clothes tossed on the floor, socks still inside-out; post piling up unanswered, while he lolled in bed, listening to his precious jazz. And his infuriating habit of burning all the saucepans because he'd wandered off to check the winning lottery numbers, or to unearth a hidden Mars Bar from his sock-drawer.

She jumped up to her feet. How had she been so blind; failed to realize that it was actually an advantage to be shot of such a loser before they'd tied the knot? Thank God she hadn't gone that far, hadn't had his kids, wasn't bound to him by a wedding ring and parenthood. Instead of moping around, ruining her Christmas Day, she ought to be rejoicing that she could bid goodbye for ever to his incompetence and laziness. If she had any sense, she'd indulge herself, for once; grab all the goodies going in this luxurious hotel; make it a time of celebration, not of grief. In fact, if she went indoors, she could search out Tina and Marilyn (who had both been pretty decent last night) and suggest they share a table for Christmas lunch – just the three of them. With the right companions, the meal could be a breeze. In fact, she was beginning to see how crucial it was to choose friends as well as lovers with the very greatest care. Victoria and Rosamund could take a running jump – along with Alexander.

She began sprinting towards the house, turning from the lawn on to the drive, which was less waterlogged and so wouldn't slow her down. Rounding the corner, she suddenly saw a figure stampeding towards her – a familiar figure, a coatless figure, clad only in shirt and trousers, despite the bitter cold.

Incredulous, she stumbled to a halt. '*Alexander*!' she whispered, not knowing whether to race towards him or bolt the other way.

'Emma, darling, *wait*! Please wait.'

He caught up with her, clasped her in his arms. 'I'm so sorry! I'm so desperately sorry! I was totally in the wrong. Please forgive me – *please*. The minute you'd gone, I realized how much you mean to me. I can't bear Christmas on my own. Come back, I beg you – *now*. I need you to be there with me – not just today, for ever.'

Pressed against his broad, warm chest, inhaling the faint but familiar smell of his skin, his hair, his maleness, she felt her heart capsizing in a tidal wave of contradictory emotions: love and fury, longing and sheer cynicism, resentment and desire.

'Emma, why the hell aren't you saying anything? What's wrong? Why don't you answer?'

Wordlessly she shook her head. What *could* she say, when she was so utterly confused? Had she over-reacted, condemned this man unfairly? Was it really a crime to burn saucepans, or leave socks inside-out, or try to make a living by writing songs and selling things on e-bay? If one viewed it in a different light, his defiance of convention could be regarded as courageous, the sign of an original mind – an artist and adventurer who refused to knuckle down and become a passive wage-slave. In fact, she was suddenly struck by the most miraculous thought: perhaps she had actually *won* the treasure hunt and Alexander's dramatic return was her longed-for, glittering prize – the prize of Christmas restored. And not just any Christmas, but an incredibly romantic one, with a proposal and a wedding ring.

And yet ... And yet ... Just moments ago, she'd been convinced that she didn't *want* his ring; didn't want her kids to be landed with a feckless, work-shy father. If he had undergone no change of heart, then this treasure might be counterfeit – what people termed fool's gold. So what, for pity's sake, did she decide?

She drew away, still silent.

She was the fool, because she simply didn't know.

Indonesians

'Goodbye then, Lynn. I'll phone when we touch down.'

'Goodbye, Pauline. Good luck!'

One final hug and she was gone – an inconspicuous figure vanishing through the departure gate, striding towards a new country and new life.

Lynn stood, fists clenched, having forcibly to restrain herself from dashing after her cousin and begging her to change her plans; turn down the prestigious American job and stay with her in London. Without Pauline, she felt rudderless and lost; indeed, could hardly even remember the way back to the flat.

She made herself turn round and walk towards the exit, impeded by the choppy tide of passengers who seemed to be bearing down on her from each and every side, armed with luggage, pushchairs, babies, children and bulky carrier bags. There was a constant risk of being knocked off-course by self-willed baggage-trolleys, rammed by wheelie-cases, or tripped up by tearaway toddlers. Did her cousin *have* to fly on one of the busiest days of the summer? And, as for airports being glamorous – as she'd assumed before she'd been in one – well, this place seemed a cross between a transit camp and an overcrowded shopping mall.

Spotting a man in uniform, she rushed over in relief, fighting a temptation to cling to him like a toddler, so that he'd pick her up and comfort her. Instead, she asked him, in a tight, choked voice, if he could direct her to the Heathrow Express. Stupid not to know the way, when she'd just come from there, with Pauline, but everything seemed different on her own.

The directions were straightforward, but it was still hard to make much progress, because she kept standing back for other people, or apologizing when *she* was pushed or shoved. She just wasn't used to crowds; found them quite alarming. Supposing someone panicked, or the whole mob ran amok? Even in the lift, she was pressed against a seething mass of warm, perspiring flesh, and jabbed by still more cases. No one said a word, she noticed, or exchanged a friendly smile. She had learned already, after just one day in London, that it wasn't done to greet one's fellow citizens, let alone strike up a conversation.

And, once she'd boarded the train, it would have been impossible, in any case, to have had any sort of chat. There was too much competition in the form of jaunty music piped throughout the carriage, and news blaring from a television mounted on the wall, alternating with announcements and advice.

'Welcome aboard this Heathrow Express to Paddington. Please have your tickets ready for inspection.'

'Passengers are advised to use the luggage-racks and not to block the aisles.'

'Please familiarize yourselves with the safety regulations. Our next stop is ...'

On the journey out, she had barely noticed the constant interruptions – too absorbed in checking Pauline's instructions, before her cousin left for New York: she must always set the burglar alarm, double-lock the front door and make sure the chain was on; put the rubbish out each Tuesday morning; pay the Council Tax and water rates, the electricity and phone bills ...

Unfolding the list, she studied it again, with increasing apprehension. Her mother, although decidedly neurotic (sometimes downright paranoid, in fact), had none the less taken care of all such household tasks. Anyway, they didn't *have* a burglar alarm at home, or a chain on the front door. Rates and bills and taxes seemed alien and daunting things that belonged to the adult realm, and secretly she still craved to be a child. Which only went to show what an utter wimp she was, considering she'd left home as well as school now, and was old enough to drive, vote, drink in a pub and have sex. Although she'd done none of those except the pub – another proof of her backwardness.

'In the interests of safely and security, passengers may be subjected to a search ...'

God, she hoped not! She wasn't carrying anything incriminating, but in London even new-born babies could probably be banged up. She peered out of the window, in an effort to distract herself, but her surroundings did nothing to inspire her. They appeared to be travelling through a wasteland of bleak industrial estates, ugly, brutish warehouses, and rows of small, mean houses, interspersed with scrubland. If only the train were heading back to Herefordshire, with its peace and space and silence, its big, brooding skies, which made you feel you could take off like a bird and fly for ever and ever – not in a lumpen plane like Pauline's, but on sweeping, soaring wings. Yet, in less than twenty minutes they had arrived at Paddington, and she was engulfed once more in the bad-tempered arms of another seething crowd. Retreating to a corner of the station, she consulted her tube-map, along with the sketch-map Pauline had drawn her, with directions to the flat.

'It's dead simple,' her cousin had said. 'Take the Bakerloo Line to Oxford Circus, change there for the Victoria Line, then just follow the red arrows on my map.'

Not 'dead simple', actually for someone who had never braved the tube before. On the outward journey, they'd taken a taxi to Paddington, because the Circle Line was suspended, for some reason, and there were delays on the Bakerloo. By now it was the rush-hour, and getting on to *any* train demanded courage and resolve. Having watched the other passengers from the safety of a bench, she realized you were meant to simply shove, and if you stepped on someone's foot, or butted them in the back, or got caught in the closing doors because there wasn't room for another single soul, well, those were just the risks you had to run.

However, once she'd let three bulging trains rattle off without her, she decided to ditch both courtesy and caution, and all but threw herself into the carriage when the fourth train thundered in. Clinging to the rail, she stood her ground while a press of people battled in behind her, until there was barely room to slide a ruler between their close-packed forms. Well, at least she couldn't fall, however much the train lurched. She had always hated being short (a pathetic four-foot-ten), but her lack of height in *this* situation meant her nose was jammed into the smelly, hairy armpit of the big hulk standing next to her.

It was sweltering in the carriage – hot enough outside, for heaven's sake – the hottest August day on record, according to the News. Her clothes felt clammy-damp; her hair hung hot and heavy down her back, and every time the train juddered to a halt, she peered anxiously through the serried mass of heads, to read the name of the station. She was terrified she'd miss her stop and land up miles from Pauline's.

At Oxford Circus, she tried to struggle out, as another throng of sweaty bodies barged into the carriage, pushing in the opposite direction. 'I'm sorry,' she kept repeating, wishing she could magic herself into a puff of smoke or wisp of thistledown, and simply float above them. 'Excuse me, can I please get by?' she asked again, politely, but most Londoners seemed deaf.

Having extricated herself, at last, she stood uncertain on the platform, as people hurtled past. No point asking for directions, since nobody had time to stop – that was clear from the frenetic way they moved, as if they dared not waste a single second in their battle to get home.

Home, she thought, uneasily. Do I even *have* one any more? The small, cosy cottage she had lived in all her life was already on the market, and once her mother moved abroad next week, there'd be no more reason to go back to Peterchurch – a village so familiar she could almost walk it blindfold. She could return for occasional visits, of course, but it wouldn't be the same without any kind of base, any place to call her own.

Looking up at the signs – Victoria Line, Central Line, Emergency Exit, Help Point – she wished there were signs for other things in life: placards in your house or in the streets, instructing you as to when to get up, when to go to bed, what to buy in the way of food, when to eat it, what to wear. And more Help Points would be valuable, in every town and village, staffed by kindly counsellors, and dispensing wise advice. For all her eighteen years, she'd had a mother, or a teacher, or headmaster telling her what to do and how to spend her day, but, in the last month or so, that structure had collapsed. It would be a relief to start her new job in three weeks. At least she'd have a boss then, someone to take over from the headmaster and give her day some shape. Pathetic, if not shaming, though, to be pining for the anchor of a timetable, when all her friends revelled in their freedom, bounded off on gap-years, lived it up, took risks, resisted even minor threats to their precious independence.

The second part of the journey was slightly less alarming and, when she alighted at Victoria, she even felt a flicker of excitement at living in such a central part of London – all thanks to Pauline, of course. Her cousin preferred to entrust her flat to someone in the family, even at a token rent, rather than risk subletting it to a careless, feckless stranger. Pauline had decided not to sell the place, in case the American posting didn't suit her and she returned to England after this trial year.

Lynn fumbled for the sketch-map and finally located Buckingham Palace Road, although there was no sign of any palace; only streams of traffic and the inevitable crowds, of course. Following Pauline's red arrows, she turned left at Ecclestone Bridge and into Belgrave Road, which was quieter altogether – a street of elegant white houses, each with a pillared portico and each five storeys high. At least this road was familiar, as she and Pauline had walked up and down it several times, both yesterday and this morning; her cousin pointing out the numerous hotels – almost more, apparently, than the number of private homes.

'Sometimes, if it's a really busy summer and everywhere else is full up, people ring *my* bell and ask if they can stay. I've even thought of re-naming the place "Hotel Pauline", instead of flat 1A!'

Lynn had laughed, although secretly she'd wished the flat was higher up the building, rather than on the vulnerable ground floor. People might break in: tramps, or drunks, or muggers. London was full of yobs with knives – everyone knew that.

She glanced around her nervously before extracting the keys from her bag, but no one was in sight except a couple of family groups, loaded down with luggage and wilting in the heat, presumably making their way to one of the many hotels.

Once she let herself in and stood in the stylish sitting-room, she had an uncomfortable sense that the flat itself was judging her; finding her too plain and dull to match its exotic oxblood walls and dramatic purple rugs. And too naïve to appreciate the offbeat objects ranged around the room: a fat-bellied, smiling Buddha, with a garland round its neck, a balding bison's head, a pair of bellows hanging on the wall, and a ship's anchor, for some reason, beached on this inland floor. At home, the cottage walls were boring-white, the carpet safely beige, and the only things in evidence were her mother's china figurines, a few faded family photographs and piles of magazines. Pauline had always been sophisticated, not only twelve years older but a high flier even at school, and destined for great things. She, in contrast, was an idiot, who'd failed to get to university, and was taking a mundane job with a high-street print-shop in Kilburn (which she'd only landed, in any case, through a friend of her mother, who was pally with the boss).

She stowed away the bunch of keys, having promised Pauline faithfully to look after them with the utmost care. Reliable she was – too much so, in fact: the kind of anxious fusspot who made twice-daily lists, double-checked each smallest thing, and still worried she'd forgotten some vital date or task.

Wandering into the kitchen (which was painted marigold, with a peculiar modern painting shrieking on one wall), she decided to make a cup of tea and try to treat the place like home. It *was* her home for this next year, so the flat would have to accept her, gauche as she might be. She took her cup back to the sitting-room and sat by the window that looked out on the street. Another baggage-laden family was just walking up the steps of the Central House Hotel, which stood directly opposite. London was swarming with tourists – she'd seen that for herself – and if people travelled half across the world to visit its attractions, then she, too, should make the most of it, now she had the chance. Tomorrow, *she'd* be a tourist, stop pining for puny Peterchurch and embark on a marathon sight-seeing tour.

She collapsed on to a bench and loosened the laces of her trainers. A bad blister had erupted from the miles she'd walked these last six days, although her mind was singing and seething from all the places she'd visited – places merging into each other now, like the pieces of several complicated jigsaws, all jumbled up together in one box. Even here, in Leicester Square, she couldn't tear her eyes away from sights she never saw at home: two gays kissing passionately in public, without a trace of embarrassment; a girl in a micro-bikini stretched out on the grass, in full view of passers-by; a middle-aged man dressed as a cowboy, complete with hat and holster and knee-length leather boots, despite the blistering heat. Every other person seemed to be a foreigner. In fact, in less than a week in London, she'd seen more different nationalities, and heard more different languages than in the whole of her life to date.

Sometimes she liked to imagine that one of those swarthy strangers was actually her dad, and they'd recognize each other through some deep, instinctive bond, despite the fact she had never met him, and probably never would. All she knew was that he 'wasn't English' and had long since disappeared. As a child in Sunday school, they had learned about the Blessed Virgin being fathered by the Holy Ghost, and she'd wondered if a similar thing had happened in her own case (although with only the haziest notion of who or what the Holy Ghost might be). Later on, she'd speculated that perhaps she had come into the world via some new technique that dispensed with men and sperm. Her mother refused to talk about the subject, although knowledge of one's father was probably a basic human right, which meant she could go to court and make a formal case. But suing a mother prone to roller-coaster mood-swings didn't seem a frightfully good idea. Besides, she found the whole thing shameful and unsettling, and preferred to pretend, as her mother did, in public, that her dad had simply died before her birth.

All at once, she jumped up from the bench and paced moodily around the square, longing for a more normal mother – or at least one she could rely on, and who wasn't going crazy over some odious new boyfriend – if you could use the word 'boyfriend' for the ancient bloke who was dragging her to Amsterdam to set up home with him.

She dashed across the road, blind to everything but her loathing for that Dutch creep, and was hooted to her senses by a stretch-limousine in gleaming silver, which came gliding round the corner. Intrigued, despite herself, she peered in through the shaded windows, but could see nothing but a blur, although the car was so fantastically long, it must have held two dozen people.

'Hey, beautiful!' a voice behind her called, as she jumped back on to the pavement. She wheeled round to see a drop-dead-gorgeous guy, who, the minute he glimpsed her front view, looked deeply disappointed and quickly backed away. To hell with him! She was used to disappointing blokes, although it still hurt to see that look of total let-down once they met her eyes. The trouble was, her hair attracted glances, being wavy, waist-length and a deep, glossy Marmite-brown. But it didn't match the rest of her: her thin, pale face and granny specs, her shaming lack of boobs. Occasionally she fantasized about meeting someone registered blind, who would love her for her self, and not for her looks – or lack of them. He and she and the guide-dog could live as a contented threesome, in a cottage of their own, with roses round the door. And he'd certainly be sympathetic about her crappy eyes. She'd worn glasses since the age of seven; an eye-patch for two years.

Still feeling somewhat mortified, as well as hot and sticky, she decided to go back to the flat. Would she *ever* meet a bloke? She wouldn't mind an ugly one, except even they liked pretty girls, she'd found to her dismay. It seemed so unfair that her mother, who was also plain and short (not to mention pushing forty), was actually head-over-heels in love, even planning marriage, for God's sake, having bitterly opposed it up till now. And, she, the daughter, was duty-bound to attend their lousy wedding; would have to watch them making fools of themselves in some pompous Dutch registry office (although she refused to be a bridesmaid – she'd made that pretty clear).

Once ensconced in the oxblood sitting-room, with a cold drink and a plate of scrambled eggs, she gazed out at the street, engaged in her nightly diversion of studying the tourists who came up and down at all hours, to or from the hotels. She had counted the hotels this morning – seventeen in total; even ventured into one or two, asking for their brochures. The pictures in the brochures had made her almost envious: romantic couples toasting each other in the hotel's candle-lit restaurant, or jolly, laughing families bouncing on the beds. Stupid to be lonely in a city of eight million people. But the trouble was she didn't know *one* of those eight million; had barely exchanged a word with anyone, except the occasional surly bus-driver, or the people clipping tickets at the visitor attractions. She couldn't phone her mother, who had already left for Amsterdam, and rarely answered her mobile anyway (probably too busy shagging loathsome Hendrik.) She was too shy to go to bars and clubs; too skint to pay for theatres; too self-conscious to eat out on her own, so the long, light evenings dragged. There was always television, of course, but she was sick of sport and sitcoms. And she dared not listen to her music when she'd promised Pauline she wouldn't disturb the people in the flat above, or below her in the basement. Actually, she was beginning to wonder where those neighbours *were*. She hadn't seen a sign of them, nor heard the slightest sound through the ceiling or the floor.

Peering down the street again, her attention was attracted by the foreign family of four (mother, father, girl and boy) whom she had seen last night and again first thing this morning, trekking up and down, apparently searching for accommodation. All four had shining caps of coarse, dark hair; all four wore spectacles, and the parents were roughly *her* height, frail and slimly built. She watched with interest as they trudged along the road once more, walking up the steps of one hotel and then the next, exactly as they'd done before. Why couldn't they find what they wanted? Were the prices too high? The kids a problem? Or were they simply trying to track down friends of theirs, but unsure of the correct address? She began to feel increasing pity for the wretched little group, who were now standing only yards away. The father was shaking his head in a hopeless sort of fashion; the mother looked close to tears; and the children seemed exhausted, with drooping shoulders, hollow eyes. She wondered where they'd slept last night. On a bench? In the park? At least the nights were warm, but if they continued living rough, the police might start to harass them.

Registering their olive skin and straight, jet-black, glossy hair, she wasn't exactly sure where they came from, but her guess was Indonesia. They'd done a school project on the country, and, as far as she recalled, it was groaning under every kind of problem: poverty, corruption, a crappy sort of government, terrorism, unemployment, and frequent earthquakes and volcanoes. Perhaps the family had fled the place, in the hope of finding a better life in London.

As they toiled up the steps of yet another hotel, she prayed they'd be successful; that they'd be ushered in, this time; welcomed, greeted warmly, maybe offered a bargain price.

But within minutes they were back in the street, looking still more miserable, and making her feel guilty about scoffing scrambled eggs, when *they* might well be starving. Should she give them food; pop out with the bread and fruit she'd bought this morning and didn't really need? Somehow, she didn't have the nerve. They might think she was being patronizing, and, in any case, she was jumping to conclusions. For all she knew, they might just have had a slap-up meal and weren't hungry in the least.

Snatching up her plate, she decamped into the kitchen, where she could no longer see the street. It was crazy to obsess about this one particular family, when there were scores of others like them, or imagine they were suffering horrors, without a shred of evidence. It was partly their own fault for not trying a different area. Why stick to Belgrave Road, for heaven's sake, when London bristled with hotels of every grade and type?

She'd make herself a hot chocolate, then have an early night, and, with any luck, the depressing little group would have disappeared by morning.

They *hadn't* disappeared. When she drew the curtains shortly after eight, they were sitting on the steps of the hotel opposite, utterly dejected. At that very moment, a small, paunchy man strode out – the manager, the owner? – and shooed them rudely off, as if they were stray dogs. She watched them stumble a few paces down the street, then the father, on his own this time, shuffled through the doorway of the Victor Hotel, despite the large 'No Vacancy' sign, which even *she* could see. But of course they probably had no English, so signs would just be gibberish. She tried to imagine being in a country where you didn't understand a single word; couldn't follow directions or take in information.

Suddenly, on impulse, she dashed out to the street and ran over to the family (now rejoined by the father, who again had drawn a blank). They shrank back at her approach, clearly petrified, as if they assumed she'd come to arrest them, accuse them of some crime.

'Look, it's OK,' she babbled nervously. 'I'm a stranger here in London, too. Oh, I know I'm English, which makes things easier – well, half-English, anyway. My dad—' No, they didn't want to hear about her father. She was meant to be offering help, nor airing her personal problems.

In fact, they looked completely mystified, all staring at her in baffled silence; the children clinging to the mother's skirts.

'I know you can't understand me. Which makes things really difficult. You see, I hoped I could sort things out a bit, maybe lend a hand or—'

A clap of thunder drowned her words, and, all at once, torrential rain began sheeting, drenching down.

'Quick!' she shouted above the noise. 'Follow me! You can't stay out in this.'

She grabbed the mother by the hand, and hustled her along the street in the direction of the flat; the children dashing after them; the father bringing up the rear, with a suitcase in each hand. She all but pushed them through the door and into the hall, where they stood huddled beside their luggage, water dripping from their hair and clothes.

The father cleared his throat, stepped forward, and addressed her in some alien tongue.

'I'm sorry, I haven't a clue what you're saying. Any more than *you* know what the hell I'm on about. But I'm just a friend – don't worry; someone trying to help.'

He responded in the same barbaric language, and she wondered (as she'd often done in French lessons) why every nation in the world couldn't speak one universal language, which would save a lot of muddle and confusion.

'Look, do come in,' she urged, ushering them into the sitting-room and gesturing to the sofa. They seemed reluctant to sit down, however, and remained standing in a stiff, silent row, as if awaiting prosecution.

She clamped a smile on her face, tried to keep it there, to put them at their ease; her muscles aching with the strain of it. She should be making tea, fetching clean, dry clothes, but she dared not leave the room, for fear they'd dash back into the street the moment her back was turned.

'Me Lynn,' she said, pointing to herself.

But no flicker of recognition in the four inscrutable faces. She fetched a piece of paper from the desk, wrote her name in large black capitals, repeating it aloud and tapping her chest as she did so. 'Me Lynn, me Lynn.'

The woman let out a sudden exclamation, catching on, at last. 'Yeyen,' she said, pointing to her own chest.

Lynn handed her the paper and made a writing gesture. Obediently the woman wrote her name down.

'And your husband?' Lynn enquired, now pointing to *his* chest.

'Mulyana,' the woman said, writing it down without even being asked. They were actually making progress – of a sort.

'And the children?' Lynn took them each by the hand, surprised and pleased when they didn't pull away but curled their small, damp fingers round her own.

'Legi and Rodiah,' Yeyen said, jotting down the names.

The introductions were followed by a further silence; the only sound the steady drumming of the rain as it pounded on the pavement, slammed against the windowpane. Lynn was beginning to feel tired herself, just from the strain of trying to communicate. 'Tea!' she suggested, finally, seizing her empty breakfast cup and raising it to her lips, to show them what she meant.

All four shook their heads. Perhaps they didn't drink tea. Indonesians were Muslim, she remembered from the project, and Muslims were forbidden certain things – pork and alcohol, for starters. But orange juice should be OK. She ran to fetch the carton and four glasses, praying they wouldn't leave in the few minutes she was gone, and ridiculously relieved to find them there when she returned, although still standing in a formal row.

'Sit down,' she all but ordered, patting the sofa once more. She'd have to be strict with them, like a teacher, however much it went against her character. Miraculously, they did sit, and she poured juice into the glasses, smiling all the while, to try to reassure them. Then, with the piece of paper as her prompt, she handed each a glass and repeated the four names in turn, muddling the girl's name, with the boy's, though. This produced a fit of giggles from both children, and seemed to break the ice.

Emboldened, she darted back to the kitchen, bringing with her, this time, a bag of cherries and a variety-pack of biscuits. Arranging the latter on a plate, she offered them around, but again all four refused. Taking a custard-cream herself, she crunched it slowly and loudly, as a sort of demonstration, in the hope they'd follow suit. The gambit seemed to work, since the mother took one, too, then the father and the kids. In fact, once encouraged, the children started gobbling biscuits at such a frantic rate, she suspected they hadn't eaten for some time, and the whole packet (of four different sorts) was demolished in ten minutes.

Next she proffered the cherries, meeting the same initial reluctance, which, she guessed, was a simple form of politeness. Perhaps, in Indonesia, you were taught always to decline, so as not to seem greedy or grasping. She solved the impasse by hanging pairs of cherries over the children's ears, as her mother used to do with *her*, when in one of her rare good moods.

'They're called cherry ear-rings,' she said, not caring if they didn't understand. At least they'd get the gist. Besides, anything was better than sitting in that tense and awkward silence. She went to fetch a mirror, to show the kids their 'ear-rings', delighted when they giggled again.

The father spat a cherry-stone fastidiously into his hand, then placed it on his plate. 'Hotel,' he said, surprising her with an English word, although he must have seen it written countless times in his search for accommodation.

'You're looking for a hotel?' she prompted. 'Yes, I realized that already. But, you know, I think you ought to try a different area. My cousin says it gets incredibly crowded around Victoria, especially at the height of the season, but if you went a bit further out ...' Useless. He couldn't follow, and was just staring at her in mute incomprehension.

The wife took over, reaching out both arms, to indicate the room. 'Hotel?' she repeated.

'Oh, I see. You're asking if *this* is a hotel.' She bit her lip, dismayed. What on earth could she say? 'No' would mean they'd leave, and how could she subject them to the deluge, still sheeting down outside? 'Er, yes,' she said uncertainly. 'It's ... called the Hotel Pauline.' Trying to swallow her sense of guilt towards her cousin, she wrote the name down; passed the piece of paper across.

Immediately, the man got out his wallet and began extracting ten-pound notes and pressing them into her hand.

'No!' she cried, all but flinging them back. 'It's a free hotel – no payment.'

He clearly thought she was turning them away. The hangdog

look returned, he said something to his wife, and all four got up and moved towards the door.

'OK, OK, I'll take the cash, but not so much. £20 is ample.' Retrieving two of the notes from his hand, she waved away the rest, then quickly led them into the bedroom, to prevent further argument. If she had assumed the role of hotelier, then the next logical step was to show them to their room. Fortunately Pauline had a double bed, and, if they didn't mind being rather squashed, it would be big enough for the children too. *She* could sleep on the sofa.

They seemed absolutely enchanted by the large, old-fashioned brass bedstead, with its heap of coloured cushions and white lace counterpane, and by the stout Edwardian wardrobe (which Pauline had kindly emptied for her.) Hastily she removed her own few clothes, her brush and comb and make-up, dumped the lot on the kitchen table, then returned to show them the bathroom.

Uncomfortable thoughts of Pauline kept pricking at her mind. Her cousin had, in fact, given her permission to invite her friends to stay, so long as they were trustworthy and didn't have wild parties. But this family might be *far* from trustworthy – even spies or crooks, for all she knew. Yet she somehow couldn't imagine them making trouble, when they were so quiet and deferential, and, as for throwing dissolute parties, that seemed unlikely in the extreme. The children, she'd already noted, were exceptionally well-behaved – nothing like most English kids, who seemed to be always squabbling and shouting. These two resembled a pair of small brown owls: solemn, shy, respectful. When she'd watched them in the street, they had never once complained or cried, however long they'd had to stand about. Besides, this was just a compromise solution, and only for one night. Tomorrow, she'd take them to Earls Court or Bayswater, or one of the other areas Pauline had said were swarming with hotels. With an English-speaking person to help, they were bound to find a room, but at least today they could catch up on their sleep.

She went to fetch their luggage from the hall, squinting at the labels on the cases. Mulyana Yahya, she spelled out, followed by an address in Jakarta. So they *were* Indonesians, she thought with a sense of strange relief. She had always hated the fact that she couldn't locate her father, and had to rely on speculation. Simply knowing that he 'wasn't English' left things horribly vague, and seemed to spread him thinner and thinner over so wide an expanse of territory, he crumbled into dust. But at least she could place this family; pin them down to one particular spot. They'd showed a map of Indonesia as part of the school project, with Jakarta ringed in red. At the time, she'd longed to ring her *dad* in red; give him a country, nationality, home and habitat.

As she heaved the luggage into the bedroom, Mulyana scurried towards her and took the cases himself, apparently horrified that she should be struggling on her own, although she could make no sense of his actual rush of words. Since communication was proving such a problem, she resorted to a mime-show for the family as a whole. First she mimed unpacking, then washing, then sleeping, and was immediately rewarded with nods and smiles. Brilliant! They were getting somewhere.

What worried her was lunch. Her mother didn't cook, and *she* had never learned, although she could just about rustle up baked beans or eggs on toast. But then most hotels in this vicinity provided only breakfast and an evening meal, and dispensed with lunch entirely. Well, breakfast had been custard-creams and cherries, and she could maybe buy in fish and chips for supper. For the moment, though, she wasn't going anywhere – not until the weather improved. The thunderstorm was still rumbling and emoting, as if congratulating itself on having brought the long, hot, dry spell to this dramatic, drenching close. Sudden bolts of lightning crackled through the sky, while the torrential rain kept lashing down with a manic sort of glee.

While her visitors unpacked, she studied her maps of London. If she proposed to act as guide tomorrow, she'd need some idea of where to go and which hotels to try. Maybe, even once they'd settled somewhere else, they could still remain in touch; she showing them the sights, perhaps teaching them some English, if they planned to stay long enough to make it worth their while. At least she'd solved their predicament, and, in the process, provided what she'd lacked herself: company, a sense of purpose and a structure to her day.

'Lynn, it's Pauline here. How are you?'

'Er, fine,' she said, glancing around her guiltily, as if her cousin was on a spy-phone and could see right into the flat.

'You sound a bit peculiar. Is everything OK?'

'Yeah, great.' Quickly she changed the subject, and quizzed Pauline about New York – the job, the Manhattan apartment, her boss, her workmates, the weather. But Pauline would keep focusing on *her*; asking awkward questions.

'Are you finding your way around all right?'

'Yes, no problem at all.' She hadn't been out, in fact – except to the nearest local shop – since the family arrived.

'Not feeling lonely?'

'Oh, no.' Actually, she did feel rather isolated, despite her visitors, who seemed reluctant to leave the bedroom, even in the daytime, let alone use her help to find a proper hotel. She suspected they were hiding from the authorities; probably over here illegally, or in some sort of trouble.

'And how are things in the flat?'

'Brilliant! I love it.' In truth, it was proving quite a strain, sleeping on the sofa every night; cooking breakfast every morning for a family of four; supper every night. It wasn't that Mulyana didn't pay her. He was continually handing her banknotes, some of which she took, if only to cover the cost of the food. But she was feeling more and more uncomfortable about having landed up in this extraordinary situation. Fortunately, Pauline's phone-call had brought her to her senses. She'd *have* to move these people out, in fairness to her cousin; just couldn't continue deceiving her like this.

'Are you remembering to double-lock the door?'

'Of course.' She kept the chain on permanently, as much to protect the Indonesians from any prying officials, as to protect herself from muggers.

'Well, look, I'll phone again next week. And you ring *me*, if you run into any problems.'

'OK.'

'Promise?'

'Promise.'

Her hands were shaking as she put down the receiver, torn between loyalty to Pauline and a sense of strange solicitude towards the Indonesians. If only she could explain to them that the flat wasn't really hers, and not a hotel at all. But her bid to teach them English had foundered from the start. They treated her with deference and respect, but as a stranger, a hotelier, which meant she couldn't sit down with them to meals, or take them out to see the sights. Yet she dared not leave them here alone for longer than her brief shopping trips, for fear of what might happen in her absence. If they *were* in trouble, the police might storm the door, or someone come to question them, or they might do some damage; steal some precious object. Again, it seemed unlikely, when, as far as she could tell, they were honest and dependable. As well as the constant terror of Pauline finding out, she faced a dilemma in her own right, in that she was due to start her job next week. How could she leave the family from 8 a.m. till 6, every single weekday? Apart from the problem of what they might get up to while she was away, she would never get their breakfast in time, before she had to leave for work, and their supper would be late, by the time she'd shopped and cooked.

No, she would have to take a stand this evening; inform them that the 'hotel' was closing for a late-summer break, or for essential renovation and repairs. Yet how the hell did she mime 'essential repairs'; make them understand that it broke her heart to turf them out, but that her first loyalty was to Pauline? She also owed a debt to her boss, for taking on a school-leaver with no experience, just because one of his friends had recommended her.

A sudden smell of burning sent her dashing to the kitchen. She'd been cooking a complicated chicken dish when Pauline's phone-call interrupted her – her first attempt at Indonesian cuisine. It hadn't looked too promising right from the beginning, and now it was a charred and blackened mess. Chucking the ruined pan in the sink, she sank down at the table and burst into tears of fury and frustration. 'Reliable,' she called herself, yet she'd been downright irresponsible in having let these people in; taking such ridiculous risks with someone else's property.

Hearing a timid tap on the door, she fought to get control, wiping her eyes on the tea-towel, and choking back her sobs. Yeyen entered nervously, then, with one sympathetic look at Lynn's swollen, tear-stained face, she suddenly stepped forward and clasped her in her arms. Lynn stiffened automatically, startled by the gesture, and only gradually relaxing as she stood pressed against the softly sheltering form. Yeyen was stroking her hair, rhythmically and slowly; making soothing, clucking noises, as she had done once with

Rodiah, when the child had cut her hand. Lynn closed her eyes, enchanted by the rare sensation of being cradled and enfolded, and wishing those small, gentle hands would hold her close for ever.

It was Yeyen who pulled away, sniffing the air with an anxious look, and, having traced the smell of burning to the sink, letting out a torrent of words as she discovered the scorched, encrusted saucepan. Although the words were indecipherable, they sounded non-judgemental; kindly words that seemed to say 'don't worry. It doesn't matter. Mistakes can happen to anyone.'

And she had now discovered the cookbook, still open at the chicken, rice and pineapple dish; its Indonesian name printed beside the English one.

'*Nasi Ayam Nanas*,' she spelled out, giving a nod of recognition, then examining the ingredients still strewn around the worktops: the remainder of the chicken, the second pineapple and second packet of rice.

'I bought double, you see,' Lynn murmured, as much to herself as to Yeyen. The reason she had got into the habit of buying double quantities was to cut down on her shopping trips, so that she could be present in the house as much as was humanly possible, to keep the strictest eye on things.

Yeyen was still speaking, and Lynn gathered from her gestures that she wanted to take over and cook the dish again herself. She nodded in relief. A native Indonesian would know about the spices – lemongrass and cumin, coriander, ginger root – things alien to *her*, which she had never bought in her life before. Lynn handed her a clean pan, showed her where the oil was kept, and the knives and wooden spoons, then sank on to a kitchen chair; tired not just from lack of sleep, but from the strain of being a security guard as well as a hotelier.

However, watching Yeyen chop and slice and simmer, she felt a sense of peace and even happiness seep into her bones. She had always wanted a mother who could produce a meal from scratch, instead of opening tins or shoving plastic pouches in the microwave. And Yeyen was a natural, as was obvious from the way she worked – swift and deft and skilful – so that, in less than half an hour, the food was almost ready and looked exactly like the picture in the cookbook (in contrast to her *own* effort).

Ashamed of doing nothing, she jumped up to lay the table – although not for four, as normally. So far, she'd been the waitress, remaining on her feet to serve the meal, but today she intended eating with them, and thus laid up for five. OK, they wouldn't understand, but she'd let them assume it was some sort of celebration.

She went to fetch the others from the bedroom. Mulyana looked seriously alarmed, as if, having heard her sobbing, he feared some new catastrophe, and even the children were crouched down on the floor in a posture of defeat. Well, there *was* bad news in store: he and his family would have to move out tomorrow – and with no delay or argument – but she wanted first to enjoy a cosy supper with them; somehow make them understand that she wasn't acting out of malice.

She let Yeyen remain in charge of the food, while she chose a seat between Legi and Rodiah. All her life, she had longed to be part of a family, with a father actually *there* – solid and substantial; not a nameless shadow. And a brother or a sister, or better, one of each. And, strange as it might seem, considering they were different nationalities, this family seemed to fit her rather well – all plain, like her, short, like her, and bespectacled, like her. Admittedly, her skin was much paler and her hair less intensely black, but her dark eyes were very similar to theirs – a legacy from her father, so she understood, and certainly nothing like her mother's greyish-blue ones. And she warmed to this new 'mother', who, instead of throwing a tantrum or being hysterical or paranoid, had simply taken charge, and was now calmly dishing up the meal, including some little side-dishes she appeared to have conjured out of nothing. It didn't matter that nobody was talking – the silence was no longer tense, but friendly and companionable, as they all sat contentedly eating, exchanging nods and smiles. Anyway, in her mind she added lively chatter, in-jokes, repartee – the sort of things she imagined would go on in a normal, loving family.

All at once, she raised her glass – apple juice, not wine, but it would still do for a toast. 'I want to drink to families,' she said, urging the parents to pick their glasses up as well, then clinking hers to theirs. 'To your family and mine,' she stated solemnly.

'Which I'd like to pretend, if only for tonight, are one and the same thing.'

'Er, hello. I'm the new girl.'

The woman behind the desk looked blank. As well she might, Lynn thought. 'New girl' sounded really naff, as if she were still at school. 'Lynn Simmonds,' she corrected, trying to be more professional. 'I'm due to start this morning.'

'Well, no one told me anything about it.'

Lynn fought a surge of panic. Had she come to the wrong place? Or had they changed their minds; decided she couldn't work here after all? Perhaps they'd sent the letter to Peterchurch and nobody had forwarded it. 'Well,' she explained, 'it *was* a bit unusual. You see, instead of being interviewed here, as I was going to be originally, I saw your Centre Manager in Hereford. He was there on business, six weeks ago, and because he knew this close friend of my mother, who also lived in—'

'Nick!' the woman shouted, interrupting the complicated story. 'Are we expecting a Lynn Simmonds?'

A tall, lanky man bounded over; a good six-foot-three to her shaming four-foot-ten. 'Yeah, you *are* expected, Lynn. Hi there, nice to meet you.'

'Hi,' she mumbled shyly, having to crane her neck to look up at him.

'I'm afraid Clifford isn't here this week – he's the guy you saw. But, don't worry, he filled me in, told me you were starting today. I'm Nick, by the way, and this is Madeleine. Maddy, would you please look after Lynn? She can answer the phone and do a bit of copying, but you'll need to show her the ropes. And if you don't mind making tea, Lynn, we're always happy to have a new tea-lady!'

Lynn forced a smile. Making tea was no problem – it was the copying that scared her. The machines looked horribly complicated, chuntering away in the background, and quite different from the simple one at school. And she'd taken an instant dislike to Madeleine, who seemed unfriendly in the extreme, hadn't bothered to say hello, and, even now, was staring at her disparagingly.

'If I was you,' the woman drawled, 'I'd wear something much more casual tomorrow. Printing can be dirty work.'

'Oh, right … I will … Of course.' She'd spent ages tarting up, in fact, trying to look worthy of her first official job, and deliberately putting on her best blue 'interview suit' – ill-advised, she realized now. Madeleine was wearing a polo shirt and jeans, as were most of the other employees she could see.

'OK,' Madeleine continued, in the same ungracious tone, 'when you answer the phone, don't just say "hello". It's always "Good morning" or "good afternoon". And then "PromptPrint. May I help you?" Got that?'

'Yes.'

'Well, go on, pick it up – it's ringing.'

'Hello,' Lynn blurted out, cursing herself for getting it wrong, and aware of Madeleine's glare of disapproval. 'Good morning,' she corrected herself. 'PromptPrint. May I help you?'

'No, you bloody well can't!' boomed a furious voice. 'It's far too late for that. You've already buggered up my order and dumped me in the shit. Put me on to the manager, and be quick about it, girl!'

'I … I'm afraid he isn't here.'

'Well, he *should* be there. That's the trouble, isn't it? – no proper management. I'd like you to know that I'm never dealing with your crappy firm again, but in the meantime …'

Lynn glanced around, distraught, but Madeleine had vanished, and Nick was busy with a small Asian guy on one of the machines. 'Er, could you hold on a moment?'

'Look here, my girl, I'm not wasting any *more* time. There's always some excuse, some useless person trying to fob me off. If the manager doesn't come to the phone within thirty seconds at the most, then I intend to …'

'Madeleine!' Lynn called, frantic as to what to do. There was still no sign of the woman, yet this guy was spitting with rage at the other end. 'Madeleine!' she shouted again, suddenly seeing her returning.

'Can't I even have a pee in peace, without you screaming the place down? What's wrong, for heaven's sake?'

'This man—'

'What man? Didn't you ask his name?'

'No, I—'

'*Always* get the client's name. I told you that.'

Madeleine hadn't, in fact, mentioned it, but Lynn passed her the receiver. She was dying for a pee herself, but no one had pointed out the toilets. She could hardly concentrate, in any case, on copying, or angry clients, or indeed on anything, when she was totally preoccupied with the problem of the Indonesians: their being in the flat at all, let alone unsupervised. She had done her utmost to explain (using gestures, dumb show, even little drawings), that she was starting work some miles away and thus forced to move them on, yet all her efforts had fallen on deaf ears. And now that Yeyen had taken over the cooking – and she herself joined them for each meal – it made things trickier still.

Physically, she was standing here in Kilburn, but her mind and thoughts were back in Belgrave Road, wondering what the hell was going on. However kind the family might be, if they were desperate to stay in England, they were bound to put their interests before hers. They hadn't even grasped yet that Flat 1A was a private home – or perhaps didn't *want* to grasp it. It seemed obvious they were hiding from the authorities, since she'd tried many times to persuade them to go out, offering them whole sheaves of brochures about places they could visit, but they simply smiled politely; clearly determined to lie low. Even after all this time, she knew almost nothing about them – their origins, beliefs, their aim in coming over here. They hadn't observed Ramadan, so they couldn't be Muslims, as she'd initially assumed. Or maybe they were *bad* Muslims – perhaps even terrorists, using the cover of being a normal, happy family to put people off the scent. No, that was quite ridiculous. They *were* a happy family – in fact, the sweetest, kindest one she'd ever met.

Which is why she'd taken no action, although she was uncomfortably aware that other, less involved people would have contacted the police, or sought advice from some official body, which knew the language and would be able to communicate. She *had* tracked down the numbers of the Indonesian Embassy and Citizens' Advice Bureau, but each time she picked the phone up, out of loyalty to Pauline, she'd immediately banged it down again, out of loyalty to *them*.

In fact, just last week, the words of Miss Mackenzie had suddenly come back to her – the Environmental Studies teacher who'd arranged the Indonesian project: 'When I visited the country myself,

I was struck by the hospitality – no, more than hospitality, genuine human kindness. Several different families welcomed me into their homes and, although I was a total stranger, refused to take a penny for my keep. Yet, most of them were dirt-poor by our standards.'

Miss Mackenzie's little spiel hadn't meant much at the time, since Indonesia seemed utterly remote – indeed, more or less irrelevant to the girls in Year Eleven. Yet now she felt ashamed of the contrast with her own country. In Peterchurch, all foreigners were regarded with suspicion – cold-shouldered rather than welcomed – and, as for London, the general attitude to everyone (herself included) seemed to be indifference. So she felt she had a duty to try to compensate, and show Yeyen and Mulyana that there were exceptions to the rule.

Besides, she had to admit that, selfishly and secretly, she was enjoying being treated as their daughter. For the first time in her life, she was living with a domesticated 'mother' who could knit and sew, make delicious meals, and turn her hand to anything in the house. Yeyen not only cooked, she had also taken over the washing, ironing and cleaning, so she herself had nothing to do except buy the food and cleaning products, the sewing things and knitting wool. Yeyen had already knitted her a gorgeous scarlet sweater and was halfway through a matching hat and gloves.

'*Lynn*!' a voice bellowed in her ear. 'Can't you listen when I speak to you? You've just upset a really important client – and on your very first day here. He's livid – and with cause. He told me you were bloody rude and—'

'Look,' she spluttered, outraged at the injustice. 'I didn't say a thing. Honestly. I swear. I hardly opened my mouth.'

'But you're *meant* to open your mouth.' Madeleine retorted, frowning in irritation. 'That's the reason you're here – to help anyone who phones, not stand there like a ninny. You'd better leave the phone to me until you've learned some sense. Do you think you can cope with some copying, or will you mess that up as well?'

Lynn stood in silence, stung by such hostility. What was *wrong* with the woman? Or was this normal practice at work? If so, she'd gladly go back to school.

She followed Madeleine to the copier, trying to take in the instructions, which seemed worryingly vague and brief.

'So I press this button here?'

'No! The *other* one – just concentrate.'

Once on her own, she did her best to focus on the task, but was fatally distracted by pictures of a cop-car screeching to a halt outside Pauline's flat; police breaking down the door; bursting in with handcuffs to arrest the Indonesians.

'Oh,God!' she cried, as, all at once, the machine whimpered to a halt. She had somehow jammed the paper-tray; fouled the whole thing up. She stood, aghast, terrified of Madeleine, who would come storming back any second now and tear her into shreds. Frantically she glanced around at the group of staff behind her, operating the other machines or poring over paperwork. They all seemed far too busy to help, and besides, she hadn't a clue who they *were*. The only name she knew was Nick's, and he was still deep in conversation with the little Asian guy, so she dared not interrupt him, for fear of further trouble. There *was* a man at the front of the shop who looked young and not too scary, but he was behind the counter, dealing with the customers. Still, he only had one couple to serve and maybe they'd leave, if she waited a sec, and she could throw herself on his mercy. She shifted from foot to foot, willing them to go, but instead, three more came in. It was too late, in any case. At this very moment, Madeleine was bearing down on her – a ship in full battle-rig.

'Christ, I can't believe it! You've not only lost us a valuable client, now you've buggered up the machine.'

'I'm sorry. I ... I wasn't thinking.'

'You're *paid* to think. Otherwise, there's no point you being here. Look, I'll give you one more chance – you can make the tea, which is all you're good for, obviously.'

Wasn't this abuse? She'd heard about harassment at work, but what on earth did she do about it, especially on her first day in the job? If she made a fuss, there wouldn't *be* a job. Madeleine had already threatened her obliquely with the sack.

'OK,' she mumbled nervously. 'But could you show me where the tea things are. And, by the way, I need the, er, loo.'

'Listen, if you think you can sneak a fag in the toilet, that's strictly forbidden, OK?'

'I don't smoke.'

'Huh! They *all* say that,' the hateful woman snorted, then, having pointed out the toilet, she marched her a little further along to a dark hole of a kitchen, with a sink, an electric kettle, a large brown earthenware teapot and an assortment of stained mugs. 'OK, all yours! And get it right, for Christ's sake. I like mine strong, with two sugars. Nadirah's on a diet – *she* has saccharine. Sean has tea with lemon, and, whatever you do, don't put milk in Josie's, otherwise she'll kill you! She's off all dairy products – silly cow!'

The minute the woman had turned her back. Lynn raced off to the toilet, now desperate for a pee – desperate altogether. How would she remember all those preferences – no milk, no sugar, lemon for Sean, saccharine for Nadirah – or tell the staff apart? And did she pour the tea into the mugs and put them on a tray, or take the teapot with her and do the rounds with it? She was in such a state of nerves, she'd probably spill it anyway; maybe even scald someone.

Madeleine was right – she was 'useless' and 'a ninny'. Besides, she couldn't really stay here any longer. Every minute that ticked by only increased her fears about the Indonesians. If anything should happen in her absence, Pauline would never trust her again – maybe never *speak* to her again. She must go back now – this instant – and evict them; never mind how kind they were, or how hospitable their country was, or how much she relished her role of elder daughter. If they tried to resist, she'd simply bundle them out into the street, along with their possessions. The thought of such brutality made her feel physically sick, but the situation had now reached crisis-point and there was no alternative.

As for Madeleine and Nick, she'd write a conciliatory note; say she'd been caught short in the toilet with a bad attack of the runs, and thought it best not to spread her germs. She'd apologize profusely; promise to be back first thing tomorrow, and rely on easy-going Clifford to smooth things over, should anyone complain or try to take her job away.

Just as the plan was forming in her mind, she spotted an exit from the toilet to an alley at the back of the building. Great! With any luck, she could make a speedy getaway without anybody observing her slip out.

'Thank you, God,' she prayed. She'd didn't actually believe in God, but she needed *someone's* help today, to oust the Indonesians.

'Happy birthday, Legi!' Lynn spelled out each syllable slowly and distinctly.

'Happy birthday, Legi!' Yeyen repeated, her pronunciation surprisingly good.

'Brilliant! Now Mulyana, *you* try.'

'Hap ... Hap ...' Clearly embarrassed, he dried up almost instantly, but at least he'd made everybody laugh, and the kids themselves needed no encouragement, but kept trotting out 'Happy birthday, Legi!' over and over and over, like a mantra, whilst gazing at the birthday cake.

She had bought the cake herself, from a baker's down the road, unsure if Yeyen would make one, or if they even had the tradition of blowing out birthday candles back in Indonesia. She craved to please this family; to cheer their sad, restricted life, in which they never saw another soul but her; never got fresh air; never enjoyed a movie or a visit to the park. In fact, arranging the celebration had pleased *her* as much as them; proved a sort of compensation for her own lack of parties as a child. Her mother couldn't cope with making cakes or entertaining guests, and if it happened to be one of her 'down' days, the birthday would literally end in tears. But today things were totally different – everyone controlled and calm – and she, the capable daughter, revelling in the goodies she'd provided. She'd bought not just the cake, but balloons and paper hats, Winnie-the-Pooh serviettes, gingerbread men, red and yellow jellies and gifts for both the kids.

It had been worth the effort and expense, because the more she did for them – and they for her – the more the bond between them deepened. The initial strain of having to squeeze a family into what was basically a flat-for-one had entirely disappeared. These people were so caring and considerate, they never hogged the bathroom or made the slightest mess. Indeed, it was they who cleared up after *her*; put her first in every way, as if she were truly their beloved child. They still didn't have the words, of course, to express affection outright, but she could feel their love in a host of little gestures: a hand on her arm, a shy stroking of her hair, a chair pulled out or cushion plumped, a dish made in her honour, the choicest piece of chicken slipped fondly on to her plate. And even her appearance had improved since they'd arrived. Compared with Yeyen and Mulyana, she wasn't short at all – just average height, in fact. And Yeyen thought her beautiful; often admired her pale complexion and long, thick, wavy hair. And, as for wearing glasses, well, this whole family had lousy sight, so she was normal in their company, not a geeky 'four-eyes'.

'Right,' she said, striking a match. 'It's time to blow the candles out. Are you ready, Legi, with lots of puff?'

He nodded, face agog. She had never seen the children so excited; both bouncing up and down on their chairs, as the eight candles sprang to flickering life.

'One, two, three,' she ordered, standing to attention. '*Blow*!'

Rodiah blew as well as Legi, but no one seemed to mind. Lynn hadn't explained about the tradition of making a wish, because, although the children's English was undoubtedly improving, they couldn't grasp something quite so complex. However, she made the wish herself, silently and solemnly. 'I wish for things to work out – for you, as well as for me. May we all find a true home, at last.'

She also dispensed with singing 'Happy Birthday', suspecting it would be a solo on her part. 'Now I'm going to cut the cake, so, Legi, put your hand on top of mine ... No, like this, over the knife. OK?'

'Shit!' she muttered, as the phone shrilled through her words. 'Excuse me, will you, please? Won't be a sec.'

As she picked it up in the sitting-room, she prayed it wasn't Pauline. Last time her cousin rang, she had almost died from worry, aware that the Indonesians had been with her now for nearly two whole months, and she'd actually accepted the fact and stopped her former efforts to eject them. She hadn't breathed a word, of course, to Pauline, although she *had* admitted she was rather short of cash and so couldn't send the sum she owed as the token rent agreed on. Pauline actually owned the flat, so at least there was no landlord going spare. None the less, she'd felt consumed with guilt, and had been investigating the chances of a loan (although terrified of landing up seriously in debt). Meanwhile, she was forced to take more money from Mulyana, every time he offered it, which meant she now felt guilt on *his* account, as well.

'Oh, Mum, it's *you*,' she exclaimed, her voice shrill with apprehension. She dreaded speaking to her mother as much as to her cousin, especially as she'd have to explain that she couldn't attend the wedding, after all.

And, just as she'd expected, once she'd broken the news, the receiver seemed to shudder in her hand from the force of the explosion.

'Mum, it's *not* that I don't love you ... OK, I promised – you're right – but things have changed since then ... No, nothing to do with Hendrik. It's just that I ... I can't afford the fare ... Yes, I know you sent me money, but I've used that up already.'

Shocked gasps, then questioning.

'No, actually, I don't *have* a job – not now. Not any more. They, er, sacked me, quite some time ago.'

More shrieks, expostulations.

'Yes, it's awful, I agree ... Yes, I know your friend will be upset. I'm sorry – honestly ... Well, maybe. I'm not sure. You see, it's not exactly easy to find another job.'

After several more exchanges about Job Centres, employment agencies and ads in the local press, her mother switched to the wedding again, now close to tears as she doubled her entreaties.

'Mum, I'm aware it means a lot to you, but it's not that simple, I'm afraid. Things have cropped up here, you see, and ... Look, please don't cry ... I *do* care ... OK, OK, I *will* come ... Yes, I mean it. 'Course I mean it ... Gosh – that's really decent. Thank you. And do thank Hendrik, won't you? I'd no idea he was loaded ... Oh, really? How fantastic! ... Well, I'm not too sure about him being "Dad". It's a bit soon, isn't it? I mean, I barely know the guy ... Look, I'm sorry, I didn't mean ... OK, OK, let's discuss it when I'm there ... Yes, I'll see him at the airport ... Yes, Friday next ... Yes, fine.'

Once she'd put down the receiver, she sank on to the sofa, head in hands. That creepy Hendrik had offered to meet her at the airport, so 'they could get to know each other better'; was dead-keen to be her *father*, for God's sake, and for her to live with them in Amsterdam. No fear! Yet how could she give him the brush-off, when he was sending her a thousand pounds – not just to cover the fare, but to help her out in general? A thousand quid – incredible!

More money than she'd ever had in her life. Well, at least she could pay her debts, but it meant she had no excuse now not to attend the wedding. And, even if she cut her visit to just a long weekend (rather than stay in Holland permanently, as her mad mother seemed to want), it would still mean leaving the Indonesians on their own.

She let out a muffled groan, feeling close to breaking-point. Despite the pleasures of being with her 'family', she still lay awake each and every night, aware of the monstrous situation she had somehow brought to pass, and wondering, would it ever end? Pauline herself was due back in the summer, and, although it was only late-October, if the Indonesians stayed on and on and on, her cousin might actually *find* them here, and all hell would break loose, with her as the guilty party – guilty on all counts.

She suddenly noticed Yeyen standing in the doorway, her face creased with concern. She came over, hesitantly, sat beside her, took both her hands in hers.

There was silence for a moment, then, '*Ibu*', Lynn heard herself saying – the Indonesian word for 'Mummy' she had picked up from the two kids. 'Please help me, *Ibu*,' she whispered. 'I need a mother – *now*.'

'What do you mean – "it's full"?'

'Exactly what I said, madam. I can't sell you a ticket, because that 15.55 departure's already fully booked.'

'But surely you can squeeze me on? One more won't make much difference, will it?'

The woman behind the ticket desk raised a sneery eyebrow. 'We're not talking about a *bus*, madam. Everyone on board a plane is allocated their own individual seat.'

Lynn bridled at her patronizing tone. OK, she hadn't flown before, but that was due to her mother's frequent panic attacks, which had put a bar on air-travel or holidays abroad. Even trips to London were ruled out, which meant she herself had been forced to lead a cloistered life, rarely going anywhere beyond the confines of their village, on account of her mother's mental state. Yet that same schizo mother had now moved house and country, and solely because of some bloke. It made her bitter, actually, the way her mum had overcome a lifelong illness just because a lover was involved. Wasn't the message all too clear? She cared more about a casual shag than she did about her daughter. Yet she still expected that daughter to show up at the wedding, with the threat of still more outbursts, should she dare refuse.

'Look, I *have* to fly today,' she said, glaring at the woman, who was now tapping her pen impatiently. 'My mother's getting married tomorrow and if I'm not there—' She broke off, unwilling to even think about the consequences. 'Is that the only flight, or is there another later on?'

'We have two more today, madam – one at 17.40 and one at 20.00 hours.'

'Fantastic! Book me on the 17.40.'

The woman spent some time consulting her computer screen, only to shake her head – gleefully, Lynn felt. 'I'm sorry, that one's full, as well, *and* the 20.00. Friday is our busiest day. It's always wiser to book in advance.'

Cheaper as well as wiser. Even she knew that. In fact, she'd been pretending to her mother that she *had* booked, just to avoid still more kerfuffle. But secretly she'd been hoping that the wedding would be cancelled. Maybe Hendrik would change his mind and decide that getting hitched to a nut-case might not be a bundle of fun. Or her mother would come rampaging home, in her usual manic state, and settle for living with a cat or dog in Peterchurch, instead of with a balding geek in Holland. No luck, on either front. So here she was, the day before the wedding, assuming she could book a flight just by turning up at Terminal Four and handing over the cash.

'So what can I do?' she demanded, aware of the queue building up behind her, yet desperate for some help.

'Well, you could fly with us tomorrow morning. There *are* seats on the first flight out – the 6.35.'

She did some calculations in her head. Two hours, fifteen minutes for the flight, plus half an hour (or more) hanging around the other end for the luggage, then at least an hour's drive from the airport. The wedding was at noon, so she'd be cutting it fine, especially if the plane was late. Anyway Hendrik would be livid, having to come and meet her when he was meant to be getting all togged up in his white suit or whatever. And, if she didn't intend spending the night in the terminal, it would mean going back to the flat, when she'd just said a long and fond goodbye to the Indonesians. They might think she was checking up on them, and didn't trust them to behave while she was gone.

'Alternatively, you could try KLM. In fact, they have more flights to Holland than we do. Their desk is just there on the left.' Dismissing Lynn with a shrug, she beckoned the next person forward.

The queue at the KLM desk looked every bit as long as the one at British Airways. Reluctantly she joined it, and stood dithering and fretting, then, after just three minutes, gave up and walked away, torn between her desire to get to the wedding and thus avoid a flaming row, and deep unease about rejoining her mother, having lived two months without her. It was Yeyen who had made her see that mothers didn't have to be so weird and unpredictable. Calm, obliging Yeyen never raised her voice, or spiralled into panic, or threw a hissy-fit because she'd lost her glasses, or the microwave had broken. And Mulyana was a saint compared with Hendrik, whom she had detested from the start. In fact, she was terrified that once she got to Amsterdam, she'd become trapped in his clutches and never be able to leave. As for him being her 'father', that was just a bad joke. Tall, fair-haired and hefty, with eyes so pale they blended ice and steel, he looked nothing like her whatsoever, and – she'd bet her life – nothing like her *real* dad, whom she always pictured as small and swarthy-dark. Yet the creepy bloke wanted to 'get close' to her, so her mother said, and, in just a couple of hours, he would be setting out to meet a plane she wasn't on.

She just had to come to some decision as to whether she was going or not, yet, after a run of sleepless nights, her mind refused to function. She'd better have a coffee, wake herself up with a caffeine-shot, then work out what to do.

Picking up her case, she began mooching towards the café at the far end of the terminal, pausing at the Departure Gate, where Pauline had left for New York. A sudden image of her cousin waving her goodbye brought another set of worries seething, surging back. Pauline trusted her completely, as a relative, a friend, yet she was deceiving her on a mammoth scale.

On the other hand, Yeyen also trusted her, which made it more or less impossible for her to turf the family out, let alone shop them to the authorities. Yeyen and Mulyana might be sent to some detention camp, the family split up, the children taken into so-called 'care'. And those children were her siblings now, so how could she subject them to such horror?

She ordered an espresso, took the cup to a table and sat staring at the black liquid – black like her thoughts; her life. She no longer belonged anywhere. Not with her mother and Hendrik. Not in Peterchurch. Not at school or at work. Not even with her Indonesian 'family'. How could she continue living in that stressful situation, never going anywhere; sharing their state of purdah, as if she, too, were in hiding? Besides, her money was running out, and it wasn't fair to keep on taking theirs, when they did more for her these days than she ever did for them. She just *had* to find a job, but how and what and where?

A tide of panic began rising in her throat, so that the one gulp of coffee she'd managed to swallow seemed to be spewing out again. If she didn't get a grip, she'd throw up here in the café, or sink on to the floor and sob in sheer despair.

Abandoning the coffee, she began pacing up and down, hardly caring if she jostled people or rammed them with her case. She barely *saw* the crowds, who were fading into a blur: faceless, voiceless strangers who didn't give a damn whether she cracked up like her mother. She'd probably inherited bad genes, and was doomed to land up in a psycho-ward, or sleep rough on the pavement, or—

'Cut it out!' she shrieked to herself, ignoring the startled couple who'd turned round to stare in horror. 'You won't crack up. You *can't*.'

Stumbling into the toilet, she splashed her face with cold water, then stood leaning against the wall, grateful for its support – grateful for the tiniest thing that might help her gain control.

'Now, look here, Lynn,' she whispered, as if encouraging a child, 'you *must* go to Amsterdam. You did promise, after all. And, anyway, it's better to do *something* than hang around this ghastly place, getting more and more hysterical.'

Dead right. Besides, going to the wedding would take care of the weekend, so she wouldn't have to think, or make any more decisions until Sunday afternoon. It would also prevent a load of frantic phone-calls, recriminations, rows.

Somehow, she struggled from the toilet and back to the KLM desk. At least the queue was shorter now – only three in front of her, all businessmen by the looks of them. She stood watching people come and go, in an effort to distract herself from the shaky, frightening feelings churning through her gut. A young couple just beyond the desk were embracing passionately, clinging to each other, as if they hoped flesh would merge with flesh and bone with bone. If only *she* had a soul-mate – someone who would accept her exactly as she was. It wouldn't happen, though. She lacked that vital quality that made people lovable.

Except she *had* been loved these last three days – an incredible experience she had stowed away in a glass case in her mind, so that nobody could shatter it or steal it. Closing her eyes, she re-created the sensation of real, rare, precious love, poured out on her by Yeyen on that desperate occasion when she'd begged her help, called her '*Ibu*' – Mummy. Yeyen *had* been *Ibu*, the perfect, ideal mother, devoting every minute to making her feel better; tucking her up on the sofa, like an invalid, a child; stroking her temples, massaging her back, bringing her little delicacies – nothing too much trouble. She could feel that miraculous love again, exulting and exploding through every cell of her body; three blissful days making up for eighteen empty years.

'Yes, the 17.10 – that's right, but I'd like to book right through to Jakarta.'

Jakarta? The word plunged her back to the present. Opening her eyes, she saw the broad, grey-suited back of the man in front of her, who had now reached the head of the queue.

'I know I've left it very late,' he continued in his deep, booming voice, 'but the damned hire-car broke down. I only hope to God you have a seat left … No, Economy, not Business Class.'

Lynn edged a little closer; her eyes riveted on the woman in her KLM blue uniform, who was checking the computer screen.

'Yes, sir, we do,' she said, looking up with a smile. 'But both flights are pretty full, I'm afraid, so I can't offer you much choice of seat. And, for long-haul flights, we do prefer our passengers to check in at least two hours in advance.' With a glance at her watch, she shook her head reprovingly. 'And it's getting on for four now.'

'Are you saying I can't fly?' the man asked, in an aggressive tone.

'Not at all, sir. It's just that you'll have to hurry, because the check-in closes in an hour. But, look, let me issue the ticket and print out your itinerary, then I can arrange for you to go through Fast Track.'

Fast Track, Lynn repeated. Exactly what she needed: a quick, immediate decision; a course of action dictated by someone else.

The woman was now going over the flight times. Lynn hung on every word. She had no choice – knew that Fate was speaking to her.

'The 17.10 arrives in Amsterdam at 19.35. And that flight connects with the 21.00 hours to Jakarta, which gets in at 16.55 the following day. All right, sir?'

The man nodded his assent. Lynn could only stare. How extraordinary, how mind-blowing, that this very service to Amsterdam was the connecting flight to Jakarta! The whole thing must be meant. The kindly Fate she had never dared believe in had come rushing to her rescue, and at a time when she was close to freaking out. She must take that flight herself; turn up at the house where Yeyen and Mulyana used to live; say she was part of their family: a new relation, if not by blood then by love and sheer desire. There was logic to the plan. Just as Yeyen and Mulyana had arrived as strangers to London and found a home and refuge, so she would go to *their* country and was bound to find the same (as even ancient Miss Mackenzie had). Of course, she knew no Indonesian, but she would have to learn the language, as *they* were learning English; model her experience on theirs. At least she had two words: *ibu* and *bapak* – mother and father – the most important words in any tongue. Maybe, in a country where everyone was kind and calm, she would find a new *ibu* and *bapak*. And it might benefit her existing ones if she simply disappeared. They would have ten months on their own, then, to sort out their affairs, before Pauline was due back, and might actually feel freer without her constant presence, her non-stop supervision. However much she loved them, she couldn't work a miracle to ensure their future safety, so best to creep away and simply leave them be.

'I'm afraid it's much too late, sir, to book you any special sort of meal. But if you're vegetarian—'

'I'm not,' the man interrupted, handing over his passport.

Lynn was barely listening now, light-headed with relief to have been given an escape-route – an escape from Hendrik and her mother; an escape from Pauline's fury and all the problems in the flat, an escape even from herself – the new London self that couldn't cope.

'Right, that'll be £530, for the round trip. Are you paying by cash or credit card?'

Lynn gasped at the size of the sum. She hadn't even considered the price – five times more than just the fare to Amsterdam. Of course, she wouldn't need a *return* ticket (no way would she come back – never in her life), but even a single would probably cost a bomb. It might almost clean her out; take nearly all the money left from Hendrik's thousand pounds (most of which she'd spent already). Suppose there was nothing spare for living: food or drink, fares or clothes? Too bad. She would simply have to trust, as Yeyen and Mulyana did. At least she didn't have two children in tow, and all the expense that kids involved.

The man dashed off with his ticket and his suitcase. There wasn't time to waste. She, too, would have to rush if she intended boarding that flight. Yet she was standing like an imbecile, her mouth opening and closing mechanically, with no sound coming out.

'Can I help you, madam?'

She swallowed. Black lumps of terror clogged her throat; lumps refusing to dislodge.

'Madam, are you all *right*?'

Suddenly, the words poured forth in one great choking rush. 'I want to fly to Amsterdam, then right on to Jakarta – like that man just said. And I'll pay by cash. And I don't want any special meals – no meals at all, in fact. *Please* say you have a seat left. Don't let me down, I beg you. It's a matter of life and death.'

The woman visibly recoiled, as if disquieted by the sheer frenzy of the plea. Then, reverting to her professional mien, she checked the screen once more. 'We should be able to get you on to the first flight. It's the connecting flight to Jakarta that's pretty chock-a-block. Hold on a minute, could you, madam?'

A minute? Whole hours appeared to dawdle past while the woman's eyes stayed glued to that cruel monitor.

Lynn gripped the counter for support, her lungs gasping for more air. Blood was careering round her body in a crazy, reckless fashion, not following its usual path through arteries and veins. If she was told there were no seats – the man had booked the last remaining one – it would mean the end to everything; mean madness and despair.

'Well, I have to say you're in luck! Just one seat left, would you believe? I'll book it for you, shall I?'

Speechless again, though this time from relief, Lynn gave a frantic nod. Already she had seized the phrase 'in luck'; was sucking it like barley sugar, rolling its sweetness round and round her mouth. Of *course* she was in luck.

Her luck would start tomorrow.

In Jakarta.

Heart-break

'So has he – you know – met anyone else?'

Mum's trying to sound as if she doesn't give a toss. I'm not fooled for a split second. Her mouth's set tight and her skin is sort of greyish, like she's going down with flu. I don't know what to say. I hate deceiving her, but even more I hate her getting hurt. I hold my breath, pick at a loose button on my shirt.

'Did you hear, love? I wondered if there was a new ... woman on the scene?'

I shouldn't lie – it's wrong – and, anyway, she'll find out in the end. I try to make my mouth say 'yes', but the word comes out as 'no'. '*No*,' I repeat. 'There isn't.'

Her whole body sags with relief. Her legs were twisted round the chair-rung, but now her feet uncurl, both fists unclench, and she gives a shaky smile. She won't drop the subject, though, and keeps plugging away, desperate for any crumb of information. Every time I visit Dad, she questions me like this.

'And did he seem OK?'

'Yeah. Fine.' *That's* true, at least. He's so besotted with Lola, he keeps smiling in this soppy way – not just smiling at *her*, but smiling at the wallpaper, smiling at the kettle. He'd probably smile at a cockroach or a turd, now that she's moved in with him. Lola – what a name! Mum's called Peggy, which is perfect for a mum, and makes you think of cosy things like home-made cakes and bedtime stories and clean sheets in the linen-chest. Lola's rubbish as a mother. She dyes her hair and has hideous long nails the colour of dried blood. And she told me off today just for taking an apple from the dish. One measly apple – I ask you! – when she's so loaded she could buy a fucking orchard.

'So what did you do? Did he take you swimming, or—?'

I ought to keep a minute-by-minute record, so I could bring it home and show Mum – minus all the Lola bits, of course. Dad *kissed* her – yes, in front of me. And stroked her rotten hair. And they played footsie under the table, when they thought I couldn't see.

'We went out to lunch,' I say, at last.

'Where? McDonald's?'

'No. A new place.' Lola at McDonald's – don't make me laugh! What Dad spent on that lunch today would have kept me and Mum in food for *weeks*.

'Was it nice?'

'Not bad.' I daren't tell her what we ate. Venison. I've never had it in my life and, to tell the truth, I'm not even sure what animal it comes from – if it *is* an animal at all. And champagne sorbet for dessert. They don't serve champagne sorbet at McDonald's.

'Did he, er, *mention* me?'

I get up, to play for time; start searching through the kitchen drawer to find a pencil or a hairclip – anything, while I work out how to answer. The way Dad is at present, I doubt he even remembers he was married. It's their fifteenth anniversary this June, but he's just blanked the whole thing out.

'I mean, did he ask how I was, or if my shoulder's better?'

Mum's voice is sort of pleading, like a dog begging for a bone. I just can't help myself and another lie pops out. 'Yeah. He said he missed you.'

'*Really*?'

What in God's name have I done? Now she's so ecstatic, she reminds me of those homeless bods who sit huddled on the pavement and almost have an orgasm if someone tosses them a fiver. I've given her £5-worth of hope, when actually there's none.

'D'you think there's any chance he might…?'

No, I think, not a chance in hell. You're forty, Mum, and showing it, whereas Lola's only eight years older than me. 'Look, sorry to change the subject, Mum, but I've lost my navy T-shirt. You haven't seen it, have you?' It's in my drawer, upstairs, but I've got to stop her obsessing over Dad, at least for a few minutes.

'It might be in the wash. Hold on – I'll have a look.'

She opens our old washer-drier and starts raking through the dirty laundry. The machine's only a quarter full, so she hasn't put it on yet. When Dad was here, she did the washing every day, because he always had a load of stuff: shirts and vests and underpants and sweatshirts and pyjamas. I liked the fact that all our clothes went whirling round together. It seemed to make us a real family – his shirts and Mum's and mine all tangled up and intertwined, then nestling close in the airing cupboard. Now the wash looks puny, and the machine's even developed a fault and started whining and complaining, like it's saying, 'Where the hell are all his socks and boxer shorts?'

I *do* have one of his socks. I found it in the laundry basket and I keep it under my pillow and sleep with it at night. Not that I need reminders, when everywhere I look there's something with Dad's stamp on it: the cupboards he built beside the sink; the spindly avocado plant he was growing from a stone; the sandwich-toaster he bought (and never used). The house looks shabby now, though, because I'm comparing it with *his* place, which Lola's tarted up. She's painted the lounge this heartless, empty white, and brought in loads of *her* stuff, including a hideous squashy sofa that looks like a cream puff. And so many cushions, there's barely room to sit down – frilly ones and fur ones and really crappy heart-shaped ones. And she's changed *him*, as well as his flat. He's grown his hair, to please her, and it's all straggling round his neck and, instead of wearing cords and baggy jumpers, he's into designer jeans and tight black polo necks. I don't want my Dad like that, but she *owns* him now, and me and Mum are just relics from the past.

Mum stuffs the dirty washing back, then straightens up, wincing at the pain in her shoulder. She's aged in just six months – never had so much as a twinge before he left.

'It doesn't seem to be here, Kirsty. When did you last wear it?'

'Let me think.' I'm not thinking about T-shirts – I'm thinking about how you can love someone and hate them, both at once. I love Dad because he's Dad, and I hate him because of what he's done to Mum. She must have lost a stone since he walked out.

'Did *you* have lunch?' I ask her suddenly.

She shrugs. 'I wasn't hungry.'

'Why don't I make us something?' I'm so stuffed with that posh nosh, the last thing I need is supper, but *she* might eat if *I* do. I don't want her fading away. I'd be an orphan then – apart from the Saturdays I spend with Dad.

'That *would* be nice. Thank you, love.'

I roll my sleeves up and dive towards the hob. Actually, I'm crap at cooking and I can't really see the point of messing about with saucepans and chopping-boards and stuff, and making loads of washing-up, when you can get a special meal-deal on a pizza. But Mum likes it if I cook. It makes her feel she's brought me up the proper way and I won't turn out a failure or a freak. I think she'd like me to get hitched to some nice dependable (boring) guy and run a home like *she* does. No fear. I wouldn't get married if you paid me. What's the point? Half my friends' parents are divorced.

I decide to make an omelette, though it's not a wild success. It starts burning on the bottom before it's cooked inside, and when I try to flip it over, it breaks up into curdled lumps, but Mum's pleased anyway.

'You're a *dear*,' she says, and gives me a hug. And when I feel her bony ribs pressed against my chest, I'm terrified I'm going to cry, so I just grunt and say, 'Eat up, Mum'.

And, miraculously, she does.

I'm here again. On my own – which hardly ever happens. Dad and Lola have gone to get some wine. It makes me mad the way they have a booze-up every single Saturday, like they can't stop celebrating the fact they're so revoltingly in love. And wasting all that money, when Mum worries herself to death about the bills. He's not paying proper maintenance – I heard her telling Auntie Jean. (They thought I was upstairs, but I came down to make some toast.)

I peer out along the street, but there's no sign of them returning. They've probably parked in a lay-by and are snogging in the back seat of the car. It's meant to be *my* day with Dad, but I never get to see him on my own now. Lola's always breathing down his neck – and mine. She told me to say 'please' this morning when I asked Dad for a drink. Bloody cheek! Does she think I'm five or something? And there's nothing left of Dad here, only more of *her*. She's replaced his cricket cups on the sideboard with these rubbish china ornaments: smirking ladies in crinolines and *angels*, would you believe? And she's bought a vile picture of a small girl on a swing, when it's obvious she hates children. Dad's not one for ornaments and the only pictures in our house are the ones I drew in kindergarten, which Mum still keeps pinned up on the wall. The flat even *smells* of Lola. She wears this sick-making perfume and, if she comes within five yards of you, you're knocked off your feet by a blast of putrid lilies.

I get up and pace around. It's impossible to relax, even though they're out. I know I don't belong here. I'm in the way – in *her* way.

I creep out to the passage and stop outside their bedroom. Since that slag moved in, I never dare set foot there. When Dad first rented this place, he bought a double bed, and, when I asked him why, he said big chaps like him couldn't fit into a single. But, of course, he really bought the bed for him and Lola, although he kept her dark, so that no one would suspect. I never saw a sign of her for at least the first two months, and, in fact, me and him used to sit together on that bed, watching the racing on TV. And he'd put his arm around me and snuggle nice and close, and it was just us two, and special. Now the bedroom door's kept shut, and I'm restricted to the lounge and that shitty cream-puff sofa, with shitty Lola sitting right beside me.

I push the handle very, very gently, open it a crack and glance around in shock. It's all completely different. Instead of the old tartan rug Dad was using as a bedspread, there's a revolting white lace counterpane that makes the bed look like a wedding cake. And loads more cushions – fancy things, all white, but with beads and tassels and embroidered flowers and stuff. And there's a brand new dressing-table, piled with all her make-up – so many jars and bottles you'd think she owned The Body Shop, or Boots. And ruched curtains at the window, so you can no longer see the park. When Dad lived on his own here, he didn't bother with curtains and you could watch children playing on the swings and squirrels darting about.

I tiptoe in and sit down at the dressing-table. The mirror's really over the top, with light bulbs round the frame, like film stars have in Hollywood. I scowl at my reflection. The only film *I'd* star in would be some horror movie. There's a vile spot on my chin, red and raised and about to pop, and my eyes are neither dark, like Dad's nor proper blue, like Mum's, but sort of boring in-between. And I've hardly any boobs at all. Every girl in my class but me has been wearing a bra for at least a year, (and Sandra takes a C-cup, lucky sod), but when it comes to breasts, I'm in the Special Needs department. Mum says not to worry – I'm just a late developer and I'll catch up in the end – but I *do* worry, all the time.

I close my eyes and pretend I'm Lola – beautiful and double-D – and that Dad worships every inch of me. He's stroking my blonde hair, and his fingers go right down to my cleavage, and he's telling me I'm the most fantastic woman in the world.

I feel better for a moment – until I open my eyes. So I hit out at the mirror, for not making me look gorgeous, like that bitch. Then I tug open the top left-hand drawer, where Dad used to keep his wallet and his chewing gum and keys and stuff. Now it's full of Lola's knickers. They're *gross* – they really are. There's a gruesome scarlet thong, and some crotchless things in fake leopard skin, and seven pairs of black bikini bottoms, with the days of the week embroidered on each pair. What happens if she wears 'Tuesday' on a Sunday? Does it make the Knicker Fairy cry? Mum buys plain white cotton underwear from Marks. I couldn't bear to see her in a thong.

I ram the drawer shut and open the right-hand one. That's crammed with tights and stockings – tarty fishnet, mostly. As I thrust my hand down into them, I feel something hard, hidden underneath: a blue padded velvet box. 'Goldcraft Jewellers' is printed on the top in a fancy sort of script. Straining my ears to make sure they're not returning, I quickly click it open. Lying on a white silk pillow is a locket on a chain: a heart-shaped locket; solid gold, and edged with tiny diamonds. I turn the locket over. On the back it's engraved with just one word – 'LOVE' – and in the box is a small white card, with my father's writing on. My hands are shaking as I pick it up and read it. 'For Lola, all my love, your Beastie.'

I just stare at it and stare. *Beastie*! How disgusting! That must be her private name for him. And 'all' his love – as well as 'LOVE' in capitals. The thing must have cost a bomb. When Sandra had her ears pierced, she chose studs with just the weeniest diamond chips, and even those set her back nearly fifty quid. This locket has – I count – fifteen diamonds round the edge. So *that's* the reason he's not paying proper maintenance. Though it isn't just the cost that hurts. What gets me is the romantic bit. Diamonds are for ever – everyone knows that – and the 'LOVE's for ever, too, engraved really deep, right into the heart. 'For ever' will kill Mum, of course.

I bite my lip, to stop myself from crying. I don't know what to do. Shall I nick the locket, so Mum can sell it and pay the electricity bill? Or sell it myself, secretly, and splash out on some clothes? Or just smash it into bits?

Then, all at once, I hear a car coming up the street, hear the engine stopping and the sound of people getting out. I almost die from terror. I stuff the locket back in its box, shove the tights on top, shut the drawer and bolt out of the bedroom – just in time. As Dad and Lola open the front door, I'm sitting on the sofa, good as gold.

'Kirsty, are you all right?'

'Yeah, fine.'

'You haven't been yourself these last few days. Is something on your mind?'

'No.'

'Is school OK?'

'Not bad.'

'So what's the trouble?'

Nothing, I'm about to say, but if I don't give Mum an answer, she'll keep pestering me all evening. 'Well, I *am* a bit worried about the history test tomorrow.'

'But, darling, you're always top in history.'

'Not top.'

'Well, near the top.'

'Maybe I'm just knackered. I can't seem to concentrate.'

'Can I help? Test you on your dates or something?'

I wish she *could* help. But we're both in the same boat. We can't stop Dad loving Lola, or make him come back here. Finding that locket really brought it home to me. The way I see it, he's given his heart away. Totally. For ever. Given her 'all' his love – every scrap, with none left over for us. Maybe Lola wears the thing in bed.

Nothing else – just his heart. I keep trying to imagine what they *do* in bed – which isn't easy when all I know is stuff I've read in magazines – but it makes me sort of sick inside, like I've eaten prawns and candy floss mixed up. And that vile name 'Beastie' really grosses me out. He never had a special name for *me* – a nickname or a pet name. '*Your* Beastie', it said, which means he belongs to her, completely.

'Tell you what,' Mum says, sitting down beside me at the table. 'Let's think up something fun to do for your birthday. Would you like to ask some friends back?'

I shake my head. Should I tell her I don't *want* a birthday – not this year, anyway, and maybe never again. What's the point of being grown-up, when most grown-ups' lives are such a bloody mess?

'Well, shall we have an evening on our own – just the two of us? I'll make you a nice birthday cake and you can choose what you want for supper. Or we could go out to a movie, if you like.'

Poor Mum – she's really trying. So I settle for the birthday cake, and choose shepherd's pie for supper (which I know is economical because you make it from cheap mince). I say no to the movie, though, because movies make her cry. Even the funny ones remind her of how she and Dad used to go to the Odeon every Friday night.

'And what would you like as a present?'

'A locket on a chain,' I mumble. Fat chance. Mum can't afford it and Dad only buys jewellery for that slag.

'What?'

'Nothing,' I say. 'I don't want anything. Just the birthday cake.'

'Mum, it's great! Did you ice it yourself?'

She's frowning as she nods. 'I'm afraid the "happy" went a bit wonky.'

I'm not surprised. How can either of us be happy when Dad hasn't even phoned? I know I've been at school all day, but he could have rung first thing, before I left. But he was probably in bed with Lola, doing 'Beastie' things. He wouldn't forget *her* birthday, I'd bet a million quid.

'The icing was too thin, I think, so I stiffened it up and the "birthday" came out better.'

'And the "Kirsty"'s really brilliant'

'Yes, by then I was gaining confidence. It's ages since I've iced a cake.'

There's a sudden awkward silence. We're both thinking the same thing. For my last two birthdays, Mum and Dad took me out to a restaurant and *they* laid on the cake. Dad made those last two parties really special. He joked with all my friends and let us pig ourselves on as much food as we liked, and when it was time to sing 'Happy Birthday', he conducted with the cake-knife and everybody laughed. I haven't laughed for months.

Mum clears her throat. 'Before I light the candles, darling, there's another present to open.'

I scoop a dab of shepherd's pie off my skirt. 'I thought I had them all this morning.' I was quite pleased, actually. I got a sparkly top from Mum, soap and bath oil from Grandma, chocolates from my other Gran, a woolly scarf knitted by Auntie Jean, and a rather brilliant hair-straightener from Stephanie next door, with its own brush and comb and half-a-dozen sectioning clips, packed in a pink storage pouch.

'No, this came special delivery.' She passes me a small, hard package, wrapped in silver paper.

'Who's it from?'

'Open it and see.'

I tear off the gift-wrap. Inside is a small box, in some sort of rigid plastic stuff. I remove the lid; see only a layer of cotton wool. Some instinct tells me to stop – stop *there* – replace the lid, return the box to its paper. But how can I, when Mum's watching?

'What's wrong, love?'

'Nothing.'

'Come on. I want to see it in all its glory!'

'Why? D'you know what it is?'

She nods.

I force my fingers to remove the cotton wool. Underneath is a locket – a locket on a chain. Silver, not gold. Oval, not heart-shaped. No diamonds, of course. No word engraved on the back. And the box is tatty plastic, not blue velvet, lined with silk. There *is* a card – a small, white card. 'For Kirsty, from Dad,' it says. Not 'all' his love. No love at all. And no special name, no pet name. I sit very, very still.

'Isn't it lovely?' Mum's burbling. 'I told him you wanted a locket.'

So it wasn't even his idea. Mum must have heard what I said (although I thought I only mumbled). He'd have forgotten the date entirely if she hadn't jogged his mind. She probably phoned him up and pestered. 'Get her a locket, Don. That's what she wants – a locket on a chain.'

'Is it real silver?' I ask suddenly.

Mum looks slightly shocked. 'I ... I'm not sure, love. But it's a pretty shape, isn't it?'

'How d'you *tell* if it's real silver?' I persist.

'Well, there's something called a hallmark, which should be stamped on it. But—'

'Where?' I interrupt.

'On the back, usually.'

'There's nothing on the back,' I say. 'I've checked.'

'Kirsty, it's not like you to be so avaricious. It's the thought that counts, surely.'

I toss the thing back in its box. Yes, it's the thought that counts – she's right. And Dad's made it absolutely clear that when it comes to me and Lola, I'm not even in the running. Lola gets the diamonds. Lola gets the gold. Lola gets the 'LOVE' in capital letters, and 'all' his love, on the card. He can't spare me even the teeniest, weeniest diamond chip of love, because Lola's grabbed the lot. And she's got his heart, of course.

'Why don't you put it on?' Mum says. 'Then you can see how nice it looks.'

No way! If I wore that rotten object round my neck. I'd be telling the whole world that I don't count as far as Dad's concerned; that he can palm me off with tat.

'I'm going out,' I say.

Mum jumps up from the table, looking quite alarmed. 'Going out? But why? Where?'

To top myself, I almost say but Mum seems so concerned, I mutter something about needing to thank Stephanie for the hair-straightener.

'Can't you phone? Or text?'

'No, my mobile's run out of credit. In fact, I was hoping you'd top it up.' It annoys her when I ask, because she says I'm wasting money texting friends I see all day. But, instead of nagging, she just says, 'Borrow mine.'

'No, I need to go in person.'

'But why *now*, for goodness sake, when we haven't even cut the cake? Can't you pop round later? Come on, darling, let's light the candles and carry on with supper.'

'No, it's urgent. It can't wait.' I'm already at the door.

'Kirsty, I don't know what's got into you! You're being quite unreasonable.'

Mum's sounding cross, but I won't give in. It's my birthday, isn't it? 'What's all the fuss about? I'll only be a sec.'

Mum returns to her seat and sits there, with her head down, rubbing her hands together, over and over and over, like they're covered with oil or dirt. 'OK,' she says, at last. 'If you *have* to go, then go, but don't stay chatting on the doorstep – invite her round to join us here. She's on her own this evening, so she might enjoy a little celebration.'

Celebration? Is Mum out of her mind? 'Fine,' I mumble, pocketing the locket. 'Won't be long.'

In case she's watching, I open next-door's gate and walk up the front path, but the minute I'm concealed from view, I retrace my steps, dart along the street, then quickly turn the corner into Ainsworth Avenue. I walk a little further to the bus-stop, where there's a drain set in the road, just below the gutter. I often drop things down it while I'm waiting for the bus: chocolate wrappers, wads of tasteless chewing gum I've been sucking for too long. Sometimes it gets blocked with gunge: cigarette ends, sludgy leaves, greasy bits of rag. Once, I even saw half a dead rat, stranded on the grating.

I shiver suddenly. It's dark and cold, and spooky shadows are flickering on the pavement, creeping up the trees. I feel them creep up *me* – ghostly fingers fumbling at my clothes. It's no good being scared, though. I have a job to do.

I scrabble in my pocket for the box, take the locket out and, if I pause, it's only for a second, before I fling it down that filthy, stinking drain. It catches in the grating, the silver glinting cruelly in the lamplight. Crouching on my haunches, I poke it down between the bars, until I hear it hit the bottom with a clink.

'You're crap!' I whisper. 'So that's where you belong.'

I'm whispering it to *Lola*, and I stay squatting by the drain as I watch her break into dirty little pieces, all mixed up with scum and gunge and bits of putrid rat, until she's part of a great pile of shit, flowing away – good riddance! – to the shit-house.

Then I straighten up and head for home. *Now* I'll have a happy birthday.

Dolce Vita

'Happy anniversary, darling!'

Rick thrust a bunch of roses into her arms – magnificent blooms, with dramatically long stems; their velvety white petals bleeding into purplish-pink.

'I chose these for their name. They're called Dolce Vita – which is how I think of our life together here.'

Life, she thought, alarmed. Hardly the word for someone she met only once a week. She buried her face in the flowers, breathing in their scent: fondant-sweet like Turkish Delight, yet unable to mask the stronger smells of the studio: oil paint, turps, linseed oil. 'They're stunning. Thank you, Rick.' The thorns were equally spectacular: triangular in shape, like tiny, lethal sharks' fins, and as sharp as a shark's tooth.

'I went everywhere to get them. Names are so important, don't you think? I mean, who'd want a rose called City of Leeds or Wolly-Dod?'

She laughed. 'Are there really some called that?'

'Apparently. But Dolce Vita says it all for me – sweetness, sensuality and' – he lowered his voice to a purring growl – 'sex with my gorgeous Diana.' Seizing the bouquet, he laid it on the table, then returned to claim his payment for the roses: unbuttoning her blouse, reaching round to unhook her bra.

She willed herself to respond. In the past, the sheer excitement of making love to an artist had been enough to turn her on. Used to mixing with pedantic lawyers and conservative accountants (with a large C and a small), Rick had seemed a true original, a tiger among baa-lambs. It was *she* who had changed, not he. Rick was still the bohemian, with his long hair and leftist views, and his paintings still surrounded them, stacked three-deep against the skirting boards, and jostling for space on the walls. Once, she had been jealous of those scores of other women, staring at her from canvases and frames; women perpetually on heat, as *she* had been, back then.

As Rick cupped his hands around her breasts, she caught the eye of a voluptuous blonde, lying on her back, her face contorted in a wild, orgasmic grimace. 'Just life-models,' he'd said, when she'd cross-questioned him about them. 'Girls who come and go. They don't mean a thing, I swear.' By then, she'd realized that he lied, so she had no idea whether it was true. The difference was, she no longer really cared.

'What's wrong, my love?'

'Nothing.' It was so hard to fake desire. Even her nipples refused to stiffen, although he was flicking his thumb against them, up and down, across and round, with his usual expertise.

'You seem a bit ... distracted.'

'No, I'm fine.' She could hardly explain that it was the actual anniversary that had brought all her ambivalent feelings to a head. Anniversaries were surely part and parcel of marriage, not of casual liaisons. She and Edmund would be celebrating their eighteenth next month, and would probably go out to dinner, as they had done for all the other seventeen; smugly totting up their years together; the fetters binding tighter with each one. Affairs should be totally different – spontaneous, impulsive and essentially short-lived: one wild night beneath the stars; one drunken, crazy coupling in the back seat of a car, then forgotten save for the memory.

'I could spend my whole life kissing your breasts, if I only had the chance. I'd gladly give up being an artist and devote every moment of my time to pleasuring each nipple.'

A year ago, she had thrilled to such extravagant remarks. Now they seemed faintly absurd, not to mention patently untrue. Rick would never renounce his art, even if Venus herself should request it. None the less, it was ungrateful, if not downright rude, to sit up in the think-tank of her head, criticizing, speculating, while he lavished his full attention on her breasts.

She gave an appreciative murmur, trying to make it sound

convincing, then leaned forward to unbutton his shirt. Slipping it from his shoulders, she ran her fingers through the coils of springy hair on his chest, admiring, as she always did, his broad shoulders and muscular build. There was no denying that Rick was an attractive hunk, with his well-toned body and his sultry, foreign air. And, to top it all, he was almost a decade younger than her, yet here she was longing to escape, just because a year had passed and their regular weekly meeting had become almost as predictable as the weekend shop in Waitrose. The problem was, she couldn't turn herself on to order every Saturday afternoon, between two o'clock and half-past four – although that was hardly *his* fault. It was she who set the terms. With a husband and a full-time job, weekdays and evenings were more or less ruled out.

He unzipped her skirt, slid it down across her hips, slipped an exploratory hand between her legs. 'Come over to the sofa, darling. I want to kiss every inch of your body.'

The first time she'd lain on his ancient, battered sofa, she had loved the feel of the cool black leather against her naked skin. Now, she was more aware of its lumpy texture, as she plumped down on her back, and of the lozenge-shaped tear in the middle that leaked little worms of stuffing. Rick crouched on top of her and began kissing from the top of her head slowly down her face (eyebrows, eyelids, nose and lips), then down lower to her breastbone, making a diversion to each nipple, before his tongue explored her navel. Again, she couldn't fault him. Generous and imaginative, he always took his time on the subtlest of preliminaries, which other men chose often to ignore. So why couldn't she respond?

'Am I hurting?' he asked, picking up on her mood.

'No,' she said. 'It's wonderful.'

She must concentrate on *him*, which would serve the double purpose of distracting his attention from her own apathetic mood. Sitting up, she unbuckled his thick leather belt and slowly eased his zip down. As his erection sprang free from the denim confinement of his jeans, she was struck, as always, by its sheer stiffness and authority. Edmund's penis had grown timid of late, with a tendency to skulk and shrink, whereas Rick's came complete with a built-in guarantee against any mechanical breakdown or defect in performance. Kneeling over him, she took it in her mouth, clamping her lips as snug and tight as possible, and using her hands in tandem with her mouth, to fondle, feather, knead, caress. He gripped her head, tugging at her hair, pulling till it hurt; his breathing deepening to a throaty, guttural rasp.

'Oh, darling, it's fantastic! I just can't tell you how ...'

Thank God she was doing something right. She *wanted* to give him pleasure; loathed this frigid version of herself that sat apart, like some disapproving chaperone. She tried to ditch the chaperone and focus on him fully, flicking her tongue across his tip in teasing little swirls, but all at once he pulled out, held her close.

'I mustn't come,' he gasped. 'Not yet. I want to save it for when I'm inside you. Let's stop a moment, spin things out a bit. It must be really special today – for our first anniversary fuck! You may not believe this, darling, but I've never had a relationship before that lasted a whole year.'

Was that a compliment to her, or were artists just more casual? She moved in different circles, so she wouldn't really know. Almost all her friends were married; some already planning their Silver Wedding parties.

Rick was tracing the coils of her ear, with his finger, then his lips. 'If only you could get away one evening this week, we could celebrate in style. Doesn't Edmund ever go out late?'

'Well, rarely on his own. He does have dinners and functions, but I usually go along to those – you know, "wives included" sort of thing.'

Pulling away, he held her by the wrists. 'Have you ever thought of leaving him?'

She kissed him as reply. He failed to understand that although she might kick against the bonds of marriage, they were impossible to break. So many things cemented her and Edmund – not just the children, but their circle of friends, their set-in-stone routines, their shared labour on the house and garden, shared grief at family members' deaths, even the in-jokes and the pet-names. Yet, if she were tied to her husband so strongly, why did she betray him, risk him finding out? Not that he suspected. The story she'd concocted – that she had signed up for a keep-fit class on Saturday afternoon, followed by a swim – had been accepted with no queries on his part.

And she *did* get her weekly exercise, although at a different location and in a rather different form than swimming and aerobics at the Health Club. She actually hated the deception; felt horribly on edge when she got out of the car and walked towards this large converted warehouse. The other units were rented by various arts-and-craftspeople, some of whom might be watching as she came and went each week. Although it was extremely unlikely, in point of fact, that any friend of Edmund would be spying on her here in Wapping.

'I'll fetch the champagne,' Rick said, leaping off the sofa. 'Then we can drink a toast to each other. It should be cold enough by now.'

He darted towards the fridge, his penis still defiantly stiff. Glancing from his body to her own, she was aware only of its faults: her breasts too full; her bush too wild and shaggy. Not that Rick complained. He liked big breasts and had expressed horror at her suggestion that she wax away the excess pubic hair. As he opened the bottle, the cork shot out and hit the wall, ejaculating a whoosh of bubbles. One of his painted women was sprayed with tiny droplets and appeared to be tonguing them up with her avid open mouth.

Quickly, he poured the wine into two earthenware mugs. Glasses were in short supply – piled dirty in the sink, or being used to hold his brushes or the turps. He kept only the basics here; his other stuff was in his flat, half a mile away. She sometimes wondered if he shared the place with one of those actual life-models he claimed 'meant nothing' to him. Wasn't it rather odd that he had never once invited her there, or suggested they make love at his home instead of in his studio? The flat was small and poky, so he said, but that could simply be a convenient excuse. Yet how could she object to his deceptions, when her whole existence was a lie? She, the faithful married woman, whose only crime was neglecting her two sons by going to a Health Club every week, instead of taking them to a movie or museum. Admittedly, Mark and Tim were in their teens and pretty independent, but should they ever discover her affair, they would condemn her out and out.

The irony was, she was beginning to wish that she *could* be with them on Saturdays, if only as a break from routine. 'Routine' seemed an appalling word for Rick's inspired and sensuous lovemaking, but if you glutted yourself too often on elaborate gourmet dishes, you could find yourself actually longing for baked beans.

'Are you OK?' Rick called, mopping up the spilt champagne from the floor.

'Yes, absolutely fine.' Thank God they hadn't invented the technology that would allow you to see into someone else's mind; gain access to their most private thoughts. She shivered at the prospect.

'You're not cold, are you, my love?'

'No, boiling.' The June afternoon was humid, and this top floor of the warehouse seemed to build up heat and hold it. The roses were lying abandoned on the table, still in their claustrophobic cellophane. *They* would wilt, for certain. 'Shall I put my flowers in water?' she asked, although the 'my' was stretching a point, since she could enjoy them for only a couple of hours. Impossible to take them home, when Edmund knew full well that she would never buy herself such exotic, pricey specimens.

'No, I'll do it. You stay there. I like to watch you with your legs apart like that. If I squat right down, I can see your labia.'

She smiled, despite herself. He looked so comic, crouching on his haunches, with a mug of champagne in each hand.

'Watch out! You're spilling it again.'

He straightened up, came over to the sofa and handed her the larger of the mugs. 'To us,' he pronounced, taking a first sip. 'And to loads more anniversaries.'

She drank the toast in silence, remembering how they'd met, exactly a year ago today, and totally by chance. She had been walking by the river, wearing a wide-brimmed linen sunhat, which had suddenly blown off in the breeze and gone bowling along the Embankment, only to plop into the water, out of reach. A tall and sultry stranger had rushed to her assistance and rescued the errant hat, drenching his shirt in the process. Then, having introduced himself as Rick, he demanded that she join him for a drink, despite the fact he was soaked. Who could resist such reckless romanticism?

He put his mug down, reached behind him, and took a small package from the shelf, slipping it into her palm and closing her fingers around it.

'What's this? Another present? But you've already given me the roses.'

'Doesn't matter. Open it!'

She undid the red-foil gift-wrap, to reveal a jewellery-box – the sort of thing Edmund might well give her, for birthdays, anniversaries. She had to force herself to remove the lid, unfold the tissue paper, discovering a gold chain-bracelet, with a tiny padlock as its clasp.

Rick was hovering beside her. 'I'd like you to wear this all the time, darling. I wanted to buy you a ring, but I was worried that your husband might wonder where it came from. But a bracelet's less emotive – something you could have bought yourself. He wouldn't be suspicious, would he? And as far as we're concerned, it *is* a ring – a symbol that we belong together.'

As he fastened it around her wrist, she heard the click of handcuffs clamping shut. A bracelet might be less emotive, but it was harder to remove than any ring. She already had the sense of manacles enchaining her, weighing down her arm.

Rick bent to kiss the inside of her wrist. 'I love you, Diana,' he said. 'Hold me very tight. I don't want anything to come between us. I want to be merged with you and part of you, breathing with your breath, sharing the same heartbeat.'

Did *all* artists say such fanciful things? And what could she reply, when she had never believed that people could be totally united, even after years of marriage? It seemed, alas, a fond delusion, like the idea of God, or the concept of eternal life.

'It's so wonderful just lying here beside you. If I could, I'd kiss every cell in your body, every vein and artery, every drop of blood.'

That, she reckoned, would take time they didn't have. Rick hadn't even come yet, and he liked to lie beside her afterwards, recovering, exulting. *She* was more concerned about the curfew; counting down the minutes till their Cinderella-hour of half-past four.

'I just can't understand why your husband doesn't worship you. God Almighty! If I was him, I'd shag you every second of the day.'

How disloyal she'd been ever to admit to Rick that Edmund's business problems made him sometimes tetchy and neglectful. It seemed a worse betrayal than the sex. Suddenly she grabbed her mug and drained it, then jumped up from the sofa to pour herself a refill. She was in such an anxious state; so full of guilt towards *both* her men, she knew she wouldn't last the afternoon without a little liquid help.

'I'm back!' she called, letting herself into the hall.

No response. The boys were bound to be out, of course, and Edmund was probably working in the garden. She was actually grateful for this time alone, so she could make the switch from studio to home. Returning from her assignation, with Rick's sperm leaking out of her and his smell all over her body, she feared everyone could tell exactly where she'd been, as if the word ADULTERESS were branded on her forehead.

She slipped upstairs, left her sports bag conspicuously on the bed, to confirm her alibi, then crept into the bathroom to remove every trace of Rick. There was no shower at his place, only an old china sink, so she never felt completely clean until she had slathered soap between her legs, cleaned her teeth, rinsed her mouth, changed her underwear.

Perching on the edge of the bath, she tried to take the bracelet off, but the tiny padlock held it fast and, although she continued struggling (breaking a nail in the process), it proved impossible to prise it open. Only now did she notice that it was exactly the same shade of gold as her wedding and engagement rings, which increased her sense of betrayal.

Retreating to the bedroom again, she glanced at the king-size bed. No lumps, no oozing stuffing, no sense of being cramped. She could see Edmund from the window, spraying the roses at the far end of the garden, totally absorbed in the task. If only there were a spray that would kill the demons in *her*, stop her making invidious comparisons. Yes, her husband's hair was prematurely grey, cut regulation short and thinning on the top. And his clothes were, frankly, dull: neat grey cords, boring khaki shirt. But an accountant couldn't go to work with luxuriant black curls rippling to his shoulders, or sporting the flamboyant shirts (purple, scarlet, peacock) that mavericks like Rick could get away with.

Moving closer to the pane, she noted how much work he'd done in one short, sweltering afternoon. The lawn had been newly mown, the verges neatly trimmed, the flowerbeds weeded, the petunias deadheaded, the whole garden spruced and tidied. He worked like that on their marriage, keeping everything in order, well-regulated, fruitful, safe; attacking any pest that might threaten its health and happiness. Yet she herself was such a pest: the weed in the herbaceous border, the black spot on the roses, the maggot in the apple – destroying what he'd planted, polluting his rich harvest.

Horrified, she ran downstairs and out of the back door; her pace slowing as she walked towards him, along the garden path. He was standing with his back to her in the middle of the rose-bed, and so hadn't seen her yet. As she watched, he paused a moment, to rub his eyes, ease his aching back. How tired he seemed, how dutiful, labouring in the heat, while she'd been lying with her legs apart, disturbing the whole warehouse with her racket. Yes, her passivity had vanished and she had come three separate times – unruly, scorching, desperate comes. But now it was confession-time, and although the confession was unspoken, it was heartfelt none the less. Silently, she assured him that the affair was over, not because it had lost its spark (that had revived, miraculously), but because she belonged here, with him, for ever. Suddenly, impulsively, she dashed forward to embrace him, allowing the gesture to express those words of shame and sorrow that could never be pronounced.

'Watch out!' he snapped, pushing her off. 'You're ruining the roses.'

Repulsed, she backed away, began shakily to retrace her steps. Edmund stumbled after her, took her by the hand.

'I'm sorry I shouted. It was totally unreasonable. You've only just got in and I haven't even said hello. Forgive me, darling. I'm just whacked, that's all, and dying for a drink. Be an angel and fetch me a beer.'

Only then did she remember the roses – the ones she'd left behind. They, too, would be ruined, and dying for a drink. She and Rick had lost all track of time, moved into a realm where nothing else existed save their two coupled, thrashing bodies. When, at last, they had pulled apart, dazed and drained and spent, they'd been shocked to see if was almost half past five, and, in the ensuing rush, had both forgotten to put the flowers in water. They'd still be lying on the table in his studio, and would die in this hot, sultry night; their petals shrivelling; their sweet scent turning rank.

'New bracelet?' Edmund was asking. 'Have I seen that one before?'

'What?' she answered, startled, yet unwilling to depart from that torrid, smouldering studio, 'Oh, this old thing? I hardly ever wear it.'

'Good,' he smiled, 'because … well, never mind. Wait and see.'

Which meant he must have bought her something similar, for next month's special day. Two sets of manacles.

'So how was your class? You're later than usual, aren't you? I suppose it must have been a bit of a drag in this heat.'

She nodded, still with Rick: his head thrown back, his face flushed and wild and wet, his hot, amazing body sweating into hers. Would he return to fetch the roses, drive over from his flat in that exhausted, languorous state, to succour them, retrieve them?

Unlikely.

The Dolce Vita was over for them both.

Worms

'Worms mustn't die,' Sam said, stopping to peer more closely at a thin, pink, slimy creature, wriggling on the tarmac.

'No, she agreed. 'They mustn't.'

'We have to put them back into the dirt.'

'The earth, you mean?'

'No, the dirt,' he repeated, still examining the worm.

Celia lodged the word in her mental English/American dictionary. So many subtle differences between two apparently similar languages, which, despite her many visits here, she still hadn't got quite straight.

'*You* put it back. *I* don't like to touch them.'

Obediently, she picked up the creepy-crawly and deposited it on the strip of grass that separated the houses from the road.

'No,' Sam objected. 'Put it in the *dirt*.'

She glanced around self-consciously. To reach any type of soil, she would have to trespass in some stranger's garden (which Sam would call a yard, of course). However, since there was no one to be seen at this early hour of the morning, she did as she was told, scratching a small hole for the worm in the middle of a flowerbed, then covering it with earth.

Sam seemed satisfied, and they dawdled on until he found another pair of worms, similarly stranded. 'Put them back!' he ordered her peremptorily.

Again she complied. At least these houses had no fences, unlike their English counterparts, so it was easy to creep into a garden with a worm concealed in each hand.

'Two more!' Sam exclaimed, coming to a halt again. 'Why do you think they're all crawling along the road?'

'I've no idea.' Road-savvy worms did seem a little incongruous in this well-heeled suburb of Seattle.

'Miss Richards said they're happy in the dirt.' Sam crouched down on a level with the creatures, half-fascinated, half-repulsed.

'Who's Miss Richards?'

'My teacher. They feel safer underground, she said, because birds can't get them there. Lots of things eat worms, you know – not just birds but frogs and shrews and moles.'

Celia nodded in accord. Just this morning, she had watched a hapless worm being eagerly devoured by a ruthless American robin, three times the size of the English species. But of course many things were bigger over here: apples, cars, fridges, cupboards (closets), even people and ideas.

Sam was now sitting on the tarmac, his clean-this-morning trousers (pants) already less than pristine. 'The dirt's happy, too, Miss Richards said. Because the worms put air in it, and water, and make it nice for plants.'

'Yes, that's the reason gardeners like them.'

'So why don't worms stay down there, in the dirt?'

Celia shook her head in bafflement. She should have packed an encyclopaedia, as well as games and toys.

'Perhaps they *want* to die.'

'No,' she said, too quickly. 'No one wants to die.'

'Did Grandpa want to?'

'Of course not!'

'Will I ever see him again?'

'No, darling, I'm afraid you won't.'

'Was Grandpa ill?'

'Not exactly ill, but—'

'*Mummy's* ill.'

'I know.'

'Is Mummy going to die?'

'Of course not,' she repeated, wishing she felt more certain of the fact. 'Now, get up, Sam, my love. We really have to hurry.'

'Why?' he asked, refusing to budge.

'Because we don't want to miss the school bus.'

'*I* do. I don't like school.'

'But you like learning about worms.'

'Mm,' he conceded, rising to his feet, at last, and resuming his slow progress. 'If no one eats them, worms can live to nine years old. That's older than me.'

'Yes, quite a bit. But you'll live much longer than nine – maybe to a hundred.'

'Grandpa didn't.'

'No.'

'How old is Grandpa?'

She warmed to the 'is'; preferred to use the present tense herself. 'He's sixty-eight.'

'That's old.'

'Not really.' Appallingly young to die, in fact. Her father was still alive, at ninety-six.

'Have *you* ever died?'

'*Me*?' she asked, jolted by the question, and about to explain that death was always permanent; that no one ever recovered or returned. Her lips, however, seemed physically unable to form such hopeless words, and, after a minute's edgy silence, Sam changed the subject – mercifully.

'Worms haven't any eyes, you know. But they have lots more hearts than us. Some of them have *ten* hearts.'

'Ten? Are you sure?' She wouldn't want ten hearts. When it came to heartbreak, one was more than enough.

'Yes, Miss Richards told us. Oh, look!' he shouted. 'Another! Put it back!'

'OK, but only if we walk faster. What will Mummy say if we miss the bus?'

'She won't say anything. She can't speak.'

'*Now* she can't, but soon she will.'

'When?'

'I'm not quite sure. Maybe in a week or so.' That was stretching the truth. According to the doctors, it would be at least a month before Katy recovered the power of speech, and even then her voice would sound distorted. 'Come on, Sam, let's run.'

If the school bus went without them, there was no way she could deliver him to Lakeridge Elementary – not without a car. She only hoped they were headed in the right direction. These streets all looked the same, with their low-slung, spacious properties, surrounded by luxuriant shrubs. Brad and Katy had moved here just last autumn, from their small Downtown apartment, so the area was new to her.

'Sam, are we going the right way?' she asked.

He gave a distracted nod, more concerned with the worms. He had stopped again, intrigued by a whole cluster of them, which he was counting on the fingers of both hands. 'Eight!' he said triumphantly. 'Put them in the dirt, Grandma.'

'I'll do it on the way back. We haven't time at the moment.'

'Yes, we have.'

'We *haven't*, Sam.'

'They'll die in the sun.'

'There isn't any sun, darling. It's only just stopped raining. Look at all that cloud!' She straightened up to study the expanse of sky, which reminded her of Sam's white porcelain cereal bowl, tipped upside down; its puddle of greyish, leftover milk solidified into scummy curds.

'Worms mustn't die,' he repeated. It had become a sort of mantra with him. Understandable.

'They won't die, Sam, honestly. The minute I've got you on the bus, I'll come back here and put them in the earth.'

'No, the *dirt*. You have to put them in the *dirt*.'

'Dirt *is* earth.'

'It isn't.'

'OK, I'll put them in the dirt, then.'

'You promise?'

'I promise. But now we have to hurry.'

They arrived at the bus stop with three minutes to spare. A group of other mothers was already waiting, with their children.

'Hi, Sam!' said one of them – a tall bleached-blonde, dressed in puce-pink pedal-pushers and a sweatshirt saying 'CUTIE'.

Sam mumbled an acknowledgement; shy in front of grown-ups.

The woman turned to Celia. 'I'm Mary-Beth,' she smiled. 'You must be Katy's Mom. Sam told me you were visiting. Great to meet you. When did you arrive?'

'Yesterday.' Could it only have been yesterday? Light years seemed to have passed since she had boarded the Heathrow Express. And, of course, the time-difference made everything confusing. In England, it would be mid-afternoon.

'How's Katy doing now?'

Celia paused. What could one say, especially in front of children?

'I hear she's still in the hospital.'

'Yes. She'll be there quite a while yet.'

'Well, if there's anything I can do to help, please call. Katy has my number.'

The yellow school bus lumbered up beside them, drowning out her thanks. The other mothers kissed their children goodbye, but Sam wriggled out of her embrace and went clambering up the steps of the bus without a backward glance. Perhaps, in some irrational fashion, he blamed her for David's death. Although he saw his grandfather only twice a year, there had always been a special bond between them. Sam even had his distinctive, slate-blue eyes.

'Do come in for coffee,' Mary-Beth was urging, as the bus began to move away.

'I'm afraid I can't. I'm going to the hospital.'

'Of course you are. That's dumb of me! But do you need a ride?'

'No, thanks. I'm fine.' She had found a way of getting there that involved three different buses: a local bus, a high-speed bus and finally a trolley bus. Brad had dismissed the plan as a total waste of time, since the journey would take an hour and a half, whereas a cab could do it in under twenty minutes. But cabs were an extravagance, and, in any case, she suspected Brad was prejudiced, like many of his compatriots, in regarding public transport as inefficient, if not quite irrelevant.

'I've nothing in my schedule,' Mary-Beth persisted, 'so I could take you right away.'

Again, she refused, politely. 'Right away' she had to put the worms back; fulfil her promise to Sam. Besides, she didn't relish company, being too keyed-up for small talk. And this friendly, cheery woman, who obviously knew Katy well, might come right into the ward with her, when it seemed imperative to be alone.

The minute Mary-Beth drove off in her armoured tank of a car, she dashed back to the worm-infested street. The creatures were still there, thank God. Sam might well cross-question her, and she mustn't let him down. He was suffering enough.

Slowly and methodically, she patrolled the length of the street, picking up each worm, slinking into a garden with it and laying it on the earth. She was surprised by the sheer numbers. A whole colony of worms must live here, improving the soil for these garden-proud suburbanites.

'Enjoy yourself,' she murmured to the last worm, imagining its contentment on joining its companions, burrowing and tunnelling in blissful safety underground. An enviable prospect to live as part of a community. The sense of isolation she was experiencing as a widow seemed worse five thousand miles away from home. Last night, in particular, had been a trial of strength. Once Sam had gone to bed, she'd sat jet-lagged and exhausted, listening to the silence. Brad was at the hospital, taking advantage of her presence as built-in baby-sitter to spend the night with Katy, camping out on a chair beside the bed. So her sole company was Theodore, the aloof and snooty cat. She had lain awake for hours, her mind darting back and forth between the desperate situation here and the problems still unsolved at home: what to do with David's stuff – his clothes, his books, his wine? (Unthinkable to give them away, when they were so intimate a part of him.) And what about the roomy flat they had lived in almost forty years? Should she sell it and downsize? And how would she cope with the whole financial side, without his expertise?

As she trudged back to the house, she tried to remove her thoughts from David (more or less impossible) and continue her search for worms. She was distressed to find *half* a worm, seemingly decapitated, which brought back instant memories of her callous little brother, who, as a child, had enjoyed cutting worms in half, claiming they could grow again into two healthy, separate specimens. Science had proved him wrong, in fact, although he'd told her since that some worms could regenerate lost segments of their bodies, or even grow new heads and tails. If only Katy had similar powers, she could have regenerated a brand-new tongue, rather than relying on a surgeon to reconstruct her own. The apparently famous Dr Tucker had taken skin from her forearm to replace that part of the tongue he'd cut out with the tumour, and stitched this skin to the remaining piece of tongue. The process sounded quite extraordinary to a lay-person like her, since, in order to do the stitching, he'd excised a string of blood vessels from along her upper arm, and used them like a length of sewing thread, then patched the arm with skin from her thigh. And before he'd even started on that complicated tongue-graft, he'd had to remove a dozen lymph nodes – some of which were cancerous – through an incision in the neck. The whole laborious operation had lasted seven hours, and left her arm and neck both badly scarred.

She hadn't seen the scars yet. To have travelled to Seattle whilst still reeling from the shock of David's heart attack had seemed beyond her capabilities, especially with a large funeral to plan. And almost more upsetting than the funeral had been the whole crass, intrusive bureaucracy of death. Confronted with coroners, solicitors, bank managers, insurance agents, her overwhelming instinct was to sink to the ground and howl. It had been weeks, in fact, before she'd regained some measure of control. And she knew it would be unfair to Sam – and an additional strain on everyone – if a grandmother who had come to help kept bursting into tears.

Soon, though, she would be face to face with a daughter not just cut about, but burned and blistered from extensive radiation, and bald from chemotherapy. And a daughter who had just lost her father, but couldn't say a word about the fact. Katy communicated by means of scribbled notes – when she felt well enough to hold the pen, Brad said – but scribbled notes were hardly adequate to convey any real emotion. And if Katy cried (wordlessly), how would *she* hold back? Yet, whatever happened, she must present a calm exterior, so that the composure won through such sheer effort and grim willpower wouldn't swirl away on a choppy sea of grief.

Having rescued four more worms, she hurried back to the house. If she didn't get a move on, she'd hardly make it to the hospital, before it was time to leave again to pick Sam up from the bus. She put all her daughter's presents in a carrier, grabbed her handbag, locked both doors, and set out for Mercer Village, where the first bus was scheduled to stop.

'I don't give change,' the surly driver said, waving away her twenty-dollar bill. 'You need the exact fare – one dollar, twenty-five.'

'I'm sorry, I haven't anything smaller.'

'Well, get it.'

'But aren't you about to depart?'

'Yeah. *Now*.' Rudely revving the engine, he gestured to her to get off. 'You'll have to catch the next bus.'

'But that's not for half an hour.'

'Correct.'

Barely had she alighted, when he pulled away – triumphantly, she felt. Blinking hard (she refused to cry on *his* account), she glanced around, in an attempt to get her bearings. Mercer Village was hardly a village in anything but name – just a nondescript square, comprising a car-park and a few large stores. Well, at least she could buy a toy for Sam and so break into her twenty-dollar bill. Wandering along the toy aisle of the supermarket, she found a wriggly rubber snake, miraculously pink – the nearest thing on sale to a worm.

The next bus had a younger, driver who was helpful and polite, and gave her what he called a 'transfer', to save money on the Express bus.

'Where you headin' for?'

'The Virginia Mason Hospital.' She consulted her hospital leaflet. 'It's in Seneca Street – number 925.'

'Yeah, Seneca and Ninth. I know it well. It's won a bunch of awards for excellence.'

Thank God, she thought, as she moved further down the bus. She was the only person on it, so the driver kept up a shouted conversation, calling out remarks about the hospital, the weather, and his sister who had diabetes yet *would* pig out on cookies.

It was a relief to bid goodbye to him, in truth. Idle chit-chat was distracting, and she needed to prepare herself. When she'd last seen Katy, seven months ago, her daughter's hair was waist-length, flowing down her back in a cascade of tawny-gold. Now she *had* no hair.

As she waited for the high-speed bus, the rain began afresh, which pleased her on the worms' account. At least they wouldn't shrivel in the sun, should they have strayed from their dank underworld once more. It might be mid-March on the calendar, but the weather refused to play along and adopt a spring-like mood. Not that she objected. Blue skies and burgeoning buds would seem cruelly inappropriate just now.

This bus, true to its name, went at quite a lick, although, once she got off, she had a long wait for the trolley bus, again in pelting rain. Far from trying to shelter, she actually welcomed the fact that she was getting soaking wet. Ever since Katy's diagnosis, she had felt guilty about her own rude health; about having a full head of hair and a tongue without a tumour. If she caught a cold or, better still, pneumonia, it would redress the balance a fraction; bridge the gulf between them in terms of vitality and strength.

'And who'll look after Sam, then?' she asked herself sarcastically. Certainly not Brad. He needed every dollar he could earn to meet the medical expenses, which, though partly covered by insurance, were still extortionate. If only Katy had stayed in England, she could have been treated on the National Health. If only she'd stayed in England anyway. But it would have been selfish – and impossible – to have overruled her daughter. Katy was in love, and not just with Brad (whom she had met by chance when he was in London on a business trip), but with the whole idea of a new life in a new country.

The trolley bus took only a few minutes and, having walked the short distance from the bus stop, she was suddenly confronted by the hospital; her pace slowing as she approached its tall glass doors. She allowed two couples to enter first, envying them, as usual. Only in the last few weeks had it struck her just how smug most couples were, regarding it as their natural right to have automatic company, built-in help and support. And she and David had been every bit as self-satisfied, of course.

More couples in the foyer, lounging on the sofas and armchairs. This elegant reception area, with not a nurse or doctor in sight, made the place seem more like a hotel. Although, once she turned into the corridor, she encountered a group of medicos, in blue baggy pants and gowns. Had they just emerged from the operating theatre; just reconstructed another cancerous tongue?

In the lift (elevator), she pressed the button for the fifteenth floor, relieved when it stopped at every floor beforehand, which gave her time to work out what to say. Never before had she been lost for words with Katy, but her daughter had moved beyond her now into a world of such extremes – extremes of pain, of danger – that she, the once-experienced mother, felt left behind, shut out. Indeed, the only time that she herself had ever been in hospital was when she'd given birth.

She stepped from the lift into a small, blue-carpeted lobby, with more armchairs and a tank of tropical fish. However, her attention was attracted, not by exotic fins and tails, but by a man in a white hospital gown, who was standing by the window, attached to a drip, with various tubes going in and out of him. His face and neck were red and raw and blistered from radiation burns. That's how *Katy's* will look, she thought, with increasing apprehension, and she'll have the same tracheotomy scar, livid on her throat; the same ominous-looking tubes and drips.

Aware of her scrutiny, the fellow turned his back and moved closer to the window. Had he escaped the ward, she wondered? Or was he planning to jump from a fifteenth-storey window-ledge, and so put an end to it all? There was no nurse with him, or relative. Would they allow her daughter to wander around unsupervised like that?

Instinctively, she joined him at the window, silently begging him not to jump; trying to tell him that there *was* still hope; that maybe people needed him and loved him.

He was eying her suspiciously, so she pretended to be admiring the view – which was indeed impressive. Up till now, she had been blind to her surroundings, scarcely noticing the thrusting heads and squared shoulders of the skyscrapers, jostling for space in the city, or majestic Lake Washington, gleaming in a brief burst of watery sunshine.

All at once, she turned on her heel and made herself walk on. Of *course* he couldn't jump. Modern hospital windows would be triple-glazed, triple-locked and completely shatterproof. She was simply putting off a moment that would test her to the limit.

Nervously, she stumbled into the ward, with its large sign, CANCER CARE – two words, she felt, which should never be conjoined. Cancer *didn't* care. It wrecked lives and bodies without justice or compunction. Katy had never smoked, drank only very rarely and was an enthusiastic member of her gym, so why should she be stricken with a tumour on her tongue at the age of only thirty-four? Most cancers of the mouth, according to the statistics, afflicted heavy smokers and drinkers, and mainly over-sixty-fives.

As she proceeded down the corridor, looking for her daughter's room – number twenty-three – she glanced in through the open doors, catching glimpses of the patients in the beds: all comatose, all ashen-faced, some seeming total wrecks.

She stood back to allow a trolley-bed to pass, holding her two bulky bags close against her chest, so they wouldn't cause an obstruction. Feeling the outline of Sam's toy rubber snake, she gripped it with a sense of dread as she met the eyes of the young man on the trolley: his skin porridge-pale, his arms as thin as twigs; an oxygen mask covering half his face.

'Worms mustn't die,' she muttered under her breath.

'Excuse me?' said the nurse accompanying the patient. 'I didn't hear what you said.'

'Er, nothing.' Blushing, she squeezed past and continued along the corridor. Yet, as she knocked on the door of number twenty-three, she fixed her total concentration on the worms: happy worms in happy dirt, ecstatically writhing and wriggling in the nutrient-rich, deep soil; worms regenerating, healing, growing strong new body-parts; worms with ten hearts each – none faltering or breaking, but pulsing with new life; worms protected from all dangers, growing fat and healthy beneath their sheltering blanket of warm, sustaining earth; worms cherished and cocooned, safe from every predator; worms living to a hundred, impregnable, unscathed.

'Worms *won't* die,' a voice said. Startled, she glanced round. No one there, except another nurse. That had been her *husband's* voice – silenced but familiar, and utterly dependable; a voice that never lied; would never try to lull her with false hope.

Smiling for the first time since his death, she walked quietly, calmly, confidently, into Katy's room.

Mystery Prize

'Would you like to buy a raffle ticket, dear?'

'No, thank you,' Frieda replied, bridling at the 'dear'. People tended to assume that because you were in your nineties, you could be addressed with demeaning endearments.

'It's a very good cause,' the girl persisted – a girl she hadn't seen before; not one of the usual staff, who wore blue overalls and lace-up shoes, but an exotic creature with hennaed hair, prancing around in high-heeled scarlet boots.

'The World Wildlife Fund. You know, saving endangered species like tigers and blue whales.'

'No, thank you,' she repeated. She believed in being generous, but she preferred to *choose* her charities, and in her particular scheme of things, human beings took precedence over wildlife.

'Here, take a look at the list of prizes. I'm sure something there will tempt you.'

A sheet of paper was thrust into her hand. Fumbling for her spectacles, she perused it with a frown. 'A weekend for two in Paris ... Two tickets for *Les Miserables* ... Two best seats for Chelsea Football Club home match ...' Everything for two. She touched her sapphire ring, which was cutting into the swollen flesh of her now crooked wedding finger. She *should* have been a couple – would have been, had fate not intervened.

Continuing on through the list, she found none of the temptations promised by the girl. What use was a Russell Hobbs toaster, when she'd had to give up toast in favour of soft sliced bread, on account of her new dentures? Or a bottle of champagne, when alcohol make her dizzy? As for the giant-sized teddy bear, it would simply gather dust. Cuddly toys were of little use without grandchildren to spoil. Besides, she had never won a prize in the whole of her long life – not at school, or sports days, and not in any raffle, despite the many tickets she had purchased over the years. Like so much else, it was probably a matter of genes. She and her whole family lacked the winning gene – obvious from their history.

'Can you *see* OK?' the girl demanded, clearly puzzled by her silence. 'If your eyes aren't good, I can read the list out loud.'

'My eyes are fine,' she replied a shade defensively. In that respect, she *was* lucky. In fact, she had only to look around at the others in the room – many blind, deaf, incontinent and wheelchair-bound – to realize just how much suffering she'd been spared in her old age.

Stooping to her level, the girl jabbed her index finger at the paper. 'I love the sound of the Mystery Prize, don't you? What do you think it could be?'

'I'm afraid I've no idea.' Mystery held no attraction. There had been too much in her early life; enigmas only solved much later on: her father's absence, her mother's constant weeping, the family's sudden, baffling change of name.

'You're the only one who hasn't bought a ticket,' the girl accused, rattling her tin of coins, as if to underline the point.

Frieda refrained from answering. She was 'the only one' in several other ways: the only one who made her own way here, walking (albeit slowly) from her flat, instead of being picked up by the mini-bus; the only one who came just once a week, instead of every day; the only one, as far as she could gather, who didn't have a single living relative.

'Well, please yourself,' the girl said, finally shrugging in defeat.

Once she'd gone, Frieda opened her book – a German book, which she was reading in the original. It still seemed strange – indeed luxurious – after a lifetime of pretending to be English, no longer to care what people thought. She had even considered reclaiming the name Beckenbauer, instead of the safely English 'Brown', chosen by her mother. Although, thinking back, she doubted if her mother had actually fooled a soul. With her thick Germanic accent, the foreign food she favoured, her drab black frock and quaint, old-fashioned hairstyle (two long plaits braided round her head), she must have seemed as out of place in Ludlow as her Bismarck herring and sauerkraut.

'Tea for you, Miss Brown?'

'Yes, please.' She accepted the stained white cup from Ann-Marie, who had served them lunch and was now doing the rounds with the trolley. The tea had spilled over, soaking into the biscuit on the saucer. No matter. Soggy biscuits were easier to eat.

As she spooned the sweet brown mulch into her mouth, she saw Veronica, who ran the place, making a beeline for her chair.

'I hope you're joining in the bingo today,' she said with her persuasive smile.

Frieda murmured something inaudible. Not only did bingo seem pointless in the extreme, but who would choose to play *any* game with people who had mostly lost their wits? Besides, as the only child of a mother on her own, she had never been a joiner; found the constant activities laid on by Veronica something of an ordeal. (Sing-alongs were embarrassing; carpet-bowls undignified.) Sometimes she wondered why she came at all and, indeed, looking round this dreary room, with its cheap cord carpet, faded curtains, and chairs as old and saggy as their occupants, she felt a sense of near-revulsion, aggravated by the potpourri of smells. The acrid tang of urine from an unchanged incontinence-pad, and the musty whiff of unwashed flesh from her podgy neighbour, Maud, mingled strangely with the tang of meat still lingering from lunch. But lunch made it all worthwhile, of course: a proper home-cooked meal, prepared with love by Ann-Marie, and different every week. Besides, without these Wednesdays at the Day Centre, time would stretch interminably, with no change of scene, no other human contact. She still missed her job, which she had managed to retain right on through her seventies, balking at retirement; that crippling sense of loss at no longer being needed, no longer doing something that made at least some tiny difference to the world.

'You'd be good at bingo, Frieda,' Veronica remarked, still smiling her encouragement. 'Your brain's so wonderfully sharp.'

Did you *need* a brain for bingo? Last week, she'd agreed (reluctantly) to take part in the Scrabble, which at least involved some element of skill, but since most of the other players had no notion of basic spelling, it had proved frustrating as well as tedious.

'There's a lovely prize, you know. And you could be the winner, Frieda, since you're so quick off the mark.'

'I don't think so,' she said tersely, settling back in her chair. 'I'd prefer to sit and watch, if that's all right.'

It took some time to set up *any* game here, as few of the participants could move with ease or speed, and had to be wheeled or coaxed or chivvied to the table, where they were issued with their bingo-cards and counters. Bill, the only man amongst them, had caught his stick in the rungs of someone's chair and was pulling at it irritably. Sad, thought Frieda, how many men died before their womenfolk, leaving shoals of stricken widows. Even in her early life, men and death had been woven inextricably – her father's death, her fiancé's death, the death of her first boss, followed by the—

'Quiet, please!' Veronica called, although no one took much notice. Iris was babbling, as ever, more or less oblivious of what was going on around her, while Maud continued running through her litany of ailments: varicose veins, high blood pressure, sinusitis, haemorrhoids ... By a certain age, everyone had ailments, but best simply to accept them rather than bore the assembled company with a whole rigmarole of symptoms, or blow-by-blow accounts of unpleasant operations. The general conversation here never reached profundity – no discussion of life's meaning, or debate about morality, only endless comments on the weather (floods and hurricanes were relished in particular), or muttered slurs about 'refugees' and 'immigrants'. As an incomer herself, Frieda hated hearing foreigners condemned as lazy scroungers. Constance was the worst in that respect, although right now she was excoriating not the usual 'wogs' and 'darkies', but the steamed jam roll at lunch.

'*My* piece had no jam on. Why call it steamed jam roll if there isn't any jam?'

'You could have had fruit salad,' Bill observed.

'I like something hot for afters, and fruit salad isn't hot.'

'Well, tomorrow it's rice pudding,' Veronica put in, diplomatically. 'And that's your favourite, isn't it?'

'Only with jam. It's not sweet enough without. If they've run out of jam, they can keep their rotten rice.'

Frieda eased up from her chair and hobbled to the door, pretending she needed the lavatory. These people were so *rude*, not to mention fussy. Most of them left half their food, despite the fact that Ann-Marie spent several hours toiling in the kitchen. Leaving food seemed incomprehensible, if not downright criminal. If you'd gone hungry as a child, the gnawing, famished emptiness never went away and, even decades afterwards, you would always scrape your plate clean, in case supplies ran out in some bleak, uncertain future. Food was precious, and precarious; couldn't be relied upon – in that respect, was similar to parents.

Once in the toilet, she opened her handbag and withdrew the piece of chicken pie she had stowed away at lunchtime. It would do nicely for tomorrow, if she wrapped it in some paper towels and thus stopped it from disintegrating and messing up her bag. She usually managed to secrete some precious piece of booty from the Day Centre – a second chop or fishcake, begged from Ann-Marie; an extra biscuit or slice of home-made cake. It took care and sleight of hand to slip them into her holdall without anybody noticing. It would indeed be mortifying to be caught red-handed; made to seem a glutton or a thief. It was nothing to do with gluttony, in fact. Food supplies were crucial – reserves against the emptiness to come.

The doorbell rang a second time. Still she hesitated, uncertain whether to answer it or not. It was far too late for the postman, who came very rarely anyway, and who else would be calling at seven in the evening? She tried to block out all the stories she'd heard of strangers turning up, pretending to be salesmen, only to cosh old ladies on the head, rob them, even rape them. Yet it wasn't very likely that such types would come in daylight, or to such a humble flat. And it would be a crying shame to miss the chance of company, if it happened to be a visitor – perhaps somebody from Age Concern, or her new neighbour popping in, at last, to introduce herself.

Limping out to the hall, she opened the door a crack. There, on the step, stood the girl in the red, high-heeled boots she had encountered at the Day Centre. Her face and half her body were hidden by the package she was carrying – something large and bulky, itself concealed in a giant-sized plastic bag.

'Hi!' she said, 'Are you Mrs Brown?'

'*Miss* Brown,' Frieda corrected, although the girl didn't appear to be listening.

'I've brought your raffle prize. Where do you want me to put it?'

'Raffle prize? But I didn't buy a ticket.'

'You must have done. You've won the Mystery Prize. My Mum was meant to bring it round, but she's gone down with this flu thing.' She dumped the package in the hall, then turned sharply on her heel. 'Must fly! I'm in a rush.'

Frieda grabbed her by the sleeve as she was about to scurry off. 'Wait! There must be some mistake. I was the only one who *didn't* buy a ticket. Surely you remember – you told me that yourself.'

The girl shook her head, having clearly quite forgotten that they had ever met before. That happened all the time, of course. To anyone under thirty, the old were interchangeable – just grey hair, wrinkled faces, veiny legs, stiff joints – no distinguishing features or distinctive personalities.

'Sorry, I sold so many tickets, and in so many different places, the whole thing's just a blur now. Anyway, you *won*, so why don't you stop arguing and let me get back home?'

Arguing? She was merely trying to establish basic justice. This Mystery Prize belonged to someone else, and should be restored to its rightful owner without any further delay. But the girl was already careering down the path and, despite Frieda's frantic calls, continued her wild dash along the street.

With a sigh of resignation, Frieda left the package by the door. No doubt someone would come to claim it soon enough, and, if by Wednesday it was still sitting in her house, she would report it to the Day Centre and leave *them* to sort it out.

Returning to her chair, she tried to continue with her reading, but now found it hard to concentrate. She kept wondering what the prize was; even wishing she could open it. But she'd been taught early on in childhood never to take what wasn't hers, be that just a pencil or a pin. However, looking wasn't taking, so she could at least remove the package from its confining plastic bag, and gain some idea of what it might contain. It had somehow claimed her interest; no longer just an encumbrance cluttering up the place; more an unexpected guest, whom she was discourteously ignoring by leaving in the hall.

Limping out to fetch it, she picked it up, with difficulty, elated by its size and sheer solidity. Then, taking it into the sitting-room, she set it on the table and slipped off the plastic bag, revealing, as she did so, a large, square-sided box, magnificently wrapped in luxurious gold-foil. The paper was printed with the word CONGRATULATIONS, repeated over and over in gleaming silver script, and yards of matching silver ribbon, looped in swags and bows, completed the spectacular effect. Well, if contents were as impressive as the wrappings, then this Mystery Prize must indeed be special.

'But it doesn't happen to be yours,' she reminded herself tartly. 'And, anyway, you didn't *want* a raffle prize.'

None the less, she drew her chair up closer and sat gazing at the box, already feeling different – the sort of pampered woman who received gifts like this as of right. Or a lucky child, perhaps, celebrating her birthday with both parents actually present, and no one spoiling the occasion with bouts of anguished sobbing. Yes, her father had chosen this Mystery Gift for his beloved little daughter – a proper living father, not a prisoner or a corpse.

She shut her eyes as his form took shape. She had never actually seen him, apart from in his photograph, where he looked stern and rather frightening, with a tight-zipped mouth and narrow slits for eyes. She exchanged that unnerving father (black and white and blurry) for an easy-going, cuddly one in brilliant living colour, and a father who was *English*. If he'd been born and bred in Ludlow, instead of in Saarbrücken, he wouldn't have been interned, which meant her mother might have had more children, rather than crying all the time. She'd have sisters, brothers – maybe aunts and uncles, and a whole tribe of friendly cousins.

Behind closed lids, the Mystery Gift began breeding like her mother, spawning further gold-wrapped boxes from her ever-growing family; gifts from uncles, aunts and grandparents, nephews, nieces, cousins – all with English names, of course, so they'd escape the perilous prison camp and the tag of 'enemy alien'.

She changed the scene to Christmas, when the presents seemed to multiply at an even faster rate; first piled beneath the Christmas tree, then opened in a golden storm by the crowd of smiling relatives. As a child, she had always hated Christmas – an empty, endless, mournful day that never kept its promises. Her mother would wear her usual black and her usual bleak expression, and was usually too sad to cook, so they'd have bread and *wurst* for lunch. And money was too scarce for proper presents (although once she'd had a jigsaw from a lady called Miss Pettifer, who lived across the street). But now presents were being showered on her, all wrapped in gold-foil paper and tied with silver bows.

She went out to the kitchen, to make herself a cup of tea, transforming the cramped cubby-hole to a spacious family room, ablaze with decorations. She could smell the roasting goose and hot mince pies; hear the voices of her visitors greeting her excitedly. And when she picked up the small teapot, with its cracked spout and missing lid, it filled a good three dozen cups, without ever running out; and even the mince pies were miraculously replenished, in the same munificent fashion.

Returning to the sitting-room, she paused to admire the box again, stroking the shiny paper, touching her stiff fingers to the gleaming silken ribbon. Then, turning the box on each of its four sides, she began counting the word CONGRATULATIONS, reaching a final total of fifty-five. It was not a word that had figured in her life. Why should anybody congratulate her when she had never excelled at anything and been a dunce at school? There was some excuse, admittedly. It was quite a strain pretending to be English when she knew deep down she was German (and spoke German at home with her mother). And the name 'Brown' didn't fit her – a short and skimpy name, like the short and skimpy clothes she wore long after she'd outgrown them. As well as the change of surname, her mother removed the 'i' from Frieda, and excised her second Christian name entirely, on the grounds that 'Wilhelmina' would give the game away. And because she dreaded her own company in this so-called alien land, she often stopped the new-fledged 'Freda Brown' from going to school at all, claiming the child was indisposed.

Besides, achievement wasn't easy when she had learned early on to hold her tongue, hide away, and avoid attracting any attention. Safer to sit silent and unnoticed in the corner than try for any honour or award. Yet, this very afternoon, things had changed dramatically. She had just won a coveted top prize at Millbrook Secondary, and the entire assembly of staff and girls were voicing their congratulations as she stepped up to the podium to receive the gold-wrapped box. The headmaster shook her by the hand, then declaimed in his deep, booming voice, 'I predict a brilliant future for you, Freda. This is just the first, I'm sure, of a whole succession of awards.'

Gliding back to her seat in the hall to thunderous applause, she saw her parents standing at the back, overcome with pride, smiling, clapping, cheering, as the rising star of Millbrook sat triumphant with her golden box.

'Silly fool!' she rebuked herself, aware she'd spent the last half-hour enacting senseless fantasies, all suggested by the Mystery Prize itself. 'For goodness' sake, stop being so absurd and get down to something useful for a change.'

But what *could* she do that was useful? Although she had volunteered her services to several different charities, she was considered far too ancient at the age of ninety-three even to stuff envelopes, let alone collect money in the street. Which meant every day dragged limp and leaden-footed from breakfast-time to bedtime. In fact, she had moved her bedtime forward from eleven o'clock to ten, and then from ten to nine, simply to reduce those stagnant hours.

It was almost nine at present, so, after a brief snack, she carried the box into the bedroom and placed it on the dressing-table. It had indeed become a sort of guest, providing instant company and upgrading her surroundings; the shiny gold of the paper contrasting with the drab beige carpet and faded counterpane. Never before had she allowed herself to indulge in make-believe, or transform her past with foolish flights of fancy, yet every time she looked at the box, new scenarios began fermenting in her mind. Even now, struggling to undo her zip with stubborn arthritic fingers, she was suddenly a girl again – as agile as a gymnast, as slim as a grissini stick. And congratulations were ringing out once more, as the guests at her engagement party raised their glasses in a toast – fifty-five of them precisely, to match the fifty-five CONGRATULATIONS she'd counted on the box. And, just a moment later, her fiancé, Henry George, slipped the sapphire ring on her finger, and presented her with an intriguing, gold-wrapped gift.

Opening it with shaking hands, she found not a dress or

negligee, but all the years denied to her – years of love, romance. And, digging deeper into the swathes of tissue paper, she discovered precious insights into the many things she'd never had the chance to learn: how he might make love (with tenderness, with passion?); the way he'd treat their children (distantly, indulgently?); the way he might have aged (mellowing as the decades passed, or cursing his constraints?).

In fact, he'd been killed in action at Dunkirk, six months before the wedding, but she passed that detail over and retrieved him from the dead, so that she could stage their romantic nuptials in the parish church in Ludlow. And, yes, there was the golden box again – the first of many wedding gifts given by their friends. Forget the war, and rationing – the wedding of her dreams was taking place in peacetime, and her loving, laughing father was also resurrected, so that he could lead her up the aisle in her exquisite white-lace gown. And although her mother happened to be dabbing at her eyes, she was shedding tears of joy, this time.

Having finally removed her clothes, she ignored her long-sleeved nightgown and, for the first time in her life, slipped naked into bed. And, although she'd switched the light off, the gold-wrapped box still gleamed with hope and promise through the soft blue summer dusk. Sleep, of course, refused to come, but not, as in the usual way, because of pain or fear of death, but because Henry George had better ideas as to how to pass the night.

Groping out her hand to locate the bedside clock, she held it close to read the tiny figures. Ten to nine. Extraordinary. She never slept so late; was normally up and dressed by half-past five or six. Sun was clamouring at the window, as if in celebration, streaming through the glass, regilding the large Mystery Box. She, a rational woman, who had never given credence to any kind of mumbo-jumbo, refused point-blank to believe in magic powers. Yet it couldn't be denied that she had just enjoyed her best night's sleep in years. And she no longer felt her normal sense of dread as another flaccid day began its stumbling progress to the evening, with no distractions, no other human presence. On the contrary, the family she had conjured up last night seemed still to be quietly breathing in the flat.

As soon as she was dressed, she took the box into the sitting-room, torn between self-reproach for creating such fictitious scenes and a desire to keep repeating them, prompted by the box itself once more. In each extravaganza it played the starring role, of course: her first wedding anniversary, the birth of her first child, VE Day, Henry's first promotion, once he was demobbed. And what about their birthdays (his and hers), and moving-house day, and the children's graduations? And on and proudly on until their Silver Wedding, followed by their Ruby, Golden, Diamond ...

The doorbell brought her plonking back to earth. That would be the milkman – she always paid him Mondays. But, opening the door, she saw not brawny shoulders and bull neck, but the frail and slender figure of the girl who'd brought the Mystery Prize. She was no longer in her scarlet boots, but wearing grubby gym shoes beneath a short, tight, mud-brown skirt.

'Listen,' she exclaimed, all but falling through the doorway in dismay. 'I've made an awful boo-boo – got the wrong address, got the wrong Mrs Brown, messed up all round, in fact. Mum's doing her nut, says I'm completely useless and she'll never ask me to do anything again. Except she *has* – insisted I get the prize back and give it to the *other* Mrs Brown. You were right all along,' she added, with a nervous laugh. 'You told me that you hadn't won, but I was in such a rush it didn't really register.' Pausing for breath, she flicked her long fair hair back from her face, before asking with a note of deep alarm, 'You haven't opened it, I hope.'

Frieda stood in silence. She had opened it so many times, her hands and mind were still aching with the awe of it.

'Christ, I'll be in trouble if you have! There'll be all hell to pay. Mum will go bananas and this Mrs Brown, whoever she is, will probably bust a gut.'

Frieda steadied herself on the doorframe. The girl was looking close to tears, and she hated people to suffer, especially on her own account. Besides, it would be morally impossible to cheat another woman of a rightful raffle prize.

Leadenly, forlornly, she went to fetch the box, feeling the air grow colder in the flat, as choking coils of black-edged grief closed so tight around her, she could barely breathe or speak. Her father was no longer close beside her, his strong arm like a bastion as he led her up the aisle, but dying in the prison camp, 200 miles away, having never seen or held his only child. And Henry George wasn't standing at the altar about to plight his troth, but being mowed down by machine-gunfire on the beaches at Dunkirk, slaughtered by her own countrymen. Which meant that the English girl and the German girl who had tried to live as one inside her were now clawing at each other in a new war of their own; a war of divided loyalties. And neither girl was winning any prizes. Indeed, neither had the slightest skill; just two dunces in the corner, who would never shine at anything. And her brilliant boss, Sebastian, had not been spared from cancer, but was dying in St Thomas's, just seven weeks after he'd first expressed an interest in her. And the hope she'd dared to entertain that love and marriage were not ruled out for ever was expiring with him, coldly, in the morgue.

'Gosh! Thanks so much,' the girl said, sighing with relief as the box was handed over. 'You're not mad at me, I hope? It's just one of those things, I reckon.'

'Yes,' said Frieda, 'just one of those things.'

The girl dashed off in her usual frantic fashion, leaving Frieda to stand staring out at the dismal, treeless street, the thick bank of lowering cloud. The earlier sun had vanished and the sky looked wan and sallow, as if it, too, were languishing.

Closing the door, she limped into the sitting-room. How different it seemed without the Mystery Box – just a cluttered space now, crammed with useless furniture. Why should one old woman need a sofa and two chairs, a table seating six, a sideboard holding nothing?

All at once, she glimpsed her face in the mirror over the mantelpiece, recoiling in distaste from her peeved and sour expression. Her *mother's* face, not hers. And she had no desire to emulate a mother who had spent fifty years living in a funeral parlour, wrapped in winding-sheets, dousing each new day that dawned with handfuls of her husband's ashes, until every hour was smudged and silted up. As a child, entombed in death, she had resolved never to repeat that cycle, or to wallow in self-pity that polluted other people's lives. So, when her own fiancé died, she had refused to weep, on principle; refused even to wear black; summoned every ounce of strength to avoid lapsing into frozen grief. And she had done the same after Sebastian's death, forcing a smile even at his funeral, then endeavouring to *live* the smile, to make it less a mockery.

Returning to the mirror, she clamped on that long-practised smile; tried to give it substance by reflecting on her good fortune. She not only had her health and strength, she also had a cosy flat and a small but useful pension; a parade of shops within less than half a mile, and the GP even closer. And her funeral expenses were already paid in full, through a special pre-death plan, which itself brought great relief. And there was plenty to look forward to, if she emphasized the positive: her new library book; the local paper – free each week – her favourite month, September, already looming into view, and a pot of English tea for breakfast, with a slice of bread and marmalade, the minute she sat down. And in two days' time it was Wednesday, which meant company and home-cooked lunch at the Day Centre. Ann-Marie had promised Irish stew, with lemon sponge to follow. *This* week, she'd make an effort, don her brightest frock, even agree to join in the bingo, just to please Veronica.

Besides, in a game of chance, anything could happen. As Veronica had said herself, she might win a lovely prize.

Perhaps.

Just once.

This time.

Peacocks

'There's a reason why I call this course "Releasing the Writer Within". The tutor's sharp grey eyes tracked from face to face, giving each of the assembled group a second's scrutiny. 'Can any of you guess what it is?'

No one broke the silence. Natasha sat rigid in her seat, praying some brave person would pipe up. Otherwise, one of them might be picked on to respond, and if – God forbid – it were *her*, she was bound to make a fool of herself – stutter like a moron, blush to the roots of her hair.

'Is it something to do with freeing ourselves?' an elderly woman suggested.

'Yes, very good, Virginia – freeing ourselves to write. You see, inside every one of us is an original, talented writer, just waiting its chance to come out and be acknowledged.'

Inside *her*, thought Natasha, was too much greasy breakfast and a load of worry about whether she should be here at all.

The tutor was now warming to her theme, pacing back and forth in the space between the window and the whiteboard. 'If you ask a child in primary school to write a story or poem, they'll do it happily, without doubting their abilities. But as we get older, we develop critical voices – often sparked by our parents and teachers – which begin to undermine us by telling us we can't do this, or we're no good at that, so we lose confidence in our natural, in-built talents. But this weekend, we have the opportunity to release our inner writer, and start believing in ourselves again.'

Natasha bit the end of her pen, thinking back to primary school. She couldn't remember ever writing poems; only doing sums and finding snails in the playground. Snails were lucky in that they carried their house around with them, so they could pop safely back, at the first sign of any threat. Even now, she was tempted to run home, despite the fact she'd only just arrived. The others had been here since yesterday evening, for the introductory session, followed by a get-together, with free drinks in the bar. She didn't drink and wasn't a good mixer, so she'd chickened out of that, and had only made it by the skin of her teeth for this first Saturday-morning session. Which was stupid of her, actually, because the rest of them had got to know each other, whereas she was the awkward stranger in their midst.

The tutor appeared to have read her mind. 'We've already introduced ourselves at last night's little party, but please forgive me if I don't remember all your names. It may take me a wee bit longer to match each one to a face. But, in order to help the process, I want you all to write me a brief character sketch – tell me who you are, where you grew up, what job you do – all that sort of thing. And, if you have the courage, then add a bit about how you feel: your hopes and dreams and fears, what motivates you in life, what you like about yourself, and dislike!'

'When you say "brief", how long do you mean?' asked a skinny man, dressed in grubby jeans – one of the few males in the group.

'Don't worry about length, Tim. Just let it all flow out. It's not meant to be a shaped piece, just something very spontaneous and free.'

Free. Natasha caught the word like a butterfly, pinned it down, examined it. Was one *ever* free? The tutor meant it in a different sense, of course, although even that seemed more or less impossible. Being spontaneous took practice.

'Right, any other questions?'

A woman put her hand up, as if she were still at school. 'Does it have to be true?'

Her words produced a ripple of laughter, although the tutor replied in serious mode. 'Actually, that's a very good point, Fatima. The whole issue of truth in fiction is one we'll explore tomorrow, but just for now, yes, let's stick to the facts. But if anyone is anxious about being too confessional, then by all means edit that truth. After the break, we'll be reading our pieces aloud, so don't divulge anything that might make you feel uncomfortable.'

'Well, that's my whole existence ruled out!' the skinny guy bantered, slamming his notebook shut.

More laughter. Natasha didn't join in. She was *already* feeling uncomfortable, just by being here. However high her hopes, suppose, in cold, hard fact, she couldn't string two words together, and was labelled the class dunce?

'OK, let's get cracking,' said the tutor. 'But if anyone feels stuck, call me over and I'll see if I can help.'

Far from being stuck, the rest of the class began feverishly scribbling away; fifteen eager pens or pencils zipping across the paper. Natasha sat huddled over her notebook, wondering how to start. 'Tell me who you are,' the tutor had said, but she hadn't worked that out yet. For all her twenty years, she'd been trying on identities – first, wizard, jockey, ballerina, cowboy, and a load of other childish ones, long since left behind. She was now considering novelist or playwright, but both seemed just as challenging as the dozens she'd outgrown. Anyway, she couldn't really admit to such ambitions, without seeming a pretentious bore. And, as for spelling out what she disliked about herself, that would fill two notebooks: her shyness and weak will, her caution and sheer cowardice, not to mention her thin legs and funny chin. Perhaps she'd skip the character sketch and start with where she'd grown up – safer and simpler altogether. Nervously, she uncapped her pen, aware that the tutor was prowling round the room, making sure everyone was working.

'I was born at home,' she scrawled, 'in a tiny village in Northumbria, on a perishing January night. The midwife's car got stranded in the snow, so Dad delivered me himself.'

Quickly, she crossed out the second sentence – too intimate to share. She could write about it in private, though, because, now she came to think of it, the whole thing was quite dramatic. First off, her mother's age: forty-six, by the time she gave birth, having tried for two whole decades to get pregnant. And the labour itself was pretty dire: her father playing obstetrician in her mother's pinny and plastic washing-up gloves, with a force-nine gale rampaging outside and snowdrifts ten foot high. And, to top it all, she was premature; a tiny, puny shrimp he'd had to wrap in a tablecloth and then in kitchen foil, to conserve every ounce of heat until the ambulance got through. So, for the first two days of her life, she and her parents were cut off from the world, clinging to each other in one tight, desperate circle, lurching between triumph and despair. She sometimes felt that her dad had forgotten to cut the umbilical cord, because all three of them were joined still, far closer than most families – more or less inseparable, in fact. Although she wouldn't dream of saying so, for fear of seeming a freak. It wasn't cool to love your parents. You were meant to kick against them, resent them, blame them for all your faults, not cherish the hope that you could stay with them for ever.

She gave a surreptitious glance at her neighbour – a stocky bloke, with a paunch and straggly, iron-grey hair. He'd already covered two pages and was still scribbling at a manic rate. But then he was almost as old as her father, so he would have much more to write about: degrees, careers, trips abroad, marriage, children, grandchildren.

Suddenly her mobile rang – an urgent, shrilling summons from her shoulder-bag, disturbing the whole room. She flushed scarlet as everyone looked up, their concentration shattered.

'I did say turn your phones off,' the tutor reprimanded.

'I ... I'm sorry,' Natasha stammered. 'It ... it may be urgent. Excuse me, could you, a second?'

Grabbing her bag, she dashed out of the room, her heart thumping in anticipation of some new ghastly crisis: a haemorrhage, a heart attack, another tumour appearing out of nowhere.

'Hello? Hello? What's up, Dad? ... Oh, I see ... Yes, of *course* I'm fine ... Yes, wonderful. Look, please don't ring me here – not unless Mum's worse.'

She rang off and stood recovering, trying to remind herself that her mother was OK. The wound was healing, the cancer was in remission, and, although she'd been suffering chest-pains and had trouble with her breathing, she was still infinitely better than she was six months ago.

Switching off her mobile, she made a move towards the classroom door, only to stop as she turned the handle. What should she say, if asked why she left the room? She had no wish to discuss the whole issue of her mother, nor reveal her wimpish decision to stay at home and be her full-time carer, rather than take a proper job.

Even her friends thought it totally pathetic that she'd chosen to play nursemaid instead of studying, or travelling, or climbing the career ladder. In fact, some of them were so frightened of the C-word, they'd dropped her, more or less, as if cancer were contagious and might spread to them as well. But, in fact, the arrangement worked extremely well. It meant her father could continue as the breadwinner, while her mother was spared the prospect of callous, bossy strangers barging in to help. As for her, she felt fulfilled and needed – far more so than if stuck in some dreary office, glued to a computer screen. None the less, it was hard to raise the subject without sounding like a martyr, so best say her dad had rung to check that she'd arrived.

Fuck it, she thought, opening the door as quietly as she could and sidling into the room. I shan't say *anything*. I don't want them thinking I can't travel fifty miles without a doting parent fearing I'll get lost.

'Are you all right?' the tutor whispered, immediately coming over to her desk.

'Yes, fine.'

'It's Nadine, isn't it?'

'No, Natasha.'

'I'm sorry, I should have remembered. It's such a lovely name.'

Once she'd moved on, Natasha completed the sentence for her: 'But you didn't think it suited me.' Her dad had actually chosen it, because its Russian tang matched the arctic conditions of her birth night. He was a romantic, anyway, and would never have opted for some ordinary name such as Jane or Jean or Pat. And, secretly, she was proud and pleased that the scrawny, red-faced, bawling scrap he'd brought into the world had seemed to him exotic and exceptional. And he had never changed his mind, despite the fact she'd grown into a mousy child and an undistinguished adult, with lank, straight hair and insipid grey-blue eyes, not the dark, bewitching beauty a Natasha might suggest. In fact, 'ish' was the word she'd use about herself: short-ish, slim-ish, fairish, dull-ish, quiet-ish.

The steady scratching of pens was the only sound in the room, reminding her that she, too, should be working. 'I feel I'm two people,' she wrote, trying to return to the task in hand. 'The one I really am, which is dull and mediocre and not much good at anything, and how my parents see me: the most amazing, brilliant daughter in the world.'

She scored that out as well. It made her parents seem biased, if not stupid, instead of merely loyal. And they had paid for this whole course (including the Friday night she'd missed), which cost almost more than her father earned in a week. The adult education centre was a revamped stately home, and charged accordingly. A swanky mansion, with fifteen acres of grounds, including orchard, trout-pond and something called an arboretum, wasn't likely to come cheap.

She gazed out of the window at the yards of lush-green lawn, the herbaceous border swoony with June flowers, and the statue of some goddess or other swanking on a pedestal. Rather different from home, where their small back-yard was given over to practical things: a washing line, a cabbage patch, a rough-and-ready compost heap and a few ancient, battered cold-frames for her father's beloved cucumbers.

If only she could do a character sketch of *him*. He, like her, was reserved and quiet, but, unlike her, had courage and determination and amazing optimism, despite her mother's illness, which he refused to see as a tragedy, but rather as a challenge the three of them must meet. And, although he'd given up any hobbies that took him out of the house, he found comfort in peculiar things like collecting Victorian codd-bottles, or mugging up on British bats on the Internet.

'In terms of age,' she wrote, selecting a clean page in her note-book, 'my parents are more like grandparents. I don't mean old fogies, of course, just—'

She jumped as an unearthly wail shattered the peace of the classroom, followed by a second, still more chilling scream. Was someone being tortured? Someone in frightful pain? Surely the class should be rushing out to help, or at least investigate, yet no one else seemed the slightest bit alarmed.

The tutor tiptoed over once more and stooped down by her desk. 'Don't worry,' she whispered. 'It's only the peacocks. They've been mercifully quiet, so far, but you should have heard them last night!'

'*Peacocks*?' she whispered back.

'Yes, they're a feature of the house – half a dozen, at least. We've all had time to get used to the noise, but it can be quite disturbing if you don't know what it is.'

The harsh, raucous screech continued – a sound that seemed to pierce through stone, indeed, through her very skull. How could the others 'get used to it', let alone continue writing? In fact, several of them had stopped, and were grinning in disbelief as two or three birds began out-shrieking one another in a wild cacophony.

The tutor raised her voice above the racket. 'Look, as we're being interrupted, I think we'll have our break now. It's almost time, in any case. Please be back here in fifteen minutes, and you can finish off your pieces then. We'll still have plenty of time for the readings before we stop for lunch.'

God, she'd forgotten about the readings! Everyone else would be spouting at impressive length, whereas her own two feeble sentences wouldn't galvanize a *flea*. But just as she'd decided to stay behind and do hers in the break, she saw the tutor bearing down on her again.

'Let me show you the way to the coffee-room, Natasha. We were given a tour of the house last night, but you probably haven't had a chance to get your bearings yet. I'm Beatrice, by the way.'

'Yes, I know.' The tutor's potted biography had been printed in the brochure. 'Beatrice Collings, MA (Oxon), has published two novellas and three short-story collections to critical acclaim. A former lecturer in Creative Writing at Northumbria University, she now lives in Hexham with her Border collie.' She had warmed to the description, feeling a natural sympathy for a fellow Northumbrian, and one without a partner. It was surely no more shameful to live with one's parents than with a Border collie. Although Beatrice *might* have a man, of course – someone with his own place or whom she preferred to keep a secret. She looked little over forty, so she wasn't past it yet. Although it was bloody hard to find a guy, whatever age you were. She herself had only been out with two, so far, and both had dropped her pretty soon. The trouble was she couldn't chat men up, or dress to turn them on, like most girls did instinctively. She knew she wasn't gay – retarded, probably.

'I'm sorry I haven't introduced myself before.'

She forced her attention back to Beatrice. 'That's OK. It was my fault for arriving late.'

'You weren't ill, I hope, or—?'

'No.' Just scared, she didn't say. And, of course, worried about her mother, whom she had hardly left all year. If she *did* go out, she was always sure to hurry back, especially if her father was at work. But for this weekend he'd insisted he could cope; told her she mustn't think of cancelling, because not only did she need the break, but she had a gift for self-expression, which would be nurtured by the course. He hoped she'd take her studies further, even do a degree in Creative Writing, once things had eased at home. His faith in her was touching, when all she'd churned out in her life were school essays and a load of crazy emails. But, for some time now, he'd cottoned on to her deep desire to write; her urge to create some new, imagined world, bring characters to life, put over her own view of things, touch readers with her way-out thoughts, leave something behind of interest when she died. It sounded horribly conceited (which is why she never mentioned it to anyone but him), yet it did actually seem possible – in her dreams, at least – to be passionate and forceful on the page, however shy and unassertive she might be in ordinary life.

'Are you coming, Natasha?'

'Er, sorry. Yes.' Hastily she caught up with the others, as Beatrice ushered them along the passage into an elegant panelled room. She stared in wonder at the ceiling, which was painted with scores of chubby cherubs lolling about on great, white, bouncy clouds. In her mind, she joined them, soaring swiftly heavenwards and choosing the fattest, softest cloud to wrap around her, like a duvet, as she surveyed the world below. She was only forced down to earth again as a small chap with a goatee beard pressed a cup into her hand. Beatrice was supervising the coffee-urn, while a weird woman in a red Hell's Angels T-shirt passed round milk and sugar, and another female (in Bermuda shorts) did the rounds with the biscuits.

'Shall we take our coffee into the garden?' Beatrice suggested. 'And make the most of the sunshine.'

'What, and brave the peacocks?' a tall, red-headed girl asked.

'Well, actually, they're worth a bit of study. They really are quite beautiful.'

'Yeah, that's the problem,' the skinny man remarked. 'If they were drab or ugly birds, they'd probably be extinct by now. People would have shot them all, just to be rid of that infernal noise. It's the same with beautiful women. They can get away with anything. Beauty gives you power – power that's often abused.'

'Do I detect a note of bitterness?' the woman called Virginia asked, flashing him a smile. 'Has some *femme fatale* broken your heart?'

'Not at all,' he countered. 'I was just making an observation.'

And a true one, Natasha reflected. *She* was nothing to look at, so she lacked self-confidence. The two went hand in hand. You saw it all the time. Her cousin Beth was stunning, with violet eyes (which real people rarely had – only heroines in Mills & Boon) and natural ash-blonde hair, so she only had to snap her fingers for every bloke in the neighbourhood to jump to rapt attention.

'It seems unfair,' Virginia said, 'that the males should be so dazzling, when the females are so drab.'

'I haven't *seen* a peahen yet. Are there any here?'

'Just one, I'm told,' the tutor said.

'So all six males are after her?'

'Apparently. I suppose that's why they make such a hellish noise – all competing with each other. Come on, let's go and see them.'

She led the way through the open French doors and out into the garden, where the group stood around in clusters on the lawn, balancing their coffee cups. Two of the peacocks were pecking for grubs in the rose-bed; their brilliant blue-green plumage contrasting with the red velvet of the blooms.

'Show us your tails, then,' Virginia commanded, tempting the birds with her biscuit. One of them came over and took it from her hand, in a series of little jerking gulps, then fixed its dark brown eyes on her, as if begging her for more.

'OK, you can have another, but only in return for a display. Go on – spread that tail!'

'It's too arrogant to bother,' the skinny man put in, clearly not a fan of peacocks, and refusing to share his ginger nut, although the second bird had come up close and was eying it with interest.

'Those tails must weigh them down,' the red-haired girl remarked. 'Imagine dragging that encumbrance around all day. It must feel worse than a train on a wedding dress!'

'The tails actually weigh just short of two pounds,' another woman informed them. 'Whereas the bird as a whole weighs roughly ten. That's quite a startling ratio, when you compare most other birds. I heard that on the box – you know, *Naturewise* on Channel 4.'

'Yes, I saw that programme, too. And apparently, the tails re-grow each year, like antlers do on deer.'

'And they said dinosaurs had a similar sort of mechanism, and used to flash their horns and spines to get attention from the females, rather like a body-builder flexing his muscles for the girls.'

'Well, why won't *this* thing do its stuff?'

'Because you're not a peahen, Meg! Actually, I'm beginning to feel quite sorry for the female.'

I'm not, Natasha thought. Fantastic to have six males in attendance, despite the fact you were boring-brown and plain. She'd blown it with both her men; refused to kiss Sandy because she didn't like the feel of his tongue, and snapped at Damian when he said her mum was exploiting her and should pay for proper help. She took a sip of coffee, wishing she could find the nerve to speak, and still frantically trying to sort out people's names. Virginia was the voluptuous one in the sort of flowing kaftan-thing; Meg the bony female with her grey hair in a bun, and Fatima the sole Asian in the group. But who the hell was the skinny bloke, or the woman in Bermuda shorts, or the Hell's-Angels-T-shirt one? All of them seemed so sociable and forthright, chatting merrily away, with no fear they'd blush or stammer or mispronounce a word. *She* must be invisible, since no one had included her in the general conversation. And, far from revelling in the gorgeous weather and glorious surroundings, she was still obsessing about her lack of success with men.

'Hey, look at that one!' Meg cried. 'It's sitting on a bench, so it can rest its tail on the ground.'

'Very sensible!'

'No, let's try to move it off. Then it might display. What's the point of having all that finery if no one gets a glimpse of it?'

'I keep telling you, Meg, it's for peahens, not for humans. They're just not interested in us.'

'Only in our biscuits,' laughed the man with the goatee beard, feeding his shortbread to a fourth bird which had materialized from nowhere.

'Anyway,' said Beatrice, 'it's time to return to class now. I'm sorry the peacocks have let you down. In fact, I ought to tell you that, although I was here three times last year, teaching different groups, not once did I see a single bird show off its famous tail. I'm beginning to wonder if something's wrong with them.'

'There's nothing wrong with their voice-boxes,' Virginia put in, wincing at a sudden hideous screech.

'Beatrice,' Natasha whispered, edging up to the tutor, under cover of the peacock's din. 'I haven't done my character sketch. I did make a start, but I crossed it out, because nothing seemed to work.'

'Don't worry. It sometimes takes a while to loosen up. And I know you had a rush to get here, and missed the partying last night, which helped the others relax. So just unwind and take it easy, and that will help your writing. It's a matter of trusting rather than trying. "Trying" suggests struggle, failure, difficulty, whereas if we simply trust, we remove all those negative overtones and are more likely to work instinctively in an open, spontaneous way.'

That word again – spontaneous. Did Beatrice have the slightest idea how difficult it was? Yet if she managed to achieve it, her whole life might be transformed. If she could stop agonizing, analysing, dithering, prevaricating – as she'd done for bloody years – she might release some energy just to act, to be, to *write*.

Lying on her back, she stared into the darkness. It was so long since she'd spent a night away from home, she hadn't realized quite how lonely it would feel. She missed the light from her father's room shining under her door, and the comforting sound of the frisky hall clock, with its energetic tick-tick-tick-tick-tick. This bed was too luxuriously large, and she'd gladly swap it for her own divan, with its lumpy mattress and mismatched, unironed sheets. She even felt deprived not to be getting up in the night to help her mother on and off the lavatory, or bring her the plastic potty if she couldn't make it to the bathroom, or sponge her down when she was feverish and sweaty. Here, at Cedar Court, she had nothing to do but sleep, and the irony was she'd barely closed her eyes as yet, although now it must be almost half-past four. Well, at least it would be light soon and she could get up and begin the assignment Beatrice had set them for this morning. In fact, why wait any longer? It would be great to get a head start on the others, and so compensate for yesterday.

Kicking off the tangled sheets, she jumped out of bed and drew aside the curtain, relieved to see the first streaks of grey seeping through the darkness. The tutor had instructed them to observe closely and intently, as if they were aliens from another planet who had never seen the world before and were approaching it with fresh, unjaded eyes. She tried to turn herself into a little green man, who was astonished by the sights and sounds just outside the window: the fading stain of the moon, the thin white mist smoking from the lawn, the chorus of twitterings and chirpings as still invisible birds tuned up in the bushes, and a sharp jangling from the colony of rooks, like bottles being clanked together.

As she watched, the black blur of the cedars sharpened into clearer silhouettes. And the sky gradually paled further to the colour of an oyster-shell, with pinkish wisps of cloud against the grey. Breakfast wasn't served till eight, so she'd have several hours to make detailed notes. A writer's notebook was essential, Beatrice said – a basic tool, like a chef's knife or a carpenter's saw – to be used as fiction-material, and a source of inspiration.

She pulled on her jeans and top – she'd shower when she came back – grabbed her pen and pad, then tiptoed along the passage and down the grand oak staircase. The house was dormouse-quiet and totally deserted, but as she crept out of the side-door to the garden, the noise of the birds crescendoed: cawings, cooings, squawkings now competing with the rooks. No peacocks' shrieks, as yet, although she'd heard them in the night, as if, like her, they couldn't sleep, plagued by endless fears and thoughts.

Now that it was light, though, she felt safer altogether. She had never liked the dark, and had continued sleeping with a nightlight until she was thirteen-and-a-half. But, with the fireball of the sun slowly climbing in the sky, who needed puny nightlights? All the different colours were beginning to sing out: clouds barred with gold and amethyst, spikes of purple iris, the acrid green of pondweed, enamelled buttercups. The air was soft and scented, and everything seemed newly rinsed, as if the countryside had been put through a giant washer, emerging sparkling-clean but damp still.

As she set out towards the pond, still uncertain what to choose as the main subject of her observation, the question was decided for her by one of the resident peacocks, which suddenly approached, gazing at her with lively curiosity, as if also primed by Beatrice to do the exercise.

'OK, we'll each observe the other,' she whispered, crouching down to the level of the bird. At least she was in practice, having been taught by her father at a very early age to use her eyes and ears. Under his tuition, she had learned to distinguish a dunnock from a house-sparrow, a common newt from a palmate newt, long-eared bats from pipistrelles, and together they'd examined beetles, earthworms, worker ants – anything that moved.

Loyal still to his methods, she decided to be systematic and start her study with the head, gradually working down to the feet and finally the tail. First she noted the little pompon crest, like a rather ritzy hat – in fact, not that different from the feathered headdress her mother wore in her wedding photo. Having drawn a sketch of it, she then described the white patch around the eye; the way it emphasized the brilliant blue of the plumage, gleaming like shot-silk. The eye itself was chocolate-brown, the beak a steely-grey. As she scribbled busily away, the bird bent its neck down to its chest, to preen and groom its breast feathers, then stood on one leg, using the other foot to scratch its chest. It seemed to be running through its repertoire, in a deliberate bid to help her, so that she could write more detailed notes. Grateful, she added a line about the neck's mobility, the ease with which it looped and coiled, as if made of India rubber. Then she penned a quick description of the chest: a more greenish shade of blue, and mottled with an iridescent sheen. The wings, in contrast, were black and white; barred and streaked and stippled, to give almost a mosaic effect.

She had never realized before just how complicated a peacock's feathers were; how many shades and markings made up the total picture. Her dad might be an expert on blackbirds, thrushes, starlings, but she doubted he'd ever been this close to a bird of such distinction. You didn't get many peacocks prancing around his pocket-hanky lawn. She wished he were here to admire the fish-scale pattern running down the creature's back; its deep-green colour so intense it almost made her eyes ache. She transferred her gaze to the feet, which were hard and dry and scaly, like the gnarled, arthritic hands of some old man, and seemed completely out of place on so glamorous a bird. Shouldn't it be clad in pure-silk stockings and stylish designer shoes, rather than strutting about on bare, ungainly legs?

All at once, it let out a piercing shriek, echoed by another peacock, somewhere out of sight. They sounded like two tomcats fighting to the death, or two new-born babies all but bursting their lungs as they bawled in sheer frustration. It was the kind of sound she'd wanted to make herself when her father broke the news about her mother's cancer: a howl of utter fury and despair. In fact, she hadn't said a word, just sat staring at the carpet, until finally she'd got up from her chair and put the kettle on, to make a pot of tea. She had never forgotten the bitter, brackish taste of that tea; the way it scalded the membranes of her mouth, adding pain to pain.

The peacock was still looking at her, its scrutiny as keen as hers. 'I'm sorry,' she murmured, 'I can't compete with you. If I was a bird, I'd be something small and humdrum, like a sparrow or a wren, whereas you're a fabulous oriental prince.'

Suddenly, amazingly, the bird began to spread its tail; the process slow and solemn and accompanied by a faint whirring sound, as if the mechanism had rusted up, through months of under-use. As she stared in disbelief, at least a hundred round green eyes seemed to be staring back at her from the great, shimmering, feathered hemisphere. The long, slender feathers supporting the tail were like the ribs of a vault, or the branches of a miniature tree, strong and taut and sinewy, in contrast to the silky lustre of the diaphanous fan arching up in front of her.

She glanced around, expecting to see the peahen, but no other bird was there – not so much as a pigeon or a crow. The peacock was putting on this show for *her*, although the notion seemed incredible, when it had refused to display its finery to any of the group – not even to the tutor on her three separate visits here. Squatting on her haunches, she let her notebook fall. It was surely ungrateful and ungracious to be jotting down her petty observations in face of such magnificence. As she continued gazing at the tail, the green roundels seemed to float free of their struts, dazzling her in a meteor-flash of vibrant, sheeny colour.

Then slowly, very slowly, the bird started circling round; flaunting every angle of its sumptuous regalia. It paused a moment, sideways on, yet still ogling her beseechingly, as if engaged in some seduction rite. And she actually felt herself grow beautiful, like a dingy Cinderella transformed by the sheer glamour of her mate.

The bird swivelled round still further, so she could see its splendour from behind; the tall, underpinning feathers now gleaming silvery-white, while the undersides of the peacock-'eyes' showed through blurry-brown. And below the great arched tail was a second, smaller tail, upturned like the main one, and no less intricate in its subtle black and white. There was still no sign of any peahen, nor had any of the writing group put in an appearance. It was *her* the bird was courting; *her* it considered worthy of this outstanding honour denied to all the rest. Never before had she been wooed with such sheer ceremony; such earnestness, persistence. Damian, on their very first date, had been listening to his iPod and only gave her half an ear, while Sandy hadn't bothered to put on a clean shirt, let alone wash his greasy hair. But this lordly bird had graced her with its full and fixed attention, and was now veering round to face her again; the exuberant blaze of spangled green replacing the striking black and white.

Then, as if to complete the mating ritual, it added sound to spectacle, letting out a sudden rapturous screech. The noise echoed through the gardens, seemed to split the sky, yet she registered, with a sense of shock, that the despair and violence of the sound had entirely disappeared. The battle-shriek, the howl of pain had changed into a love-cry, an ardent serenade. And she realized at that very instant that *she* could change, as well, from a doubting, fearful, indecisive nobody into a genuine Natasha. Was there any reason why she couldn't be exceptional – in reality, not just in name; couldn't be exotic, despite her mediocre looks; couldn't fulfil her parents' faith in her and achieve some little brilliance of her own?

'I *will*,' she said, out loud, so that the grounds and gardens, and even the sweep of wooded hills beyond could bear witness to her vow. 'And I'll start this second, to show I truly can.'

Then, watched by her proud peacock-mate, she seized her pen and notebook and flung herself full-length on the grass. By now, the sun was crimsoning the sky; gilding the open page in front of her;

streaming down in dazzling, fierce approval as she began to write swiftly and – yes, spontaneously – the first chapter of a flamboyant peacock's tale.